Midnight Is a Place

OTHER YEARLING BOOKS YOU WILL ENJOY:

ARABEL AND MORTIMER, *Joan Aiken*
FOOTSTEPS ON THE STAIRS, *C. S. Adler*
THE STONEWALKERS, *C. S. Adler*
THE HOUSE WITH A CLOCK IN ITS WALLS, *John Bellairs*
THE FIGURE IN THE SHADOWS, *John Bellairs*
THE LETTER, THE WITCH, AND THE RING, *John Bellairs*
THE BOOK OF THREE, *Lloyd Alexander*
THE BLACK CAULDRON, *Lloyd Alexander*
TARAN WANDERER, *Lloyd Alexander*
THE HIGH KING, *Lloyd Alexander*

YEARLING BOOKS are designed especially to entertain and enlighten young people. Charles F. Reasoner, Professor Emeritus of Children's Literature and Reading, New York University, is consultant to this series.

For a complete listing of all Yearling titles, write to Dell Publishing Co., Inc., Promotion Department, P.O. Box 3000, Pine Brook, N.J. 07058.

Midnight
Is a
Place

Joan Aiken

A YEARLING BOOK

Published by
Dell Publishing Co., Inc.
1 Dag Hammarskjold Plaza
New York, New York 10017

Yearling® TM 913705, Dell Publishing Co., Inc.

ISBN: 0-440-45634-7

Reprinted by arrangement with The Viking Press/Viking Penguin, Inc.

Printed in the United States of America

September 1985

10 9 8 7 6 5 4 3 2 1

CW

Contents

Night's wingèd horses
  No one can outpace
But midnight is no moment
Midnight is a place.
                    —*Denzil's Song*

PART ONE

Evening

IT HAD BEEN raining all day. Even in good weather the park around Midnight Court was not a cheerful place. Smoke from the city's many chimneys had blackened and half-killed most of the great chestnut trees which stood like chess pieces from a half-finished game dotted at distant intervals over the sooty grass. It seemed hard to believe that sheep had ever grazed or ladies lolled with parasols under those branches, now so grimy and dripping, or that children had climbed the rocks which came like bared teeth through the ground as if it were too scanty to cover them. And the smoke was always in the sky. Even on a clear day it hung like a thin layer of tissue above the hollow which held the city of Blastburn.

The boy who sat curled up on a window seat looking out at this dismal view had remained there for the past two hours only because he could think of nothing better to do. On a shelf to his right stood a row of schoolbooks. A partly written composition lay on the ink-stained table. The composition's title was "Why Industry Is a Good Thing." Under this heading the boy had written: "Industry is a good thing because it is better to work in a carpet factory than to be out in the rain with nothing to eat." Having written these words he had stopped, wondering to himself "Is that true?" and had turned to look out at the rain-swept park.

Dusk was beginning to fall. A faint strip of stormy light showed for a moment where the sun had set and seemed to be reflected in the pools of sodden yellow leaves under the trees; then the light faded and was gone. The trees looked more than ever like sulky phantoms, obliged by an unkind spell to linger shivering out there in the wet. It would be doing them a kindness, the boy thought, to cut them into logs and set them ablaze on some welcoming hearth. But not in this house. He glanced over his shoulder at the meager attempt at a fire smoldering under a black polished mantel. Across the dusky room he could hardly see it. Large fires were unknown in Midnight Court, as were bright lights, or gay voices, or lively music, or laughter.

The boy blew on the wide rain-streaked windowpane and wrote the words "I'm lonely," then added his name and the date. Tomorrow would be his birthday. He wondered if anybody had remembered the fact. The words *Lucas Bell, October 30, 1842*, faded as the vapor from his breath dissolved. No one in the future would know that they had been written.

He gave a sigh that was half a yawn. Moving from his cramped position on the stiff brown velveteen window seat, he was about to cross the room and employ his breath more usefully in blowing the wretched fire when, far away across the park, he caught sight of the first interesting object he had seen all afternoon. A carriage, its twin lights flickering in the downpour, had come to a halt while the lodgekeeper unbolted a pair of massive iron gates in the high wall that encircled the park. Now the carriage was in motion again and crept slowly over a slight rise and down the long curving drive that led round to the front of the house, which lay in a shallow saucer of grassy ground.

The boy watched intently. Visitors to Midnight Court were almost unknown. But during the last few weeks there had been four. Two riders on horseback, two carriages. Here came a third carriage. No information had been given to the boy about these arrivals. Business affairs of your guardian, the tutor, Mr. Oakapple, had said impatiently, no affair of yours.

Nothing was ever explained to the boy; sometimes he

felt like a ghost in the house. Now, impelled into action by boredom, he jumped up, crossed the big shabby room, quietly opened the door, and ran, stealthily but at a rapid pace, down a series of chilly stone passages. Nobody saw him quit the schoolroom quarter and make his way to the main hall.

This was a bare, looted-looking apartment. Paler patches on the painted walls showed where pictures had been taken down. A hole in the ceiling was all that remained of a chandelier. Somebody had hung a torn fragment of brown holland over the carved stone coat-of-arms above the fireplace. Although it was a large room, the hall contained no furniture except for an umbrella stand holding a rusty sword, and a small oval loo-table with one broken leg.

Nobody was to be seen. Moving silently to the half-open front entrance, through which rain was drifting, the boy looked out and saw the lights of the carriage already retreating into the wet night. Who could have come and gone so rapidly? Or had the driver decided not to stop? Or had somebody alighted? In which case, where were they?

It seemed to the boy, straining his ears to catch any sound in the silence of the big empty hall, that the ring of unaccustomed voices had perhaps only just died away, that the long marble stairs had only just stopped echoing to the clatter of feet.

Hesitant, chewing his thumbnail, Lucas came to a halt by the foot of the stair. For many nights now he had slept badly, tossing in his lumpy four-poster, getting up to stare out the window at the livid glare over Blastburn, where by day and night the factory chimneys vomited red-hot vapor and the air was filled with a sour metallic smell. Something was wrong in the house; he felt sure of it. Something, he hardly knew what, an unsettled feeling about the place made him uneasy. Although he was told nothing, he had a sense of trouble; he spent much of his time listening—as now—for some sharp voice, some explosion, some clap of thunder which would explain his anxiety.

He looked up the staircase. If he were caught at the top, it would mean punishment, for he was strictly forbidden to stray outside his own quarters; Sir Randolph detested children. But the chance of being caught was not very great, much less than it would have been six months ago. Lately the staff at Midnight Court, never large, had been much reduced. Six footmen, eight maids, the steward, the coachman, the head stableman, and most of the grooms and gardeners had been turned off. The great house stood half-empty; thirty rooms had been closed. Many of the windows were broken. Walls were crumbling. The roof had begun to leak here and there.

Lucas ran upstairs.

At the stairhead a thin strip of brown drugget still remained, leading as far as the door of his guardian's study. It was possible to creep along this without making any sound. A few candles, not many, had been lit and burned flickeringly in the wall sconces, but there were big patches of shade in between, and the boy slipped from one shadow to the next, moving with great caution, listening alertly, tempted by the faint sound of voices from behind the closed study door.

As he drew closer, he could hear the words more distinctly.

A quarrel was going on inside.

"Idiot! Sapskull! How dared you write and give any such permission? You had no authority to do so!"

A thin, high, rusty, snarling voice—that was his guardian, Sir Randolph Grimsby. The reply, in a much lower tone, was not audible to the boy; he could not be certain yet who was speaking.

Sir Randolph interrupted the speaker. "Thought it best

be damned! Who asks you to think? Who pays you to think?"

There was a furious thump on the floor. Sir Randolph in his younger days had broken both legs trying, for a wager, to make his horse jump a row of six twelve-pounder guns; and he now walked very lame with two sticks, which were also frequently used to demonstrate his displeasure.

"Keep your thoughts to yourself, sir! What has the boy to do with the matter? He is enough of an encumbrance as it is. You exceeded your warrant, sirrah—you took an outrageous liberty. Now what the devil am I supposed to do? Is this an orphanage? Or a poor farm? I am plagued to distraction as matters are by those prying jumped-up interlopers from the tax office—not to mention the ill-conditioned rabble at the Mill—bedeviled at every turn—and now to add to all this, *you* have to meddle where you've no business and harass me with yet another infernal burden—damn it, sir, damn it, I've a good mind to turn you off—"

Another angry thump was succeeded by an equally fierce volley of barking—evidently Sir Randolph, laying about him with his sticks, had accidentally landed a blow on his wolfhound, Redgauntlet, who mostly lurked, molting and snoring, under the big mahogany desk.

"Quiet, will you! Curse it, man, now look what you made me do! Give over, damn your eyes, let go! You, fellow, kick the dog out. *Will* you let go of the cane, rot you—"

It was difficult to decide whether Sir Randolph was addressing the dog or his companion, but it was plain that he was in his customary bad temper.

The door flew open, and Redgauntlet was propelled backward, growling, into the corridor. Mr. Oakapple, the tutor, who had pushed him out, stepped back inside, closing the door. The boy retreated hastily—quite apart from his fear of discovery, there had never been any love lost between him and the surly-tempered hound—but Red-gauntlet had started in the other direction and continued that way.

During the moment that the door had been open, Lucas had caught his tutor's eye. Would Mr. Oakapple inform on him to Sir Randolph? Or were the pair of them on such angry terms that he would choose to remain silent?

Either way, there was little purpose in remaining so dangerously close to the door now that the tutor knew of his presence. Lucas turned and started slowly back in the direction of his own quarters, kicking the brown carpet moodily as he went. He took an upstairs passage, risking the very slight possibility of encountering one of the few remaining servants; at this hour they were mostly below stairs.

Halfway along the passage, however, he paused in surprise outside the door of a chamber that was usually unoccupied. Inside it he was almost sure that he had caught the sound of a high unfamiliar voice.

As he stood straining his ears, the door handle turned, and the housekeeper, Mrs. Gourd, came out. At sight of the boy, she quickly slammed the door to behind her.

"Mester Lucas! What the pest are you doing here?" she said, giving him a sour look.

"Measuring the distance from the east to the west wing for my arithmetic lesson," he answered glibly. "Mr. Oakapple ordered me. What's wrong with that?"

Even if she did not believe him, he was not much afraid of old Gourd; at the most, all she could do was cuff his head and deprive him of jam with his breakfast.

"Wrong? You'll wear out the carpet, you'll raise dust, you'll make a noise and rile Sir Randolph—dear knows, we've trouble enow in the house without *your* doing owt to make matters worse. Get back to your schoolroom directly, and don't let me find you up here again where you've no road to be. Look sharp, now!"

Muttering and shaking her gray head, she hurried off in the other direction. She was carrying, strangely enough, what appeared to be an immensely long loaf of bread, made in a shape quite unlike any that Lucas had ever seen before, no thicker round than his wrist but as long as one of Sir Randolph's crutch sticks. As she went, she muttered to herself, "*Goo-tay, goo-tay*—what like of a word's that when it's at home?"

Lucas ran back to the schoolroom where during his absence the fire had gone out completely. To remedy this mishap (a frequent occurrence due to the poor quality of the coal) he kept a secret hoard of candle ends and sulphur matches stored in an empty wine bin in the disused butler's pantry next door. Now he fetched some from his hoard, burrowed a small crater in the top of the dismal heap of black slag, inserted two fragments of candle, and carefully lit them. A slow pale flame curled up. "Goo-tay, goo-tay," he thought, blowing on the flame. "*Goûter?* The French word for lunch?"

But Mrs. Gourd knew no French. He must have misunderstood her.

While he was coaxing up the fire, Pinhorn, the head housemaid, came in with his meal. It was plain that she, like Sir Randolph, was in a bad mood. Sometimes she could be persuaded to stay and talk a little while he ate his supper, but today she slammed down the tray on top of two schoolbooks and was retreating with a crackle of starched apron over long black bombazine skirt when Lucas asked, "Who came in the carriage, Pinhorn?"

"Them as asks no questions lives longest!" she snapped and flung the door to behind her, but opened it again and put her head round it to say, "You'll learn soon enough, I dessay, if Sir Randolph thinks fit. Drat that meddlesome Oakapple!"

Lucas sighed and looked distastefully at his supper. It consisted of a plate of cold mutton chops, a glass of weak beer, and two slices of brown bread. He was hungry, for he had eaten nothing since noon, but the meal was far from appetizing. The chops lay in a puddle of cold gravy, skinned over with congealed fat, and the beer had slopped onto the bread.

He set the tray on the floor and considered the two books on which Pinhorn had placed it. *Double-Entry Book-keeping* and *How to Run a Factory*, they were called. He opened them listlessly, shut them again, turned back to his unfinished composition, and wrote, "Industry is a good thing, because if you don't work you may get bored."

Then he chewed his quill pen for a few minutes. Suddenly he pushed aside the composition and pulled toward him a thick, shabby brown leather book with a brass clasp. Opening this in the middle—it was half filled with writing already—he began scribbling very fast:

Sir Randolph is like an old gray condor with sharp beak and talons. I have seen pictures of birds like him perched on crags, with fierce little red eyes; they live in the wilderness and tear their prey untidily. He is a good man; he built three churches and brought prosperity to the town of Blastburn. He is my guardian; I should be grateful to him. I am afraid of him. This must be because I am bad. Why am I bad? Heredity? Upbringing in heathen country? Is it because I have bad dreams?

The door behind him opened suddenly, and his tutor came in. His hand jerked guiltily, and the bottle of ink toppled over and rolled off the table, leaving a trail of ink over the unfinished composition and falling on to the supper tray below.

"You've spoiled your supper," said Mr. Oakapple irritably, stepping forward and looking down at the ink-splashed chops. He was a ginger-haired young man with a long serious face. The skin of his face was pale, dry-looking, and covered with freckles. He had pale sandy eyelashes and pale gray eyes, which generally held an impatient expression when he looked at his pupil.

"It—it wasn't very nice to start with," stammered Lucas, hoping that the tutor could not from where he stood see the unfinished task, hoping that the spoiled meal might be considered sufficient punishment for his eavesdropping upstairs.

Surprisingly, Mr. Oakapple did not mention this incident.

"Get your hat," he said abruptly. "You can't eat that stuff anyway; you may as well leave it. And Sir Randolph wants us to go out."

"Out?" Lucas was amazed. Sir Randolph never sent him anywhere.

"Yes. Down to the Mill. Fetch your hat—hurry."

Mr. Oakapple plainly had no taste for this errand, whatever it was.

Lucas fetched his hat and jacket from his bedchamber upstairs, and rejoined Mr. Oakapple, more mystified than ever. Momentarily he had had the wild fear that because of his listening outside the study door he was to be expelled from Midnight Court, turned out into the world to fend for himself. He was not happy at Midnight Court, but the unknown world outside was more terrifying still. However, if they were being sent to the Mill—but *why* were they being sent to the Mill? Such a thing had never occurred before.

Lucas knew, his knowledge having been acquired from Pinhorn and a young groom called Bob who had lately been dismissed, that what money Sir Randolph possessed came from the Mill. Its real name was Murgatroyd's Carpet, Rug, and Matting Manufactury, but locally it was always known as Midnight Mill. Its extensive premises occupied a central position in the town of Blastburn, and its chimneys belched out more smoke than any other. But Sir Randolph himself never went near the place, and nor had Lucas. He entertained very little notion of what the Mill was like, beyond a vague general dread of it, born from

Bob's dark saying: "Ah, there's more folk dies at Murgatroyd's, think on, than at all th'other mills put together. They'll allus take on new hands at Midnight, for they go so quick, but chaps looking for work'll try anywhere else first."

Perhaps Sir Randolph, at no time a kindly or welcoming guardian, had decided to get rid of the burden of his ward altogether by sending him to earn his living in the Mill? Children much younger than himself, ones of nine or ten, and even of seven or eight, did work there, Lucas knew.

Unhappily, following Mr. Oakapple, he went out to the stableyard, which lay to the rear, between the east and west wings of the E-shaped house. A governess cart stood waiting, with an old cob called Noddy, one of the few remaining horses, already between the shafts.

They set off in silence, Mr. Oakapple driving.

"Why are we going to the Mill?" Lucas finally summoned up courage to ask. He always felt ill at ease with Mr. Oakapple whose manner was invariably short, preoccupied, as if the center of his thoughts were a very long way off. Although the two of them spent hours together every day doing French, arithmetic, and geography, Lucas did not have the least knowledge of what went on inside Mr. Oakapple's head.

"Oh"—Mr. Oakapple turned slightly at the question, then concentrated once more on the dark road—"I thought Sir Randolph had told you. We are going because it is your birthday tomorrow."

"I don't understand."

Lucas knew that he ought to have been pleased at his birthday's being remembered, but he could only feel cold, wet, and anxious. They jolted on through the rainy dark. By now the lodge gates had been left behind; they were descending the broad main hill that led into Blastburn. Gas lamps flared at intervals; the mare's feet slipped and rang on granite cobbles.

"Well"—Mr. Oakapple drew a sharp, impatient sigh—
"You know that your father was Sir Randolph's partner."

"Yes."

"And after he died, it was found that he had left a will
appointing Sir Randolph as your guardian."

"Yes," Lucas answered despondently, remembering his
journey back from India to England last year, after the
death of his parents from smallpox, and the miserable arrival at Midnight Court.

"It was also laid down in your father's will that from the
age of thirteen you should be permitted to learn the business, in order that when you were of age you could take
your father's place as partner. Your father stipulated that
some part of each day should be spent in the Mill, studying
how it is run. And I have to go with you."

Mr. Oakapple's tone indicated that he did not in the
least relish this program, but Lucas did not notice the tutor's shortness for once.

His great relief at learning that he was not immediately
to be put to work as a stripper or fluff-picker was mixed
with another anxiety. How, he wondered, did one set
about running a carpet factory? He found it quite hard
enough to perform the tasks in geometry or history prepared for him by Mr. Oakapple, who often called him a
slowtop; he was unhappily certain that learning how to
look after a whole factory would be completely beyond
him.

They had reached the town. There were very few shops,
taverns, or dwelling houses. The buildings for the most
part were factories, workshops where articles were made—
nail foundries where clanging lengths of iron were cut into
strips, gasworks where coal was baked in huge ovens, pa-
permills where wood pulp and clay were boiled into a porridge that was the raw material for books and magazines—
jute mills, cotton mills, potteries, collieries. None of these
places looked as if they were built by human beings or

used by them. Huge, dark, irregular shapes rose up all around; they were like pinnacles in a rocky desert, like ruined prehistoric remains, or like the broken toys of some giant's baby. The potteries were enormous funnels; the gasworks huge flowerpots; the collieries monstrous pyramids, with skeleton wheels the size of whole church fronts which stood above them against the fiery sky.

Every now and then the roadway was cut by sets of iron rails, and sometimes a clanking train of wagons would run slowly across in front of the governess cart, and the mare would sweat and whinny and shudder her coat at the sudden loud noise, and the smell of hot metal, and the spark-filled smoke.

"Why do we have to go to the factory at this time?" said Lucas nervously in one of these pauses while they waited for a train to cross. "Won't it be shut for the night?"

"Factories never shut." The tutor glanced at him briefly. "Didn't you know about shift work? When the day workers leave, the night workers come on, so that the machines, which cost a great deal of money, need never stand idle. We shall get there just as the night shift comes on duty. It makes no difference when we arrive—people are always at work."

Somehow this idea filled Lucas with dismay. He thought of the machinery always running by night and day, the great fires always burning, the huge buildings always filled with little people dashing to and fro—never any darkness, or silence, or rest. He felt a kind of terror at the thought of wheels turning on and on, without ever stopping.

"Don't the machines ever stop at all?"

"Oh, perhaps for one week in the year, so that they can clean the boilers and put a new lining on the main press. Here we are," said Mr. Oakapple with gloom, turning the mare's head in at a pair of huge gates through a wall even higher than that around Midnight Park. Tram rails ran right through the gates and across a wide cobbled area beyond which was lit by gas flares.

Mr. Oakapple brought the mare to a halt and found a place to tether her in a line of stable sheds at one side of the factory yard. As he did this, they were passed by a dismal little procession going in the opposite direction. Two or three women with checked shawls over their heads accompanied a pair of men who were carrying something—a small shape—on a plank and covered by a blanket.

A short distance behind them walked another shawled woman. Her arms were folded, her head bent. She walked draggingly, as if she had been dead-tired for more weeks than she could remember.

As she passed near Lucas and Mr. Oakapple, a man in a black frock coat came out of a small brightly lit office and spoke to her. "Mrs. Braithwaite—ah, Mrs. Braithwaite! Mr. Gammel said to tell you that the compensation will be sent up tomorrow morning—you may be sure of that—ten shillings and a free doormat. The very best quality!"

"Ten shillings?" The woman flung back her shawl and stared at him for a moment in silence. Her face was very pale. Then she said, "What do I care about your ten shillings? That won't bring my Jinny back, that had the sweetest voice in our lane and could make a bacon pudding to equal mine, though she was only eight."

The frock-coated man shrugged. "Say what you please, there's not many turns up their noses at ten shillings and a free mat—why, you could sell *that* again, if you already have one, for double the factory price."

"Have one?" she said bitterly, her voice rising. "Why, we have *three,* already. Three fine free doormats. What do you say to that, Mr. Bertram Smallside?" Then she drew the shawl over her face again and followed the plank-bearers out through the gate into the rainy night.

"What did she mean?" whispered Lucas uneasily, as he

and Mr. Oakapple left the cart and walked toward the frock-coated man, who had turned back in the direction of his office.

"Oh"—the tutor's voice was low and dry: he spoke hurriedly—"I suppose her child may have been injured by the great press—she was one of the fluff-pickers, maybe; it does happen from time to time, I have heard—"

He entered the office. Lucas remained outside, looking toward the gateway, which was empty now. He remembered the words of Bob the groom: "Nineteen or twenty a year, regular—specially fluff-pickers—even more than falls into the soap-plodders at Lathers and Smothers—"

Inside the office he heard his tutor saying, "Mr. Smallside? Good evening. I believe Sir Randolph has already sent word. I come from the Court; I have brought down young Master Lucas Bell, as arranged, to be shown the works."

Mr. Smallside's manner changed completely. He had been looking irritably at the visitors as if he had little time for them. Now he smiled, and the brisk, matter-of-fact tone he had used with Mrs. Braithwaite was replaced by obsequious, hand-rubbing civility, as he came out into the yard.

"Young Master Bell? Yes, indeed, yes, *indeed.* Sir Randolph did graciously think to mention it. He sent a note. Delighted to meet you, Master Bell, delighted indeed! What a pleasure, what a pleasure! How well I remember your dear father, at least I almost remember him, for in fact he left to look after our Indian supply office just the year before I became manager here, but I've heard his name spoken so often that it's much the same. Such a sad loss when he passed away. And so you're his son—young Master Bell! Well, well, well, young Master Bell, what can we do for you?"

"I—I don't exactly know," stammered Lucas, quite taken

aback by all this politeness, so extremely different from his usual treatment. In spite of it—or even because of it—he was not sure that he liked Mr. Smallside, who was a lean, pallid man with a balding head and a face the color and shape of a bar of carpet soap. His hand, also, with which he grasped that of Lucas and shook it up and down very many times, had a kind of damp soapy feel to it. Lucas withdrew his own as soon as possible, and, when he could manage it without being observed, rubbed his palm vigorously against the skirts of his rough frieze jacket.

"Now," said Mr. Smallside, leading them into his office, which was a kind of little hut in the middle of the yard, cramped, hot, piled high with dusty papers and lit by hissing gas globes. "Now, what can we offer young Master Bell? A bit of parkin? A drop of prune wine? A caraway biscuit? Young gentlemen usually have a sweet tooth, *I* know!"

"Nothing, thank you," Mr. Oakapple replied for Lucas. His tone was brusque. "I think we should commence our tour straight away. The boy still has his schoolwork to do as well."

"Dear, dear, dear!" Mr. Smallside shook his head sorrowfully. "Don't stretch the young shoot too far, though, Mr. Oakapple? All work and no play won't make the best hay, we used to say when I was a young lad—" Putting his head on one side, he smiled at Lucas so much that the smile seemed likely to run round and meet at the back of his head. Lucas felt more than ever that he could not possibly be at ease in the company of Mr. Smallside and hoped that they would not have his escort while they went over the Mill.

He soon discovered that he need have had no anxieties on that score. It was suddenly plain that Mr. Smallside felt he had kept his smile on long enough; it dropped from his face like melted butter, and he went to the door of his hut and bawled across the yard towards a group of men engaged in unloading a truck: "Scatcherd! Scatcherd! Where are you? Hey, one of you trimmers— Barth, Stewkley, Danby, Bloggs—send Scatcherd to me directly. Make haste there!"

His tone was quite different again—bullying, loud, sharp, as if he enjoyed showing off his power.

A man left the rest and ran across the yard.

"There you are then," Mr. Smallside addressed him disagreeably. "Took your time, didn't you? You're to show young Master Bell here over the works, anything he wants to see."

"What about the new load o' wool?" said the man, who had come into the hut. His tone was not quite insolent, but it was by no means humble; he stood in the doorway, panting a little, and looked squarely at Smallside. He was a thin, white-faced, muscular youngish man with sharp features and black hair, a lock of which had fallen across his forehead, partly obscuring but not concealing the fact that he had one eye covered by a black patch. It might have been the reflection from the red flares outside, shining through the unglazed window, but Lucas thought that Scatcherd's other eye held a spark of something bright, fierce, and dangerous. He looked like a circus animal that had not been very well tamed.

"Bloggs can handle the wool," Smallside answered shortly. "Show the young gentleman round, anywhere he asks you to take him."

"Where shall I start?" said Scatcherd in a sulky tone.

"At the beginning. Show him the wool intake. And then the cutters. And then the looms. And the gluing. And the trimming. And so on—good heavens, I don't have to wet-nurse you, do I?"

"Shall I show him the press?" Scatcherd inquired. There was nothing out of the way about his manner, but the question somehow fell oddly.

Smallside's answer took a moment in coming. "Later—that can come later. After the rest. If there's time. Get on, man! I have all these orders to countersign."

Mr. Smallside turned with a preoccupied busy air to the papers on his desk, and Scatcherd by means of a sideways jerk of his head indicated that Oakapple and Lucas were to follow him. They hurried after him across the cobbled yard. Lucas, glancing back, felt sorry for poor Noddy, the mare, left alone in the dark, noisy, dreary place, and highly apprehensive for himself as to what lay ahead.

He was to dream, that night and for many nights to come, of what he saw during the next couple of hours.

It was not so much that the sights were frightening, though some were that; but they were so strange, so totally unfamiliar from anything that he had ever seen before; the shapes and movements of the machines were so black, quick, ugly, or sudden; the noises were so atrociously loud, the heat was so blistering, the smells so sickly, acid, or stifling.

"This here's the melder"—or the grabber, the sorting-press, or the tub thumper—Scatcherd kept saying, as he dodged nimbly under great metal arms, round swiftly-spinning enormous screws, by wheels that were almost invisible from speed and ever-whirling belts, through arches of pistons that rose and fell like the legs of some great insect, the body of which was hidden in the forest of machinery above them. Scatcherd never bothered to turn his head or to raise his voice while he imparted information about the work. Often Lucas could see his lips move but could catch less than a tenth of what he said. Could those be the right names for the machines, or could Scatcherd be deliberately misleading them? In either case, Lucas felt that at the end of the two hours he would be no wiser than at the start; he was totally bewildered by all he saw.

The wool intake was the only part of the process that he could really grasp: raw wool, as taken from the sheep's back, came clanking into the works on the trains of trucks that ran through the forecourt. The wool was in huge bales, corded up like outsize parcels. Men slashed through the cords, and the bales immediately exploded apart into masses of springy fluff which was sent sliding down a great chute into a kind of hopper where it was washed and graded; then it was teased, to have the knots and lumps and prickles taken out; then, according to the grade, some wool was dyed, some was bleached. The men in charge of the dye vats were a strange sight, for they were splashed all over in brilliant colors, their hair was colored, their arms were green or blue or crimson to the elbows.

Some of the carpets were woven with shuttles on looms. The looms, with their high and complicated machinery, occupied several of the large central buildings. But other carpets, the more inexpensive ones, were made in a new way, invented, Scatcherd told them, by Sir Quincy Murga-troyd, the original founder of the factory. He had devised a means of sticking short lengths of wool onto canvas, which was both faster and cheaper than the weaving process. And if the carpets tended to come unstuck after a few years, what did that matter? They were not the kind of carpets that were bought by rich folks. Imparting this information, Scatcherd gave his audience a malicious, side-long glance.

"T'glue's not t'best grade, you see," he remarked, pausing beside a huge vat which contained a frothy brown vile-smelling brew that was just coming to the boil. "Very poor glue that is, and joost as well, for when chaps falls into it, which happens from time to time, they stand a better chance o' coming out alive. Which they never did, mind you, in owd Sir Quincy's day; the glue he used would ha' stuck Blastburn Town Hall oopside down on top o' Kilnpit Crags till the week after Joodgement Day."

"People fall in *there?*" said Lucas faintly.

"Ah, it's slippery roond the edge, you see; you don't

want to step too close, yoong master, or you'll get those nice nankeen britches splashed," Scatcherd told him with a mocking smile.

Oakapple opened his mouth as if he would have liked to put in some remark, but Scatcherd led them on, talking all the time, past wide rollers, which spread the glue on the canvas backing, and complicated mechanical arms which, working back and forth on hinges, sprinkled the chopped-up wool over the gluey surface. Then there were implements like rakes, or combs, which straightened the pile, teasers to remove any dots of glue, sponges to mop away loose hairs, and a sucker-fan to draw the wool up so that it stood on end while the carpet was whirled round on a platform called a swiveler.

"Had enow, maybe?" Scatcherd inquired drily as they stood by the swiveler which spun and rocked so giddily that it made Lucas feel dizzy just to watch it. "Reckon you've looked at as mooch as you can take for one shift?"

Lucas did feel so, but his pride was pricked by Scatherd's tone. "What was that thing you spoke of to Mr. Smallside—the press? We haven't seen that yet, have we?"

"Oh, I think we've looked at quite enough for one evening—" Mr. Oakapple was beginning, but Scatcherd, again without seeming to have heard the tutor, said, seeming to find this a most unexpected request, "The press? You want to see the press? Eh, very well"—and he turned on his heel. "Down this way then. Pressing's the end o' the manufacturing process. After that the carpet's ready for sale. This here's the pressing room—careful down t'steps. They're slippery—t'glue gets all over."

The pressing room was a huge place like the crypt of a church. Steps led down to it on all four sides.

"Where *is* the press?" Lucas began, and then, looking up, he saw that the whole ceiling was in fact a great metal slab which could be raised or lowered by hydraulic machinery.

A carpet was being unrolled and spread at feverish speed in the square central part of the room. The very instant it was laid out flat the men who had done so bounded up the steps, not a moment too soon, for the press came thudding down with a tremendous clap of dull sound.

"Toss a cob nut in there, you'll get it cracked free gratis," Scatcherd said briefly.

Lucas could well believe him. If anybody slipped and fell under the press, they would be done for. It rose up again much more slowly than it had come down, and the carpet was snatched away by a mechanical grab; then half a dozen overall-clad children with brooms, who had been ready waiting on the steps, darted out onto the floor and swept it with frantic speed and assiduity before the next piece of carpet was unrolled.

"Why can't the floor be swept by machinery?" Lucas asked.

"Childer's cheaper," Scatcherd answered laconically, with another of his sidelong glances. "Machines has to be kept cleaned and oiled, but there's always a new supply o' kids."

A question trembled in Lucas's mind; but Scatcherd, as if hearing the unspoken words, went on, "That bit's not *so* risky, but what does come up chancy is when there's a bit o' fluff or dirt discoovered on the carpet when it's spread out—ah! Like there, see?"

A new carpet had been spread out, brown and gold; in the middle, clearly visible on a circle of gold, was a clot of black oily wool, seemingly left from one of the previous processes.

"The chaps on the swiveler work too fast, you see; it often happens," Scatcherd said. "Now someone has to go get it off, o' course, before it's ground in by t'press. The quickest one on the shift has to do it—the one they call the snatcher. Watch now—"

A barefoot girl dashed out onto the carpet, snatched up the bit of wool with a pair of metal tongs, and leapt back to safety on the steps just before the great press thudded down again. She slipped a little on the steps, but recovered by throwing herself forward onto hands and knees, while two mates grabbed her arms.

Lucas took off his hat and rubbed his forehead with the back of his sleeve.

"O' course, they gets paid a bit extry for snatching," Scatcherd said "Ha'penny an hour danger money. Most of us has bin snatchers at one time or another when we was yoonger, but not for long—you can't keep on long at it—you gets nervous. You begin to dream at night, then your legs begins to shake and you can't run so fast."

Lucas could imagine it. Just having seen the snatcher at work made him sick with fear. Mr. Oakapple evidently shared this feeling.

"We have to go back," he said abruptly. "We have seen enough for this evening. Thank you."

Scatcherd nodded; with a shrug that showed he perceived how they felt, he began moving away toward a pile of unopened bales of wool.

At that moment a man in a wheelchair spun past Oakapple and Lucas with almost uncanny speed. Veering his chair toward Scatcherd, he called, "Ey, Davey! Coom to t'singsong at t'Mason's Arms tonight?"

Scatcherd turned. Without replying to the invitation, he said, "Two o' thy lazy, feckless, cack-handed swivel hands left clots on this afternoon. Has tha heard aboot t'Braithwaite kid?"

The man in the wheelchair made no reply; the silence between him and Scatcherd seemed condensed, like the air before thunder. Then the wheelchair turned and shot away. Mr. Oakapple walked into the forecourt, and Lucas followed.

"There will be no need to say good night to Mr. Small-side—he's busy," Mr. Oakapple said, and untied the mare. They climbed silently into the trap. The mare was eager to be off and broke into a trot, jolting the wheels over the cobbles and the tram tracks. They rattled briskly through the open gates and then slowed down for the long climb out of Blastburn.

Halfway up, on the other side, stood the Blastburn Municipal Infirmary, which, Lucas knew, had been built at the expense of Sir Quincy Murgatroyd. As they passed the gates, he wondered if the Braithwaite child was in there.

But near the top of the hill he was surprised to perceive ahead of them what seemed to be still the same sad little procession of men and woman, still slowly carrying the hurt child.

"Where can they be going?" he demanded of Mr. Oakapple. "No one lives up here so far out of town—do they?" he added, as his tutor remained silent.

"No—nobody lives up here," Mr. Oakapple said reluctantly, after another pause. "I suppose they are going to the cemetery."

The cemetery gates, guarded by large granite pillars, each topped with a stone angel, stood to the right, just over the brow of the hill.

By the time the governess cart had reached the gates, the group of mourners had passed through, but the shawled woman whom Mr. Smallside had addressed as Mrs. Braithwaite remained outside. She was sitting on a milestone by the roadside, rocking herself back and forth, repeating the same words over and over. "They got my Jean; they got my Nance; they got my Jinny. But they shan't get Sue; they shan't get Betsy—I'd sooner see them starve. I'd sooner see them starve."

One of the men returned from the graveyard. "Coom along, then, missis?" he said awkwardly. "Doesn't tha want to be there?"

"Coom on, Emma lass," said another woman, putting a hand on her friend's shoulder. But Mrs. Braithwaite shook her head.

"I seen it three times. I know what happens," she said. "I said my good-bye to Jinny the day she went through the Mill gates." And she returned to her rocking and murmuring.

Mr. Oakapple whirled the reins sharply and slapped them against the mare's withers. She had been going slowly but broke into a trot, and soon the cemetery gates were left behind.

Neither of the passengers in the cart said anything more until they were back in the stableyard where Garridge, the head groom, was waiting to take the mare and rub her down.

"Sir Randolph wants Mester Lucas in t'stoody," he said briefly.

Lucas felt his spirits, already lowered by the evening's happenings, decline still further. Would Sir Randolph be waiting for an account, a report of all they had seen? Would Lucas now be obliged to answer a whole series of questions on the carpet-manufacturing process? He tried in vain to assemble his thoughts and to recall the sequence of actions that turned wool into carpets. All he could think of was the snatcher, dashing out from under the murderous weight of the press, and Mrs. Braithwaite, sitting huddled in her shawl by the graveyard gate.

"Well, bustle along then, boy," Mr. Oakapple snapped with a sudden return to his usual impatient manner, which had not been evident during their visit to the Mill. "You know Sir Randolph can't abide being kept waiting. Here— I'll take your hat and coat. You may go up the front stair, it's quicker."

Lucas nodded, with a dry mouth, and made his way to the main hall. His heart had begun thudding uncomfortably in his chest. Slowly climbing the marble stair he was weighed down by the whole burden of the day, which seemed to have been going on for about twenty hours already. For a moment he stood outside the study door, reluctant to knock. He had not entered this room above three times during the year he had spent at Midnight Court, and on none of these occasions had his guardian appeared at all friendly or pleased to see him. There seemed little chance of any difference on the present occasion.

It must be very late—nearly midnight. But Sir Randolph kept late hours, everybody knew: he was a poor sleeper; often throughout the hours of dark, his lamp could be seen shining out over the blackened grass of Midnight Park.

No sound came from behind the door, and Lucas tapped softly with a stifled hope that perhaps his guardian had dozed off since issuing the summons, but the high irascible voice called, "Come in—come in. Don't dawdle on the threshold, damn you!"

Lucas quickly opened the door and walked in.

The study—a room almost as bare and shabby as the schoolroom—was lit by only one candle, which had burned down to a stub. A couple of red coals glowed faintly on the hearth. An almost empty decanter and tumbler stood on the desk by the guttering candle. There was a powerful smell of brandy in the room.

Sir Randolph, with all his face and body in shadow, sat half curled, half crouched, in the big leather chair by the desk, with the folds of a plaid rug wrapped round his shoulders and spread over his knees. His two knobbed canes leaned against the arm of the chair.

"Well—don't just stand there. Come forward, boy!" he ordered sharply in his high voice that was like the croak of some angry bird.

"Shan't I put some more coal on the fire, sir?"

"No, rot you! Coal costs money—perhaps you hadn't

heard? Leave it alone! Stay—you may light another candle. Then come here."

Lucas found a candle, set it in place of the stub, and lit new from old. As the yellow flame grew taller, he noticed with part of his mind that the carpet on Sir Randolph's study floor was of the very same brown and gold pattern as the one he had seen an hour ago on the floor of the pressing room.

"Well—have you been down there? Have you been over the Mill?" Sir Randolph demanded as the light was placed in front of him. The strength of his voice seemed to rise and fall with a variability like that of wind or the sea. He leaned forward abruptly and drank, splashing some of the contents of his tumbler onto the leather top of the desk.

"Yes, sir."

"Understand it?"

"Not—not altogether, sir—" Lucas began.

"Be quiet then! I don't want to hear about it. Don't—want—hear 'bout it," he repeated in a kind of snarling singsong, though Lucas had not ventured to speak. "Jus' learn 'bout it—that's all. You are to go there every day until you do understan' 'bout it—every day—that's what you have t'do."

"May—may I go now, sir?" Lucas was confused and alarmed by his guardian's manner, which seemed half angry, half absent, as if his attention were directed to matters far away in the distant past.

Sir Randolph was gazing at the new candle dreamily. In the dim light little could be seen of his deeply-lined face but the outline of the hooked nose, heavy eyelids, and thin mouth, of which the lower lip was set somewhat behind the upper one, making his profile even more like that of a bird of prey. Although not much above sixty, Sir Randolph could have been taken for a man ten or fifteen years older than that. Troubles, and his own nature, had aged him early.

"Go? No! Who said you could go? Stand still—don't fidget." Sir Randolph's head lifted sharply. He took off his worn black-velvet smoking cap and looked into it as if he hoped to find a memorandum written inside. "I'll tell you when you may go, and it isn't yet. 'Was something else I had to say t'you."

He fell into a brown study again.

Lucas waited nervously.

"Ah—know what it was—yes." Sir Randolph roused himself again. "Fellow said you'd been complaining of loneliness. Wanted comp'ny—something of th'sort—" His next words sank into a mutter, but "puling milksop" seemed to be detectable among them.

"Loneliness? Sir—I never—" Lucas began, very much startled. Whom could Sir Randolph have meant by that "fellow"—surely not Mr. Oakapple to whom Lucas had never spoken of his longing for a friend or companion of his own age?

"Quiet, boy! I don't fesh—fetch you here t'entertain me, do I? Deuce knows you don't do that. Where was I? Yes, comp'ny. Well, now you've got comp'ny, due t'that fellow's int'ference. Company you have got. So don' let me hear word'f any *more* complaints, d'unnerstan'?"

"I have company? What company, sir?" Lucas was completely puzzled.

"Turned up today's evening. Old Gourd been seeing t'arrangements. Oak Chamber. So no more moaning, no more grouching, hear? Now, *go*—d'think I want you staring at me with that cheese-faced look all evening? You put me in mind—can't stand it. No matter. But *she* was beautiful," he muttered to himself; then looked up at Lucas and said, "Get out of my sight."

"May I—may I go to the Oak Chamber?"

"Oh, certainly—go an' play billiards t'll cockcrow if you wish, don' let me detain you," snarled Sir Randolph, dragging savagely at his crimson wool bellpull. "Skate, play marbles, ride the farmhorses, break the windows, pull the whole *house* down—only clear out of here!"

Lucas waited no longer. Leaving his guardian muttering, cursing, and hauling on the crimson rope, he slipped out of the room and sped along the passage in the direction of the Oak Chamber, from which he had seen Mrs. Gourd emerging earlier that evening.

It did briefly cross his mind that the hour might be somewhat late to disturb the newcomer, but his eagerness and his loneliness were too great to bear any delay. A companion! A friend with whom he could share lessons and exercises, a friend to talk to, read with, accompany on scrambles up Grimside, the great black hill to the north of the town—perhaps even farther. If the other boy was older, and sensible, they might, at holiday time, be allowed to take the governess cart out by themselves with food for the day. They could go fishing or crag climbing, things Lucas had never done but dreamed of doing. They might even get as far as the sea. They could play tennis and battledore in the old tumbledown court; they could climb the sooty chestnuts and explore the old icehouse in the park— there seemed no end to the possibilities that might be achieved, with a real companion.

In the most secret corner of his mind, Lucas already had such a companion, an invented one. When he went out for his solitary trudge across Midnight Park to the town moor, when he munched his lonely meals, when he lay sleepless at night with the silence of the house around him, words inside his head automatically flowed into an accustomed pattern:

Once upon a time, Lucas and Greg started out for a walk. They had left their horses behind for once, because they were going to cross the dangerous quagmire known as Scroop Moss; in their knapsacks they carried a scanty but sufficient repast of bread, dried meat, and a handful of dates; their quest was to locate the huge and dreadful monster said to lurk at the bottom of Grydale Water. . . .

The features of Greg were as clear to Lucas in his mind's eye as those of Sir Randolph or Mr. Oakapple. Greg was tall, with dark hair and blue eyes; he was fifteen or sixteen, quick-minded, with a ready smile, fond of riding, reading, and swimming, better at some things than Lucas—algebra; knew more about wild birds and music, but didn't know so much French and couldn't draw so well. . . .

Of course it would be stupid to hope that the exact image of Greg would be waiting in the Oak Chamber. Lucas knew better than that, but still—And whatever he was like, almost certainly the poor fellow would want cheering up, Lucas thought, knocking gently on the door, remembering his own solitary and uncomforted days when he had first arrived at Midnight Court, the period of utter misery before even Mr. Oakapple had been brought in to instruct him.

I'll just go and introduce myself, he thought, simply say a friendly word or two, and then I'll leave him to sleep. He's possibly come a long way. I wonder where from?

He knocked at the chamber door. To his great surprise he heard Mrs. Gourd's voice rather tartly bidding whoever it was to come in and not make too much noise about it.

Lucas turned the handle and entered. The Oak Chamber was one of the few bedrooms in which any furniture was left. What remained was somewhat stiff and old-fashioned: a four-poster bed with thick dark hangings, an iron-bound chest, a carved oak grandfather clock, a high chair, a large old clothespress; the walls were covered by aged, worn tapestries over which Lucas had occasionally exercised his mind, if Pinhorn chanced to be in a good mood and let him in while she cleaned the room, but he had never decided to his own satisfaction if the embroidered scenes depicted Hannibal crossing the Alps or the Israelites crossing the Red Sea.

The Oak Chamber was looking slightly more cheerful than usual, due to the fact that a bright fire blazed on the hearth. In other respects the somewhat somber furnishings were unchanged. But an air of gay disorder was given by the quantity of clothes and belongings which were strewn about the room. Several boxes, uncorded, spilled their contents onto the carpet; traveling wraps hung over chairs; hairbrushes and shoes lay scattered at random; a bottle of rosewater, set down by the fireside, sparkled in the light of the flames; a canary in a half-covered cage let out a sudden, loud, sweet snatch of song.

"My gracious, Mester Lucas! What in the plague's name are *you* doing here at this time of night?" demanded Mrs. Gourd in a tone not much above a whisper. "I thought you were the maid with the warm milk, or I'd never have bidden you come in—"

"It's all right. I have leave from Sir Randolph," Lucas put in quickly. "Where is—"

"However, now you *are* here, I daresay it's for the best," Mrs. Gourd pursued without heeding him. "You can stay a moment while I go below stairs, for I forgot to ask Fanny to put a pinch of spice in the milk. Any road, you study the French lingo, don't you—wi' that tutor of yours?" she added cryptically as she made for the doorway and passed through it. She put her head back to say, "Bide till I come again—I'll not be long," and then vanished from view.

Lucas moved toward the fireplace, mystified by this reception, looking about him for the newcomer. At first he thought that no one else was in the room; then he perceived a shadowy shape on the bed, huddled among cast-off capes, shawls, and pelisses.

Who lay there? Was the person asleep? He waited silently by the fire, unwilling to disturb whoever it was, but also itching with the wish to speak, to start the new friendship. His problem was solved by a half-burnt log, which broke in the middle and fell on to the hearthstone with a sudden crackle and blaze. Lucas heard a movement from the bed, and a yawn that was half a sob, followed by a low cry: "Papa?"

Wholly taken aback by the sound of this voice, so completely different from what he had in his mind, Lucas nevertheless started a step or two in the direction of the bed. There, illumined by the blaze, he saw a child, a tiny girl, who looked—to his inexpert guess—not more than five or six years old, staring at him with huge black eyes. Her dark hair was cut in a straight line across her forehead, and dangled on either side of her small face in two untidy plaits; the traces of recent tears showed on her pale cheeks, and as she saw him, she began to cry again.

"Oh," she wept, "*you* aren't my papa. Go away, go away, I hate you! My papa is dead; he is dead! And Sidi fell off the boat, and I wish I was dead, too. Go away, hateful boy!"

Lucas had turned almost as white as the child on the bed; the shock of this reality, after his hopeful imaginings, had been very great. Who was this strange ghostly little creature? Where could she have come from? He stared down at her with a feeling of something like rage— wretched, useless little midget—who wanted her here? Could she really have been the company Sir Randolph had promised him? Was the whole thing a kind of hateful joke on his guardian's part?

But the little girl had thrown herself down on the floor and was crying so wildly, in such frantic hiccuping sobs, that Lucas felt a twinge of compunction mingled with his shock of disappointment. If Mrs. Gourd were to come back now, she would be sure to think that he had said something unkind to her and been the cause of this outburst.

"Come," he said curtly, "You can't lie there, get up! Stop crying so and get back on the bed. I'll move some of these things—"

He did so, and tried to lift her up, but she shook her shoulder out of his grasp and flung herself away from him with more abandonment, crying, "Papa—Papa! I don't want you—I don't want anybody but my papa!"

Only then did Lucas realize with total astonishment that she was speaking in French. But what amazed him even more was that, although she had spoken French, he had understood her. True, for the past ten months he had studied French for two hours every day with Mr. Oakapple, but the lessons had not seemed to add up to anything or make sense to him. Now, suddenly, he realized that French was a *real* language in which people spoke, and thought, and understood one another—and it also suddenly struck him that perhaps Mr. Oakapple might be quite a good teacher. But all this passed through his mind with great speed; meanwhile he was leaning over the child, and saying, in a tone that sounded more reasonable than he felt, "Don't lie there, you will get cold and make yourself ill. It is stupid to lie on the floor, it does no good. It is useless. *C'est inutile,*" he repeated, listening to himself in amazement. He was speaking French; and much more fluently than he ever had when conversing with Mr. Oakapple. With his tutor it had seemed like a silly game, since they could understand each other so much better in English.

What was even more remarkable, the little girl evidently understood him. She looked at him with dislike, indeed she put out her tongue at him, and said, "Why should I do what *you* say? You are only a great ugly boy!" But she allowed him at length to pick her up and put her back on the bed. There she sat and stared at him with hostility through her tears.

He looked longingly toward the door and wished that

Mrs. Gourd would reappear; he was dying to get away, back to his own room. But the silence drew on, and he could hear no footstep in the corridor.

"What is your name? And where do you come from?" he asked the child presently.

At first she looked as if she did not intend to answer. But at length she said, "*Je m'appelle* Anna-Marie Eulalie Murgatroyd." This last she pronounced very slowly and carefully, Mur-ga-troyd. "*Et je suis venue de Calais aujourd'hui.*"

"Is that where you have been living—Calais?"

She nodded. "I and papa at the house of old Madame Granchot. But"—her little face crumpled again in desolation—"papa is dead, and Madame is too old to look after me, and a lady brought me from Calais to here, and Sidi fell off the boat, and the man would not stop it to go back, oh, oh, oh, oh, oh—"

"Who is Sidi?" Lucas asked, hoping somehow to stem this new outburst.

"My cat—he is my cat. The boat frightened him, and he was strong—he got away from me—"

With a sudden pang, Lucas remembered his dog Turk, left behind in Amritsar last year.

"Have you come to live here? I daresay Sir Randolph would let you keep a cat—" He was not at all sure about this, but in any case the comfort failed to work.

"I do not want another cat, I want my Sidi!"

"Oh, don't be so silly," Lucas snapped, his patience evaporating. There is nothing so tiring as a person who cannot be comforted, and Lucas already found himself much more tired than usual. Too many things had happened.

Luckily at this moment Mrs. Gourd reappeared with a mug of hot milk. She clicked her tongue in disapproval at sight of the child's tears.

"It's not my fault—" Lucas began rather defensively.

"Oh, I daresay not. She's been going on like this all the time about her papa and some *Seedy* she keeps calling for, I don't know who Seedy is—"

"Her cat."

"Oh, is that it? *I* can't make head or tail of what she says. We'll have to get Mr. Oakapple to teach her English right off; she won't get far with that lingo living at Midnight Court. And not a bite of food have I been able to get down her since she set foot in the house. Come, miss, drink up your milk like a good girl. *Milk*," she repeated loudly and slowly, holding out the cup.

The child, who was evidently hungry after her nap, did finally begin to drink the milk, holding the cup in both hands, looking first at Mrs. Gourd, then suspiciously at Lucas over the rim.

"I'll be going then. Good night. *Bonne nuit*," said Lucas, seizing his chance to escape. Mrs. Gourd looked as if she had half a mind to ask him to stay on and interpret Anna-Marie's talk, but he had had quite enough. He slipped out and closed the door behind him.

Not until he was halfway to his own bedroom did the full blow of his loss and dissappointment strike home.

A portrait hung at the head of the back stairs which led up to the room where he slept. It was a picture of some bygone son of the house, a faded representation of a boy in Cavalier dress who stood smiling, holding up a falcon on his wrist. This boy, with his dark hair and laughing eyes, had, though Lucas hardly realized it, formed the model on which he had built his imaginary friend. Passing it now, he was suddenly stabbed by a sense of loss, a feeling that he had been cheated. The pain was so sharp that he involuntarily pressed his hand to his chest with a kind of sigh that was almost a groan. Hardly aware of what he did, instead of proceeding to his own room, he turned in the other direction, passed along a complicated series of landings, galleries, and corridors, and came at length to Mr. Oakapple's door.

A light showed underneath, and he knocked.

"Come in?" called the tutor's voice. He sounded surprised.

Lucas, pushing open the door, stopped short in almost equal surprise, forgetting the urgency of the impulse that had drawn him there.

The tutor lay half-reclined in an armchair, facing the door, with his feet on a stool; a violin rested on his left arm and shoulder, in the position for playing, and his right hand held the bow. But Lucas was certain that he had not been playing. No sound of music had been audible as Lucas approached the door.

"I—I didn't know you played the fiddle, sir?" Lucas blurted.

"I don't," Mr. Oakapple replied shortly, putting the instrument on a table with a somewhat hasty action, covering it with a velvet cloth.

"Are—are you learning?" Confusion made Lucas want to fill the silence.

"Don't be a fool," said the tutor with great ill humor. "How could I possibly play with two fingers missing?"

Only then, far too late, did Lucas recall the injured fingers which Mr. Oakapple invariably kept concealed by a leather glove. The tutor himself never alluded to his disability, but Bob the groom had told Lucas of a household rumor that it was the result of a duel, fought long ago when Mr. Oakapple was younger; now he was quite old—at least thirty-five.

"I—I ask your pardon, sir. I didn't think," he stammered, hot-faced.

"You never do think about other people, do you? Always shut up in your own world."

The tutor's tone was depressed, weary, not angry. To Lucas, staring abashed at his own feet, a novel thought came pricking through his depression: Was the somewhat chilly relationship between them his own fault, rather than Mr. Oakapple's? Would the tutor really prefer it if he, Lucas, tried to be more friendly?

"Anyway, it's of no importance," the tutor added dryly. "I used to play—once—that's all. But what brings you here? Why aren't you in bed?"—with a return to his usual severe manner—"Did you not see Sir Randolph?"

"Yes, sir, I saw him." A recollection of his grievances rushed back over Lucas, and momentarily forgetting this new light on his tutor, he exclaimed, "Was it you, sir, who told Sir Randolph I'd been complaining about being lonely?"

"Not exactly," Mr. Oakapple said coolly. 'I have certainly said to him that it might benefit your studies if you had a companion."

"Then was it your idea to bring that—that girl—that *child* who has just come? to be a companion for me?"

"Oh, Anna-Marie?" Mr. Oakapple began to laugh. "No, no, I am not quite such an optimist as to hope that *she* might encourage you in your work. Was that what Sir Randolph suggested? He likes his little joke."

"Who is she? Why has she come here?" Lucas demanded.

"Well, as you have begun learning the business at the Mill, I don't imagine there is any reason why you shouldn't hear the whole story," Mr. Oakapple replied, looking at Lucas thoughtfully. "And it might give you something to think about besides your own fancies. She is little Anna Murgatroyd, granddaughter of the original owner, Sir Quincy. But I suppose I had better make sure that Sir Randolph has no objection before I tell you about all that—he might prefer you to hear the history from him."

"Oh I'm sure he wouldn't," Lucas said hastily. "At least, I would much rather hear it from you."

"Well—you may be right. But at any rate, I had better

obtain his permission. And tonight is too late. Look at the time! Nearly one. Go to bed, and if Sir Randolph agrees I'll tell you about it tomorrow. Run along. You must be tired after the visit to the Mill.—and hungry. You missed your supper. Do you want a piece of pork pie?"

"Why—thank you, sir." Surprised, awkward, mumbling his thanks, Lucas took the solid heavy hunk of meat wrapped in pastry.

"I get them in the town. Old Gourd's cooking doesn't tempt me above half. Good night then."

With a nod, dismissing his pupil's stammered thanks, Mr. Oakapple almost pushed Lucas from the room.

Deep in thought, absently biting off chunks of meat as he walked, Lucas wandered back through the long bare stretches of passage until he reached the schoolroom.

So many things had happened to him since that afternoon—since he wrote his name and the words "I'm lonely" on the window—that he felt as if half a year had gone by, as if he were six months older than the boy who had looked out so hopelessly at the driving rain. He was still lonely, true, but his thoughts had taken a different turn. They were now reaching out in all directions; like the tendrils of Jack's beanstalk, they had found things to grasp and grow on.

He pulled his leatherbound book toward him, righted the fallen bottle of ink, found with relief that it still contained enough to write with, picked up his quill, and began:

Dear Greg: So many things have happened since I last wrote to you yesterday that I hardly know what to tell you first. But perhaps I'll start with the Mill. This afternoon Mr. Oakapple suddenly came into the schoolroom. . . .

He wrote on for almost an hour, until his hand was numb with cramp and the last of the ink was gone.

Then, closing the book, he went upstairs to his bedroom,

undressed, splashed his face and hands with cold water, climbed into his lumpy bed, and blew out the last of his candle stubs.

Faces, faces, faces, swam before his mind's eye—smiling Mr. Smallside, the mocking Scatcherd with his sidelong look, the haggard, tear-streaked face of Mrs. Braithwaite, rocking herself on the milestone. And the little girl, the snatcher, who had darted out so intrepidly as the press descended. And Sir Randolph peering with brandy-reddened eyes into his smoking cap. And that other sad waif, little Anna-Marie, with her pale cheeks and her great black eyes.

But all the time, behind all these faces, were the never-ceasing wheels, the relentless hammers and pistons of the Mill, and those were what he saw last, for a long, long time, before he finally slept.

LUCAS HAD HOPED to hear the story of Anna-Marie Murgatroyd from his tutor first thing next morning, before lessons began for the day. But he was only halfway through the basin of porridge with black treacle on it, which Pinhorn had brought for his breakfast, when she returned to say, "Missis Gourd asks if you'll be so good as to step along to the Oak Chamber, Mester Lucas. Seemingly, she's having a bit of trouble making herself understood wi' the little lass."

"Why doesn't she get Mr. Oakapple?" Lucas rather peevishly inquired, shoveling down his last three spoonfuls.

"Mr. Oakapple's not to hand; he's with Sir Randolph, reckon."

When Lucas arrived at the Oak Chamber, he saw that last night's scene of confusion had not greatly altered. The traveling gear had been tidied away, but the room was still littered with immense quantities of small garments— muslin chemises, petticoats, fichus, heaven knew what; the place looked as if a hurricane or snowstorm had blown through a forest of handkerchief trees. In the midst of this chaos, the small Anna-Marie sat like a white double hollyhock, in two petticoats and a cambric jacket, with a sulky, rebellious expression on her wan face and her mouth set in a mutinous line.

"I declare, I'm clean out of patience with whoever packed up for this child to send her to England," Mrs. Gourd exclaimed to Abby, the chambermaid, who was searching through a wicker hamper of thin white dresses, which seemed to be all different sizes. "Don't those French know what the weather's like over here? Not a frock in that lot would keep out the cold for ten minutes; there's a reet nip in the air today."

It was true. Yesterday's relentless rain had stopped in the night, and a sudden frost had transformed the view of the park, for once, to immaculate beauty; each blade of grass, each twig of the chestnut trees, shone outlined in dazzling brightness against a pure, pale sky. The air was crisp and icy.

"Look at yon!" In disgust the housekeeper held up a diaphanous gauze underskirt of pale pink. "What good's that to a body?"

Although it was evident that the child did not understand the exact meaning of her words, Mrs. Gourd's countenance was so expressive of disapproval as she held up the little garment that Anna-Marie indignantly snatched it from her and carefully smoothed out its folds.

"I—will—this," she announced slowly and emphatically. "This, and this!" She found a pink muslin dress and began taking off her jacket.

"*No*, miss!" The housekeeper was scandalized. "Why, you'd *clem* before you'd even set foot outside. Haven't you anything that's made of decent linsey-woolsey or alpaca or even merino? How do you say those words in French, Mester Lucas?"

Lucas had not the least idea. "Have you no thick woolen clothes?" he asked Anna-Marie.

She put out her tongue at him. "I will not *you*. Go away!" she informed him.

"Besides, the pink color's not fitting, even if it were warmer," Mrs. Gourd said to Abby in a low voice, removing the unsatisfactory pink dress from Anna-Marie, folding it, and returning it to a dressing basket.

Anna-Marie snatched it out again. It tore on the wicker edge of the basket, and she began to cry.

At that moment a bell started ringing elsewhere in the house.

"Dear! Servants' dinner—is it that time already?" exclaimed Mrs. Gourd. "I'll have to go—else the grooms'll be throwing bread pellets at the kitchenmaids—there's no one to keep them in order since Master turned off Mr. Flitch—you'd think *whoever* he dismissed he'd keep the butler. But I'm in a fair puzzle what to do about this child. We can't leave her in her shift all day."

"I've a notion," said Abby. "What about Madge Pickens, the undergardener's wife? Didn't she lose a little 'un at t'Mill a couple o' weeks since? She might still have some things put by."

"True for you. And she's a decent sort o' woman—her yoong ones were dressed none so badly. Roon down to her, Abby, and say I'd take it as a kindness, if she's any things yet, if she'd let us have them—they'd be the right color, any road," with a significant look. Abby nodded, and hurried off.

"Mester Lucas, do you please to bide here a few minutes, and I'll send back Miss Pinhorn with the little one's breakfast—she slept so late I didn't like to wake her before. I declare, things are all at sixes and sevens in the Court these days"—and Mrs. Gourd bustled off, shaking her head over her difficulties.

Finding that no one regarded her, Anna-Marie had stopped crying. With a resigned, business-like air, which impressed Lucas against his will, she inspected the torn dress, evidently decided that it could not be worn, so folded and carefully put it by.

Almost immediately the door opened, and a bent old man entered, carrying a tray of breakfast. Lucas was surprised to see him there; normally he was employed out of doors as a yard man and log carrier. It was believed that long ago he had been the butler, in old Sir Quincy's day, until he had taken to drink. His name was Gabriel Towzer.

He came in very slowly and carefully. From somewhere—Lucas could not imagine where—he had managed to find a number of silver dishes and had carefully arranged them on the tray; they were somewhat dented and battered, but lovingly polished until they shone like satin. There was a silver porringer, containing the same oatmeal-and-treacle mixture that had been served to Lucas, a silver mug of milk, a silver plate with slices of brown bread and butter, a withered apple in a silver fingerbowl, even a torn but clean napkin in a silver ring.

Gabriel's fingers were black with silver polish, and so was the front of his ancient baize apron.

"There!" he said proudly, setting down the tray. Then he came round to stand in front of Anna-Marie.

"Be you really little Missie Murgatroyd?"

He knelt down and put his hands on either side of her face—leaving black marks—and carefully tilted it up. "Yes!" he said after a long, grave scrutiny. "You've a look of the old man, owd Sir Quincy, an' a touch o' the young one, young Mas'r Denzil, too; ah! 'tis a comfort to have ye back among us, Missie, even if there was broke hearts as'll never be mended now."

"I don't understand," said Anna-Marie in French. "What is the matter with the old man?"

"She speaks no English," Lucas explained to old Mr. Towzer.

"Eh, my! That I should see the day when a grand-daughter of owd Sir Quincy couldn't pass the time o' day with Gabriel Towzer," the old man said mournfully.

"Say to him, 'How do you do,' " instructed Lucas. "That is the proper thing to say to a person in England when you first meet them."

"*Quoi?* I cannot say it." Anna-Marie seemed inclined to resent Lucas's suggestion, but then, on a sudden change of impulse, she turned to the old man and said, " 'Owdoo eeyu doo?"

"Spoken just like young Mas'r Denzil!" he said triumphantly. "Just like his own self! Now eat your breakfast, do, Missie, afore it gets cold."

"Bah! What is this lump of earth?" inquired Anna-

Marie, inspecting the porridge. "It looks like stuff they mend holes with. I cannot eat it."

"Try it. It's not so bad," Lucas advised. "You might as well. You won't get anything else."

"Be quiet, you!" She turned on him in a sudden flash of fury. "I do not need you to order me. You do not like me, I know, and I do not at all like you. Go away! You are a great ugly boy, of no use at all, and I do not want you in my room."

Fortunately at that moment Mrs. Gourd returned, so Lucas was able to take his departure.

What a spoiled brat, was his main conclusion about Anna-Marie, apart from the continuing bitter regret that she was not older, that she was not a boy, that she was so hopelessly unsuited to be his friend or companion. Anyway a few days in Midnight Court would soon knock the vapors out of the self-willed little thing. Pampered and coddled all her life, no doubt. Well, no one would pay much regard to her whimsies here; she'd have to learn to stand on her own feet.

He dismissed her from his mind.

Bounding along the corridor, he cleared the back stairs in a couple of leaps and entered his schoolroom.

Mr. Oakapple had arrived already and stood at the window, with his back to the dull room, staring out. Beyond him, a greenish-white frosty sweep of landscape went smoothly up to meet the luminous pale early-morning sky.

"Right: to work then," said Mr. Oakapple, turning with a sigh when he heard the click of the door.

"I—I'm sorry I'm late, sir. Mrs. Gourd wanted me—"

The tutor accepted Lucas's excuse with a nod and gestured him toward the desk. "Simple and compound interest. Followed by quadratic equations. Then principle parts of Latin verbs."

"Oh, but sir—"

"Well?"

"You did say you'd tell me about Anna-Marie."

After the words had left him, Lucas had a sudden feeling of—what was it, a kind of guilt? As if he were stealing a mean march on the child, whom he did not even like, by employing her as a pretext to get off lessons for half an hour. But why should he feel guilty? He had been as friendly to her as he could. It was she who had been rude and hostile. Anyway there was no reason why he should not ask about her history; what harm could that do?

"Oh, very well. Sir Randolph didn't seem to have any objection to my telling you the history of how he came to own the factory; in fact he was surprised you didn't know it already," Mr. Oakapple conceded. (In fact, Sir Randolph, gray-faced and red-eyed after a long night spent drinking brandy, had growled, "Tell the boy what you please, and the two of you can spend the day at Jericho for all I care!")

"How did he come to own it, then?"

Lucas did not quite see how the history of the factory could be connected with that of Anna-Marie, but anything was preferable to a morning of compound interest and Latin principle parts.

"Can't we go into the park while you tell me?" he suggested with a flash of inspiration, as Mr. Oakapple turned regretfully from the view. "Just for a few minutes? It's such a fine morning. And there aren't many."

This was true. For two hundred and fifty days out of three hundred and sixty-five, according to local lore, cloud or fog hung low over Blastburn, Grimside, Midnight Park, and Grydale Moor. And during his year of residence there, Lucas had seen no reason to doubt the theory. Today was a rare and beautiful change.

"As you wish!" Surprised but not unwilling, the tutor put on his hat while Lucas quickly found a jacket, and the two of them went out into air like iced nectar. They walked

over the crisp grass, leaving a trail of black footprints behind them as they crossed the gentle saucer of land which
encircled Midnight Court. From the top of the ridge they
could look west, back at the house whose gables were just
beginning to catch the first rays of the rising sun, or east,
into the smoke-filled valley where the city of Blastburn lay
wrapped in the foggy reek from its chimneys.

Lucas had asked no questions while they walked, content
to enjoy the clear morning, sniff the keen air, feel the
frosted grass crunch under his feet, and make the most of
this unusual respite from lessons. He felt, too, an unaccustomed sympathy toward Mr. Oakapple—unspoken but
somehow comfortable.

When they stood at the park's highest point, the tutor
began of his own accord: "As you probably know, some
twenty years ago, when your guardian was younger, he belonged to an extremely dashing and notorious sporting
club known as the Devil's Roustabouts."

The tutor's measured manner held neither admiration
or disapproval.

"What sort of things did they do?"

Lucas had not known this; indeed, he had never heard
of the Devil's Roustabouts.

"Oh—they used to give very wild parties, wager large
sums of money on anything from horse races to whether
the king would take coffee or tea with his breakfast next
day, and they fought duels on the slightest provocation."

Lucas longed to ask Mr. Oakapple if it was true that he,
too, had fought a duel, but did not like to interrupt.

"One of your guardian's greatest friends at that time was
a very much younger man, Denzil Murgatroyd, whose father, Sir Quincy, was the owner of this house, not to mention a great deal of land on which coal had been found
and mined, making him one of the richest men in England.

"Denzil Murgatroyd had not been trained for any profession, but was considered very brilliant, even as a lad; while still at college he constructed a scientific instrument for measuring the depth of potholes; he had discovered several new stars, had a beautiful singing voice, and had composed an opera which was performed before the king. Also, he had devised the carpet-manufacturing process which brought Sir Quincy Murgatroyd's mill to the forefront of the industry and greatly enlarged the family fortune."

"What happened then?"

"Denzil Murgatroyd was only twenty when he left college. He met your guardian—who, as I have said, was a much older man, about forty then—made fast friends with him, abandoned all his scientific pursuits, and led a life devoted to sport, betting, gambling, and doing his best to shock all the more respectable part of society. The two friends were inseparable, outvying each other in their wild escapades. It was your guardian who smuggled an alligator into the House of Lords; Denzil Murgatroyd had himself flown up on a kite to the cross at the top of St Paul's, and attached a small carpet there; Sir Randolph introduced ten Glasgow sailors into the Court of St. James's as the Bey of Tunis and his suite, and had them entertained at the palace for a week before the imposture was discovered, for no one could understand a word they said; Denzil hired a gang of workmen to remove the Monument to the Fire of London from its place and lay it across the Derby racecourse just before the race was due to be run; however I will not weary you with further tales of their goings-on. Besides, it might put ideas into your head."

Lucas would very much have liked to hear more, but the tutor sounded so disapproving that he did not suggest it and asked instead, "What happened about the factory?"

"Denzil's father, old Sir Quincy, violently objected to his

son's friendship with your guardian, and to his association with the Devil's Roustabouts. He wanted Denzil to live at home and pay attention to the family business. Several times he threatened to disinherit Denzil if he did not break off the connection." Mr. Oakapple sighed.

"But he didn't?" Lucas inquired.

"No. Young Denzil was, in fact, very fond of his father, but he was a wayward, reckless, spirited youth who could not bear to be coerced. After some months, though, he did promise to give up his membership of the club, since he was in love with a beautiful young lady, Miss Eleanora Featherstonehuff, and she refused to become engaged to him unless he did so. But he had made arrangements to attend one last meeting of the society."

"And so?"

"Denzil went to the meeting. It was held on midsummer night, in the ruins of Bellemont Priory, not far from here."

"What happened?"

"It was a very fancy affair. All twenty members of the Devil's Roustabouts turned up for it; immense quantities of wine, champagne, and brandy were consumed; they had a whole orchestra playing, and dancing—and so forth." Mr. Oakapple's tone of disapproval deepened.

"I wonder what sort of food they ate?" Lucas said dreamily.

"They had a fire and roasted an ox, among other things. One of the delicacies provided was a particular kind of ginger pie, made in the village of Clutterby-le-Scroop. This pie, when taken together with wine or spirits, greatly intensifies the effect of the alcohol. The pie prepared for the party measured twenty feet across and had been specially baked in a grain hopper. All the club members had large helpings of it. They became extremely drunk."

"And?"

"A good many of them had been making fun of Denzil Murgatroyd, twitting him with the fact that he had been forced to promise to leave the club. Goaded by their taunts, and particularly by those of Sir Randolph Grimsby, he entered into a last wild wager."

"What was it?"

"Sir Randolph had been particularly free with his mockery all through the evening. And when the pie was served, he called out, 'Hey, young Denny, hey, Stargazer! Since you're so fond of your old man, don't you want to trot home and take him a helping of Clutterby Pie? It wouldn't take you very long!' At this young Denzil, who had drunk much more than was sensible, became enraged beyond bearing and shouted back, 'If I did so, I'll wager I could do it faster than you could!' 'Done!' shouted Sir Randolph. And so the bet was on."

"What did they do?"

"There are two roads from Bellemont to Midnight Park; you can go through Canby Moorside or through Mucky-under-Edge—both ways are exactly the same distance. Sir Randolph was to ride by Canby, and Denzil by Mucky: each was to carry a piece of the pie weighing a measured ten pounds, to enter Midnight Court, ascend to Sir Quincy's bedroom, leave the pie on his bedside table, and return to the gathering at the Priory. The first to return was the winner."

"What was the amount of the bet?"

"Denzil had suggested a thousand pounds, but Sir Randolph, cool as a cucumber, called out, 'Pooh! Why deal in trifles? I'll wager all that I have.' Several club members privately shrugged their shoulders at this, since it was generally known that Sir Randolph hardly had two brass farthings to rub together at the time; however Denzil, who was hardly better off since he lived on an allowance from his father which he had always spent even before it came in, shouted, 'As you wish!' So they mounted their horses and rode off in different directions."

"Who got back first?"

"Nobody had reckoned on seeing either of them again within about an hour and a half. So there was general amazement when Sir Randolph returned, his Arab mare fresh, hardly sweating, in less than sixty-five minutes; another forty minutes elapsed before Denzil galloped back, his horse heaving, badly winded, and frothing at the mouth. It was later learned that his father had woken up when he entered the bedroom and there had been a violent, angry scene from which Denzil had stormed out and ridden away at top speed, but too late to win his wager. In any case, he had found Sir Randolph's piece of pie already there on the bedside table when he arrived."

"What happened then?"

"Sir Randolph was waiting in the center of the circle, in the moonlit Priory ruins, when Denzil rode in on his exhausted, gasping horse. Sir Randolph looked the pair over calmly and said, 'You need to get a better nag, Denny.' Denzil jumped down, flung over the reins, and said, 'Take him, he's yours.' He stripped off his clothes, threw them over, too, and borrowed a shirt and a pair of breeches from one of the musicians; they were all rigged out in fancy dress as spooks and specters, so they had their daytime clothes with them."

"Good heavens," said Lucas, imagining the scene: the moonlit ruins; the fire, the circle of half-drunk, mocking men, the two in the center, the audience of ghosts. "Then what did Denzil do?"

"He walked off into the dark. The party went on for a while longer, but it broke up fairly soon. The musicians were paid off. Local people collected the remains of the food next day. And next day also it was heard that Sir Quincy had died in his bed of a seizure not five minutes after his son had left him—of rage, it was thought. So Sir Randolph, through his lawyers, sent a formal message to the effect that, since Denzil had inherited the estate the minute his father died, the house and the land, like his horse and clothes, were forfeit to the winner of the wager."

"My goodness. The whole estate? That would mean the Mill, too, everything?"

"The Mill, the house, the land, the coal mines, every-thing. It was said by many people, fairly openly, that Sir Randolph must have found some means of cheating. But it could not be proved. He had been seen to ride through Canby, and back again; the pie was there, in Sir Quincy's room."

"Did Denzil say he had cheated?"

"He said nothing at all. Sir Randolph, getting wind of what people were saying, became very angry; said he'd not be called a cheat without getting satisfaction, and chal-lenged Sir Denzil, as he had become on his father's death, to a duel. But Sir Denzil refused."

"Refused a duel? Wasn't that rather a cowardly thing to do?"

"In those days it was thought shocking, yes. They had met in Midnight Park for Sir Denzil to hand over the title deeds of the estate. Sir Randolph accused Denzil of having spread slanderous stories, and challenged him. But he replied, 'My dear Grimsby, I have not said you cheated. For all I care, you borrowed the Devil's mare; I think it quite probable. I am not interested in how you achieved your end. And I have no intention of fighting you; the cause is not worth five minutes of my time. Here is your slice of Clutterby Pie; I hope you enjoy it.' Sir Denzil then walked away, said good-bye to his mother, Lady Murga-troyd, got into a borrowed carriage, went to Dover, and from there to France. The fishing boat in which he crossed was wrecked in a storm, and he was thought to have been drowned, but this was a false rumor as it turned out. A message was recently received, simply addressed to Murgatroyd House, Blastburn, England, to say that he had been living in France, but had died, and his little daughter was left destitute."

"I wonder how he lived?"

"Taught music, I believe. And English," said Mr. Oakapple, shrugging. "Apparently he died in very reduced circumstances. But enough money was collected to send his child to England, where it was thought she might have relatives."

Questions were struggling together in Lucas's mind like sheep at a gate. "Then Anna-Marie—is she the daughter of the beautiful young lady—Miss Eleanor Thingummy?"

"Featherstonehuff? No, *she* called off the engagement as soon as she heard of the wager, and of Sir Quincy's death. I believe that in the end Sir Denzil married a French girl, who died when the child was born. But that cannot have been until many years later."

"And Sir Randolph came to live at Midnight Court?"

"He came to live at Midnight Court. Many of the old servants left. A few stayed. But in society the suggestion that he had somehow managed to win the estate by underhand means became more and more widely circulated. Sir Randolph was invited nowhere; people began cutting him in the streets of London. Neighbors refused to meet him. It soured his nature as you have seen. He shut himself up here, took in a partner to manage the Mill—your father— and spent his days in playing solitaire and drinking brandy. For twenty years he has hardly set foot outside the park."

No wonder he isn't very pleased to have little Anna-Marie Murgatroyd in the place, Lucas thought. Even suppose he did not cheat in the wager, he must feel fairly mean at living in the place that would have come to her.

"Perhaps he was ashamed of the way he won Midnight Court," Lucas said, half to himself.

"Oh, wagers of that kind were perfectly respectable then, "Mr. Oakapple assured him. "Larger fortunes changed hands over the card table every day."

A new thought occurred to Lucas. "Mr. Oakapple—how do *you* come to know so much about it? The Roustabouts' party—you told the story almost as if you had been there."

"I *was* there." Mr. Oakapple brought his pale eyes back from the horizon and turned them on Lucas. "I was a fiddler. When I was quite young—five or six—my parents found I had a great gift for violin playing, so I was sent to a choir school in York where there was very good tuition; my father was the rector in Sutton Grimsdale. We were very hard up; by the time I was nine or ten I was earning quite a bit of extra cash playing my fiddle at balls and parties. So I was at Bellemont on the night of the party."

"You know all about it." Lucas wished he had the courage to ask about the accident—or duel—that had brought an end to Mr. Oakapple's playing, and whether that too had any connection with the story of Denzil Murgatroyd. But a set, bleak expression had come over the tutor's face as he remembered those old times, and Lucas knew that he did not have the courage.

"I wonder if Anna-Marie knows all this?"

"Very likely not," Mr. Oakapple said indifferently. "On the whole, if she does not, it would be best for her to continue in ignorance."

"Yes, it might," Lucas began, thinking that Anna-Marie would not be one to take matters calmly if she believed that somebody had deprived her of her rightful property by unfair means. Then he broke off, "Look, isn't that her?"

They looked back toward the house.

By daylight Midnight Court was visible as a big, light-gray mass, built of Grimshead Moor stone, which neither storm nor rain could darken; the fiercest gale only bleached its pale smooth surface so that, from a distance, the house appeared to be covered by the same frosty coating that whitened the park. But the roof looked ruinous, with many tiles awry, and most of the windows gaped black and broken.

Now from this large pale mass a small black object emerged, and came slowly toward them.

"Poor child—it will be strange for her here," Mr. Oakapple muttered, and started toward her, with Lucas following him more slowly. But they had not gone more than half the distance between them and the black-clad Anna-Marie when the figure of Mrs. Gourd appeared, red-faced and flustered, in the doorway from which the child had issued, and came hurrying after her.

They heard the housekeeper's voice calling: "Miss! Miss! Come back here directly! You are not to go off by yourself!" Anna-Marie ignored the summons and walked on determinedly.

"Miss! You are to come back here at once."

Then Mrs. Gourd perceived Mr. Oakapple and Lucas. Her face cleared. "Oh, Mr. Oakapple! I was just searching for you when this little madam wandered off. You are wanted in master's study. The gentleman from the tax office is here again, and Sir Randolph isn't himself. He won't answer the gentleman's questions, and he threw an inkpot. Could you come?"

"Oh—very well." Mr. Oakapple showed no relish for the interview. He muttered what sounded like a bad word under his breath, and then turned to Lucas. "You may be excused lessons for the rest of the morning. You had—you had best show Anna-Marie over the place and find something to amuse her."

"Aye, that's a good notion." The housekeeper plainly approved of this proposal which would relieve her of her difficult charge. "You'll keep a good eye on her, won't you, Mester Lucas? Such a mardy little one!" Lucas heard her say to the tutor in an undertone as they turned back toward the house. "There is no doing anything with her. Willful! And obstinate! Let alone she doosn't speak a word o' the King's English."

Lucas gazed in dismay at the responsibility that had been thrust on him. Anna-Marie returned his stare with her underlip thrust out. Then she hunched her shoulders, turned away, and walked as fast as she could toward the top of the slope. She could not go very fast because of her clothes. Somebody had found her an outfit of black—black hat, black dress, black petticoat, black stockings—But everything was too big. The hat kept slipping down over her eyes. The petticoat dangled below the dress, and the coat flapped round her calves, hindering her progress. The stockings, much too loose, kept sliding down, and at every few steps she had to stop and impatiently haul them up. It was not hard for Lucas to overtake her. But when he did so she pushed him off with a furious little black-gloved fist, shouting, "Away! Go away! I do not want you at all."

"You have got to have me," said Lucas crossly. He saw that her pale face under the wide black brim of the hat was streaked again with tears. "Either me or Mrs. Gourd."

"*Hein?* That woman? I do not like her. She smells of sneeze."

"Of *what?*"

"Sneeze," she repeated impatiently in French. "When one goes *attishoo!*"

Utterly baffled by this, Lucas walked beside her, frowning.

"Where do you think you are going?" he asked.

"I am going away. I do not wish to stay here. I do not like it."

"How can you go away? Who will look after you?"

"I will go back to Calais, and Madame will look after me."

"But you cannot. You have no money. How can you go on the boat?"

"Oh, be quiet! I do not wish to talk to you."

She pulled a small china doll out of the large pocket of her oversize coat and walked doggedly on, cradling it in her arms. Lucas perforce accompanied her; she was too big to pick up and carry back, and he was reluctant to drag her by the hand against her will. So they went on unwillingly together. And Lucas suddenly thought, If Anna-Marie's father had not made that rash bet, he would still be living here now, and Anna-Marie would have been born here; this place would be her home. Maybe she would have brothers and sisters to play with. Sir Randolph would not be here. *I* would not be here. How queer it seemed that a dozen words, spoken in a temper, could travel so far, like a tidal wave or an earthquake, could alter the lives of people in distant countries, people who were not even born at the time when the words were spoken.

"How old are you, Anna-Marie?" he asked presently, in a more friendly tone.

"*J'ai huit ans.*"

"Eight! You don't look as old as that."

"I am small," she said with dignity. "My mother was like this also, they say. There is nothing wrong with being small."

"Of course not."

"Napoleon was so. And he was a great man. He beat the English in many battles."

"They beat him in the end, though," Lucas put in without thinking.

She turned around and faced him, her eyes flashing, her face red with fury. "Will you go away from me! I did not ask you to follow. I do not want you with me."

"Oh, don't be so stupid," he said irritably. "You are too small to be out on your own."

"I am not too small!" she shouted in a passion, stamped her foot, tripped over a protruding wedge of rock in the hummocky ground, and fell in a tangle of black cloth. Her hat came off and rolled down the slope. Shrugging, Lucas went after it.

When he came back, he found that Anna-Marie had made no effort to get up, but was lying as she had fallen, crying bitterly, with her face pressed into a tussock of brown, frost-covered grass. Half of the doll was clutched against her heaving chest. The legs, broken into three bits, lay separately.

Oh, dear, Lucas thought. It wanted only that. Now what do we do? He sat down beside her and said nothing, because he could think of nothing to say.

Anna-Marie went on crying. After some time her sobs died down to a gulp every other minute. Then the spaces between became longer. Finally she was silent; the heaving of her shoulders stopped. She lay so still that Lucas began to fear she might have fallen asleep.

"Hey, Anna-Marie!" he said anxiously, at length. "You can't go to sleep out here. It's too cold. You'll freeze."

"I do not care," she said in a muffled way through the tussock. "Then I will go to heaven and see Papa and play on a trumpet, with the angels."

"Oh, don't be silly!" he snapped. "You can't lie there till you die! Come on. I'm sorry your doll broke. We'll go back to the house and find Garridge in the stables and ask him for some—some jelly"—he could not think of the French word for glue—"and perhaps we'll be able to mend it."

"Her, not it! And you do not mend things with jam, stupid."

But she sat up, exhibiting an earthy, tear-stained face. Lucas drew out his handkerchief and wiped her cheeks, none too gently; she pulled away from his grasp, sniffing, and picked up the broken bits of the doll's legs. Her lip quivered again and a great sigh shook her from head to feet, but she had cried all the tears that were in her just then.

"Right," said Lucas. "Come on."

"I do not wish to come." She stood stubbornly still.

"Oh, for heaven's *sake!*" He looked around him in despair at the frozen, empty park, at the distant silent house. The sky had clouded over to its customary leaden gray. A cold wind was beginning to numb his face and fingers. They seemed to have been out a terribly long time. "Listen, as we go along I'll tell you a story about Greg." He took her hand, giving it a gentle tug.

"Who is Greg?" She came after him with slow, reluctant steps.

"Greg is a boy who rides on a big black horse called Sultan. And he has a lot of adventures. I'll tell you about how he fought a dragon."

"I do not wish to hear. I do not like boys," Anna-Marie said ungratefully. "Tell about a *girl* who has adventures."

"Girls don't have adventures."

"Yes they do! Just as much as boys."

"Girls stay at home and do sewing," Lucas began to say, but suddenly, out of nowhere, there flashed into his mind the image of the little snatcher, yesterday, at the Mill, dashing out under the huge descending press to gather up the fragment of cotton waste in her metal tongs. And another, stranger thought struck him: if Anna-Marie's father had not made that wild bet, then this child here beside him would own that carpet factory and be the employer of all the people in it, including the snatcher.

"Tell a story about a girl," Anna-Marie repeated, standing still and pulling back on the hand that clasped hers. "I will not come unless you do."

"Oh, all right. Once upon a time there was—*il était une fois une jeune fille*—a girl who was a snatcher."

He used the English word because he did not know what the French would be, and Anna-Marie asked at once, "What is that?"

"She worked in a factory." Lucas was proud that he remembered the word *usine*. "A big house where they make carpets."

"What was it like?"

As well as he could, with many gestures, Lucas described the Mill: its great machines, its noise, confusion, blackness, smoke, whirring wheels, heat, danger, and muddle.

"So what did the girl do there? What was her name?"

"Let's think. Her name was Mary," he said, using his mother's name, which was the first that occurred to him.

"No it was not, it was Michelle."

"If you wish. Every day Michelle stood on the steps waiting to pick up any bits of cotton that might have been left on the carpet. Or dirt."

"Well? And what happened?" Anna-Marie said impatiently as Lucas paused.

He racked his brain. What *did* happen?

"She used to bring her dinner to work every day in a red cotton handkerchief," he said, improvising, marking time.

"What did she have for her dinner?"

"Brown bread and cold bacon."

"And cherries."

"Very well. Then one day," said Lucas, the wheels of the story suddenly beginning to turn in his mind as he remembered the scene in the Oak Chamber last night—"I had forgotten to tell you that this girl called Michelle had a pet bird in a cage, a yellow bird—"

"*Un canari*—like the one Madame gave me—"

"*Oui, un canari*—and this canary was very fond of cherries, and one day when Michelle was getting her dinner ready, the canary saw her putting the cherries into her bundle, and it pulled and pulled with its claws at the door of the cage, and at last pulled it quite open, and flew after Michelle all the way down the street and in at the gate of the factory where she worked, and it came to perch on her shoulder just as she was waiting in the pressing room. And when she ran out under the press to pick up a piece of cotton, the bird flew after her."

"*Ciel!*" Anna-Marie grabbed hold of Lucas's arm with both hands in fright. "What happened then?"

"Oh—" Inspiration had left him again. "Then Michelle's fairy godmother looked down and saw what was happening—"

"*No,* she did not, idiot! There is not such a thing as a fairy godmother."

"This is *my* story that I am making up, and if I want to put a fairy godmother in it, I shall have one."

"Then I shall not listen." She pulled her hand out of his and stuck her fingers in her ears. "Fairy godmothers are nothing but stupidness and make-believe. If there was such a thing as a fairy godmother, mine would come and take me away from here. What *really* happened to Michelle's bird?"

It was on the tip of his tongue to say, "The press came down and squashed it flat," but her hopeful expression, like that of the bird itself, looking up for crumbs, pricked his conscience. He glanced around him for a new idea.

They had been wandering, not toward the house, but rather away from it, and had reached the corner of the park nearest to the town. Here a belt of trees screened the high stone wall from view, and a little round, artificial hill rose in front of the trees. On top of the hillock a miniature thorn tree had been planted, and by its roots lay a couple of boulders, poised near the edge of a dark, crevice-like opening in the side of the mound.

"The carpet factory where Michelle worked," Lucas continued, strolling on past the little hill, "was at the foot of an enormously high mountain, so high that its top was almost always covered in cloud."

They passed the cleft in the hillside, which, as Lucas knew, contained a door. But he had never been inside.

"The cherry tree from which Michelle picked her cherries grew on top of this high mountain."

"*Eh bien?*"

"Well, that morning when she picked her cherries, Michelle had kicked a small stone. And it slowly rolled nearer and nearer to the top of a cliff down the side of the mountain, until at last it lay right on the edge of the cliff. And presently the wind blew hard, and the stone fell off the edge of the cliff. It fell to the bottom and started a whole lot of other stones rolling, and they all went roaring down the side of the mountain."

"*Une avalanche, alors! Et puis?*"

"The avalanche roared down to where the factory was."

"And knocked it down?"

"Well, not quite," said Lucas. "But the stones fell into the machinery and stopped it. So the press stuck halfway down, and Michelle's canary was safe."

"And it flew back to her shoulder, and she gave it a cherry out of her red bundle," said Anna-Marie with satisfaction. "I think I will let *my* canary go free. It makes me sad to see it in a cage."

Lucas opened his mouth to say, No, you should not do that; it will die of cold or be caught by a hawk. But then he decided to wait. Perhaps she would forget this impulse. And in the meantime she was looking more cheerful, swinging on his hand, from time to time trying to take little skipping steps; there was no sense in upsetting her over a trifle.

They walked round to the side of the house and entered

the stableyard, for Lucas thought Anna-Marie might like to see what horses were left.

Garridge was there, setting Noddy between the shafts of the governess cart. As they approached him, Mr. Oakapple came out of the house. He was carrying a large bundle of papers and wore a harassed expression.

"There you are," he said to Lucas. "I have to go down into Blastburn to take this note to the tax office. You might as well ride in with me and pay your second visit to the Mill; then I will pick you up on my way back."

"*Et moi?*" said Anna-Marie. "What is to happen to me?"

"Garridge will take you indoors to Mrs. Gourd," Mr. Oakapple said to her in French.

"I will not go with that man," Anna-Marie said loftily. "He smells of dirty straw and besides I do not like his face. I will come with you."

"Certainly not. The place where we are going is not at all suitable for you," Mr. Oakapple said hastily, but without conviction.

Lucas could see that Anna-Marie was going to get her way, and in fact she did, by stubbornly refusing to go into the house, and finally by simply climbing into the governess cart and sitting there, defying anyone to remove her.

"She'd best have a comforter," said Garridge, who had watched this scene in silence with a sardonic expression. And he fetched out a musty-smelling carriage rug and wrapped it round Anna-Marie, muttering, "Proper chip off the owd block *you* be; a'body can see that."

"*Qu'est-ce qu'il dit?*" asked Anna-Marie as they drove away.

"He says that you resemble your father, who lived in this house when he was a boy."

Mr. Oakapple sighed, glancing at Anna-Marie as if he wondered whether she had inherited her father's abilities along with his willful disposition.

Over in the distance to their right lay the little hillock with the thorn tree on top and the opening in the side.

Anna-Marie glanced at it as they passed it again, and inquired, "Is that a cave? Who lives in it?"

"A witch—" Lucas was beginning, but Mr. Oakapple interrupted him with a frown. "What nonsense. Don't let me hear you frighten the child with such tales."

"But Bob the groom always used to say so. An old woman who only came out in the dusk—"

"Then Bob the groom talked a lot of rubbish and I am glad that he is no longer here. That cave was once an ice-house," Mr. Oakapple told Anna-Marie. "It is not a real cave, but was built by your grandfather."

Lucas kept silent, deciding not to say that once or twice in the twilight he personally had seen what, in the distance, looked like the figure of an old woman dressed in gray slipping into the cave. What could she possibly be but a witch? However he was sure that Mr. Oakapple would dismiss this as mere invention, and unsuitable for Anna-Marie's ears at that.

"What is an icehouse?" Anna-Marie was asking.

"When your grandfather was young he used to have big parties, and all the visitors would drink wine and eat ice pudding. In the winter, when the lake on the other side of the park froze solid, your grandfather used to send men with axes and carts to chop out the ice and pack it away in that cave. Then it would stay frozen all through the summer."

"And they could come whenever they liked and take some to put round their pudding."

"I suppose so," said Mr. Oakapple. "I'm not quite sure how you make ice pudding."

"*I* am sure. You take eggs and cream and sugar and lemon and beat all together and put the basin in a bowl of ice, and you beat it and beat it and beat it. Madame Hortense who keeps the Auberge du Cheval Blanc has often shown me," Anna-Marie said triumphantly.

"Er—very likely." The tutor seemed a little taken aback. "Now here we are at the Mill. I'll leave you two with Mr. Smallside and drive back to collect you in an hour or so."

"Can't Anna-Marie go with you?" Lucas murmured in an undertone, but Mr. Oakapple shook his head.

"It would be out of the question to take her into the tax inspector's office."

Lucas felt that it would be equally out of the question to take Anna-Marie over the factory. It had been bad enough going round with Mr. Oakapple, meeting the hostile, curious, or sneering glances of the workers, trying to ignore the veiled mockery of Scatcherd, but with the small Anna-Marie it would be far worse. He would be reduced to her status, made to look like a child.

However he was given no choice; Mr. Oakapple pulled up by the door of Smallside's office, lifted Anna-Marie down, waited briefly for Lucas to alight, then whipped up the mare and drove off.

The moment that Lucas set foot inside Mr. Smallside's little office he felt again the prickling sensation of approaching trouble that had visited him so often, and with so little cause, it seemed, during the last few days. And yet he could hardly have said what caused the feeling. Mr. Smallside was talking in a low voice to a big black-haired man at the other end of the room; the two men's heads were bent close together.

"If it should come to a strike, whom can you trust?" Lucas heard Smallside demand softly. His pale soapy face wore an even yellower tinge than it had on the previous day.

"Noakes and Goadby are staunch," the big man returned in the same tone. "But I'd not trust Bludward farther than I could push him in that chair o' his."

"You are certain of those two?"

"I'll go bail for 'em."

"Then tell them to keep by the big gates, ready to shoot the bolts, the very minute the last of this shift's out. There's a feeling around the works I don't like; mischief's afoot, or my name's not Bertram Smallside. I've sent for the dragoons, but dear knows how long it'll take 'em to come"

"A strike's not the only form that mischief can take."

Both men looked over their shoulders, nervously, at this, and then for the first time Smallside caught sight of Lucas and Anna-Marie. With considerable difficulty he creased his face into the ingratiating smile that Lucas had found so annoying the day before.

"What a surprise!" he said with false heartiness. "Young Master Bell and a young lady. Just fancy that, now!"

"I've come for my lesson," Lucas said stiffly. He felt foolish at having to say this, particularly since Mr. Smallside quite plainly had not been expecting him at all, and seemed decidedly put out by his arrival.

"Indeed? Is that so? Well, now, can you imagine it?" Smallside spoke at random, quite mechanically, as if his mind were not at all concentrated on Lucas, but were occupied with something else entirely.

The black-haired man addressed a question to him, in a voice too low to be heard.

"Young Master Lucas Bell from up at the Court," Smallside replied. Lucas might not have heard this if he had not caught his own name. The other man looked extremely startled, and made a gesture as if he were shutting a door.

"Unfortunately," Mr. Smallside went on smoothly, addressing Lucas as if he had never stopped speaking, "most unfortunately it won't be convenient for you to be puttering around here today, Master Bell. For one thing the young fellow, Scatcherd, you see, is not available."

"Perhaps somebody else—"

"And—and other reasons make it just not a suitable time for young ladies and gentlemen to come sight-seeing. Another day, perhaps."

Lucas felt very annoyed with Mr. Smallside, who seemed to be behaving as if a visit to the Mill were a handsome treat, which he might or might not kindly allow Lucas, instead of the professional instruction it was supposed to be.

"I'm afraid it's not convenient for us to leave just now," he said rather shortly.

"Young gentlemen and ladies have to learn that sometimes their convenience is not the most important thing in the world," Mr. Smallside said, always smiling.

"Who is that man? What does he say?" Anna-Marie demanded. She was becoming bored with standing in the office doorway and was looking about her impatiently.

Both men looked a good deal surprised at hearing her speak French.

"Is the young lady a foreign young lady then?" asked Mr. Smallside.

"Eye amm Mees Anna-Marie Murgatroyd," said Anna-Marie with her usual dignity.

"Murgatroyd!" The black-haired man opened his eyes wide at this name. "Will she be soom kin to owd Sir Quincy, then? I thowt there was noan o' that stock left."

"She is his granddaughter. She has lived in France all her life," Lucas said.

"And now she's come to live up at the Court?" Smallside inquired. Lucas nodded.

"If the hands knew about Sir Randolph taking the lass in, think on—" the black-haired man began dubiously.

"Nay, it's many a long year since Sir Quincy died. Tha cannot put back the clock," Smallside said. "—Let alone Sir Quincy himself was a bad enough master, by the end. —The men are in a flaysome mood; mere sight of a child's face will not change them." His manner, for once, was neither hectoring nor obsequious, but merely weary and practical, and his accent was much broader than it had been. "This is no place for childer, my young master and miss; you must joost gang off, the best road you can. That's all there is to it."

He made shooing movements with his hands, urging them out of his little office, across the yard.

Lucas noticed that a great many of the workers, both men and woman, seemed to have left their tasks and gathered at one side of the big yard, where they formed a restless muttering group, which swayed to and fro as some people joined it and others left. A man was standing on a bale of wool, addressing such of the crowd as were nearest him. Lucas recognized Scatcherd but could not catch much of what he said.

A few of the workers turned to glance with curiosity or hostility at Lucas and Anna-Marie as Smallside urged them toward the gate.

Annoyed at being hustled in this manner, Lucas hung back, and caught a few sentences of Scatcherd's harangue: "Well, friends, there we are: Sir Randolph has chosen to cut our wages by half. What are we to do about it, eh? Are we to take it lying down?"

There was a growling mutter of response from the crowd.

Anna-Marie and Lucas walked out through the big gate, with Smallside behind them.

"What had we better do?" Lucas said, half to himself.

"Do? Why, make the best of your way home," Smallside said shortly. "You've got legs, haven't you? Think yourselves lucky you've got whole skins—"

Not a trace of his fawning servility was left; he turned back into the yard, evidently dismissing them at once from his mind.

Lucas felt rather aggrieved; he had not intended his question for Mr. Smallside.

"It must be nearly five kilometers home and almost all uphill," he said to Anna-Marie. "Can you walk as far as that?"

"Not in these shoes," she said positively. "They are grown too small for me and they are not comfortable at all—*du tout, du tout!*"

"Then we had best inquire our way to the tax office and find Mr. Oakapple. He will be there for quite a while yet. Besides, I think it may rain."

All memory of the bright morning had vanished. The day was dark and lowering. The town of Blastburn, not a cheerful place at the best of times, in this murky light seemed suitable only as a dwelling place for trolls or hobgoblins. Gas flares had been lit in the cobbled streets, and the foot passengers came and went out of a thick obscurity, half smoke, half dark.

"Can you tell me the way to the tax office?" Lucas asked one man.

"Nay, it's noan a place I'd be fain to visit," he said unhelpfully, and walked on.

But another said he thought it was near the Town Hall— "Down along t'Micklegate, past t'prison, go left when ye see t'workus, ower along by t'insane asylum, alongside t'stocks and t'ducking stool, cross t'Market Square into Brass Gate and ye canna miss it."

He gestured down the wide busy road on which they stood.

However it was plain that, after going some distance in the deepening fog, they must have taken a wrong turn, for instead of arriving at the Market Square, they found themselves among narrow, mean streets where a carriage could not possibly have passed; even on foot it was hard enough not to slip into the filthy gutter than ran down the middle of the way.

"I do not like the air here," said Anna-Marie, wrinkling her nose. "This place smells of cheese that has gone bad."

It smelled worse than that among the decaying little houses with squalid heaps of rubbish outside each door, and Lucas began to be anxious for Anna-Marie; he hoped that she might not pick up some noxious disease in this slum. He would have liked to ask the way again, but hesitated; they were receiving unfriendly glances from the shawled women on doorsteps, the men in clogs who stood lounging at corners.

But they were certainly lost; each turning seemed only to plunge them deeper into the heart of the maze.

At last Lucas perceived someone whose face seemed vaguely familiar—for a moment he could not think why, but he knew he had seen her recently—at all events she looked kindly enough, though sad. He started toward her, firmly gripping the hand of Anna-Marie, who showed a disposition to loiter and gaze about her.

Before he reached the woman he was approaching, however, she had been accosted by a friend. They stood deep in talk while Lucas hesitated, feeling it would be impolite to interrupt, yet impatient to learn his direction before it should be too late, before Mr. Oakapple had finished his business at the tax office and started for home.

The two women were talking in low voices.

"Eh, I'm reet sorry not to oblige thee, Bess, I'd take in the liddle 'un, and gladly, wi'out a thought, if it were only me. But it's my owd man, he's a tippler, as tha knaws, and when he's a drop taken, he says there are ower many mouths to feed a'ready—he'd break ivery bone in my body if I took on another—"

"Never fret, Annie lass. I knaw tha would if tha could. I'd take the bairn wi' me on the ship, but they tells as how bairns dies quick as windflowers on those transports. I'm afeared even for Sue, that she'll never see Van Diemen's Land."

"Eh, Bess, woman, 'tis a long way—" the second woman sighed. Then, plainly glad to change the subject, she gave her friend a nudge and said, "Reckon the lad yonder wishes to speak to thee."

The first woman turned, pushing back her shawl with a familiar gesture, and now that he was close enough to recognize her, Lucas would have liked to back away. He felt ashamed to trouble her. For she was Mrs. Braithwaite, the woman he had seen mourning by the roadside on the previous evening. Her face was still pale as death, but it was resolute and firm; she gave Anna-Marie and Lucas a kind glance and said simply, "Well, my lad, how can I serve thee?"

"I—I'm sorry, I didn't wish to interrupt—" he stammered. "I only wanted to ask the way to the tax office—"

"*Oh, oh, le joli bébé, tout en riant!*" exclaimed Anna-Marie at his elbow.

For Mrs. Braithwaite held a baby in her shawled arms, and it was giving Anna-Marie a broad grin.

"*Comment est-ce qu'il s'appelle, madame?*" Anna-Marie inquired politely.

"English, English, Anna-Marie! And it's not polite to interrupt. She is asking about your baby—what he is called," Lucas apologized to Mrs. Braithwaite.

"It's Betsy, my little lady—she's a girl, bless her."

Then the woman looked fully into Anna-Marie's face and started. She said, hesitantly, "You'll excuse a poor woman asking, my little lady—I can see you're quality—but what might your name be? I wouldn't take a liberty, mostly, but it's a hard time for me, joost now—if you'll not think it amiss—"

"*Je m'appelle Anna-Marie Murgatroyd, madame.*"

"Murgatroyd! Why didn't I think on it mysel'?" Mrs. Braithwaite murmured. Then, unexpectedly, she dropped a slight curtsey and kissed Anna-Marie's cheek. "Bless your

bonny face, lassie. You came by in time to put a good notion into my head, and maybe the saints sent you. . . . May
you have a long life and a happy one, happier than poor
Bess Braithwaite's. Murgatroyd," she murmured to herself
again. "I'll go see the old lady directly. If ony can give me
good counsel, she can." Then, remembering she had been
asked a question, she gave Lucas clear and explicit directions for reaching the tax office, nodded kindly to them,
hastily kissed her friend, and hurried off in the opposite
direction.

"I'll see thee again, Bess, afore tha takes ship—" the
other woman called anxiously.

"Happen—if there's time—" her brief answer came back
before she vanished round a corner.

Lucas and Anna-Marie turned the other way. Anna-
Marie had not understood Mrs. Braithwaite's remarks, but
Lucas had, and he wondered if there were still some rela-
tive of Anna-Marie's living in the neighborhood—who
could "the old lady" be? Who would know?

However this question was banished from his mind almost at once by the situation in which they now found
themselves. It had been plain, from the unfriendly stares
they had been receiving as they walked along, that strangers were not welcome in this part of the town. They caught
muttered remarks: "Jack Puddings! Fancy boots! High
nebs! What do they think they're faring t'do here? Let 'em
goo back where they coom from while they'm still got
their boots on!"

The angry looks and hostile murmurs increased; they
were jostled several times and Anna-Marie who had shown
a tendency, earlier, to tug away from Lucas's protective
clasp, now seemed glad enough to keep close by and clutch
his hand.

At one corner a fairly large group of boys had been
playing a kind of football game, using a lump of wool tied

with string for their ball. As Lucas and Anna-Marie approached, the ball, whether by design or accident, struck Lucas on the side of the head. The boys gave over their game and moved, half mocking, half threatening, into a solid phalanx in the middle of the path, so that it was impossible to get by. Some of them were big and heavy—nearer men than boys.

One of them—a large, lumping fellow of eighteen or nineteen, with a shock of fair, frizzy hair, thick lips, and pale blue eyes—called out, "Look a' the dainty bonnets. Eh, what a lace-edged pair! Knaw who they are, mates? Tak' a good peer at the high-belted mimsy scratlings!"

"Nay, who are they, then?"

"Divven't tha knaw? Old Randy Grimsby's foundlings from oop at t'Court all fatched oop i' hog's leather an' silk velvet!"

In fact the clothes of Anna-Marie and Lucas were by no means luxurious, but they certainly seemed so in comparison with the rags worn by most of the boys.

"Gan on home to where tha belongs, whey face!" one of them shouted.

"Glad to, if you'll let us by," Lucas replied curtly, doing his best to conceal his anxiety for Anna-Marie; and, indeed, for himself: most of the boys were twice his size.

"A' reet, gan on, we aren't stoppin' thee," replied some of the boys, while others cried, "Let's run 'em t'gantlet, eh, lads?"

The group broke up to form an irregular pair of lines, between which Anna-Marie and Lucas would have to pass.

"Ne t'inquiète pas; reste tranquille," he whispered to her, though far from tranquil himself.

Hand in hand, Lucas leading, they began to thread their way between the staring, jeering boys. They were jostled, pushed; Lucas received a couple of kicks; he could only hope that Anna-Marie did not understand the language that rained down on them. Insulting allusions to Sir Randolph were numerous; it seemed plain that he was about the most unpopular man in Blastburn.

Lucas longed to speak up and say, "We don't like him any better than you do!" But instinct told him that this would be no help, might only further antagonize their attackers.

Anna-Marie suddenly let out a sharp cry; a stone, thrown from the rear, had struck her on the cheek.

Up to now she had remained subdued, wary, but uncertain how to behave in this hostile, unfamiliar situation. Now, suddenly, her temper blazed out.

She snatched up the stone, which had fallen ahead of her, and hurled it, with astonishing strength and unerring aim, back at the boy who had thrown it—a big red-faced, red-headed lout who stood sniggering well to the rear of the crowd. It struck him full on the ear and made him stagger. Anna-Marie, meanwhile, screamed out a startling flood of insults, which lost nothing in force and ferocity from being all in French.

"*Ah, cochons, canaille,* pigs, trash, idiots, rats, garbage, offal, vermin! Just because you are many and we only two, you think to bully us!"

Utterly disconcerted by the vigor and unexpectedness of this defiance, most of the group fell back. Lucas caught muttered exclamations: "Nay, what a little spitfire! Who'd a thowt it? Yon lass is a reet hullum-skullum—"

Only one boy still seriously opposed them, a big but somewhat stupid-looking lad, better dressed than the rest, in leathers and a velveteen waistcoat with brass buttons. This boy squared up to Lucas, who, now that open battle had been declared, had no hesitation in making use of a wrestling throw that Bob the groom had once taught him; momentarily letting go of Anna-Marie's grasp, he flung an arm around the other boy's neck, kicked his legs from under him, and laid him full-length in the gutter.

"Aha! That has taught you a lesson, pig-face!" screamed

Anna-Marie triumphantly, and, to Lucas, "Bravo! Well done, very good! I did not think that you were so *habile!*"

"Come on, quick, let's get out of here," grunted Lucas, grabbing her arm again, and he hurried her down the alley to the next corner, which, luckily, proved to be an opening into a much wider street, which in its turn led to the Market Square. They crossed it into Brass Gate and then saw, directly fronting them, a building with a door bearing a painted legend:

TAX AND REVENUE DEPARTMENT
OFFICE OF HIS MAJESTY'S CUSTOMS AND EXCISE

Outside the building, to the immense relief of Lucas, they also observed Mr. Oakapple, standing by the governess cart and still deep in discussion with a man in a dark-blue uniform and brass buttons.

Lucas hurried across the road with Anna-Marie panting and expostulating behind him. As they reached the cart they heard a snatch of the two men's conversation.

"Well, there it is, Mester Oakapple. I'm afeared I can't do any more. If Sir Randolph cares to coom down in person, I'll tell him the same. The taxes are long overdue, and if he cannot pay, there'll be noothing for it but to lay a distraint. As an official of the Crown, that is my last word. Nowt against you, persoonally, Mester Oakapple, you onderstand—"

"Yes, yes, I quite understand, thank you, Mr. Gobthorpe. I'll tell Sir Randolph exactly what you have said. But I fear he's in a very difficult mood at the moment. I doubt if he'll listen to reason—" Then, seeing Lucas, Mr. Oakapple broke off to exclaim in surprise, "Hey! What are you two doing here? I told you to wait at the Mill—"

"They wouldn't let us—" Lucas began, but at that moment his words were drowned by a tremendous clatter of hoofs and the sound of drums, as a whole detachment of mounted troopers galloped across the square, sabers ready drawn, to vanish almost as quickly as they had come into the foggy dusk.

"Croopus! What's amiss i' the town? Who's called oot the militia?" exclaimed Mr. Gobthorpe. "Nay, if there's going to be trooble, I'd best shoot oop t'office; I'll bid ye good day, Mester Oakapple." And he vanished indoors, while Lucas and Anna-Marie followed the tutor's example and hastily climbed into the cart.

"We'd better go home by Peggoty's Piece; it's round-about, but there's not likely to be any disturbance that way," muttered Mr. Oakapple, and turned the mare's head in the opposite direction from that taken by the soldiery.

"And now, why are you here? Why did you disobey my instructions to stay at the Mill until I called for you?" he inquired. "With this trouble in the town—if I had already left—if you had failed to find me—"

"Mr. Smallside wouldn't let us into the Mill. He said it was not convenient," Lucas began, thinking that his explanation sounded extremely lame and unconvincing.

But the tutor hardly seemed to heed his words; with lips pressed tight together and frowning brow, he drove on through the dim, deserted side streets of Blastburn, past the rows of little mean houses; he was evidently almost wholly preoccupied with the problem of Sir Randolph and his taxes. And after a few more unheeded sentences of explanation, Lucas, too, was glad to fall silent. As for Anna-Marie, she had wriggled back under the old carriage blanket and pulled it round her so that it almost completely covered her; Lucas could just see that she was sucking her thumb, and that her eyes held a thoughtful, far-distant expression.

"Tell me a story, Luc-asse?" she invited.

"Hush! Not just now," he said rather crossly, embarrassed in case Mr. Oakapple had overheard.

Anna-Marie was silent after that.

She's only a baby, he thought. It's lucky she didn't realize what a tricky situation we were in, back there.

And for the rest of the silent, gloomy ride he did his best
to cheer himself by the recollection of the neat hip throw
with which he had disposed of the boy in the velveteen
waistcoat.

ANNA-MARIE WAS found to be asleep by the time they arrived back at Midnight Court, so the chambermaid, Abby, came out and carried her indoors without waking her.

Mr. Oakapple hurried away, presumably to report to Sir Randolph on the outcome of his discussions with the tax officials, and Lucas wandered rather disconsolately to his own quarters. Although the day was so dark—indeed it had begun snowing on the drive home and the storm promised to be severe—it was still only midafternoon. Lucas found a cold luncheon laid out in his schoolroom: mutton, pickled onions, and a bowl of bread pudding. The slices of bluish-pink underdone mutton, accompanied by three large pale wet pickled onions, looked most unappetizing, and he left them, but ate the bread pudding; it was a dry and tasteless lump but he needed something to chew on after the day's doings.

Munching the dull stuff he remembered that while waiting to speak to Mrs. Braithwaite he had noticed a most appetizing smell of rabbit stew floating from the doorway of one of those miserable little houses. He had a notion that old Gabriel caught rabbits in the park and sold them in the town; or perhaps people from the town occasionally snared their own rabbits in the park on moonless nights?

He knew that he ought to be getting on with his schoolwork and brought his mind back to it with an effort. There lay his unfinished composition: "Industry is a good thing, because it is better to work in a carpet factory than to be out in the rain with nothing to eat."

But suppose the owner of the factory cut your wages by half? Suppose you had six children? Suppose three of them had been badly injured by the press? Would you think industry was such a good thing then?

He wrote a few paragraphs—slowly, with as much effort as if he were cutting the words in marble. Then his eyes strayed toward his leatherbound book. He pushed the composition away, opened the book, and wrote, "Dear Greg: Since I last addressed you, I have had another adventure. . . ." His hand raced. Lines flowed out from his pen. Three quarters of an hour later, he wrote, "Anna-Marie had gone to sleep," stretched his cramped hand with a sigh, and closed the book.

Glancing out the window at the park, dimly visible behind whirling snowflakes, he suddenly remembered that he had promised to try and repair Anna-Marie's broken doll. He jumped up, ran from the room, and made his way to the Oak Chamber, feeling rather pleased with himself for his kindness.

He entered the room cautiously, in case Anna-Marie was still asleep. She had woken, however, and was sitting by the fire in a small wicker chair which must have been fetched out from some forgotten lumber room; she was very carefully stitching together the frayed edges of the pink dress that had been torn that morning.

"*Qu'est-ce qu'il y a?*" she inquired, biting off her thread in a preoccupied manner, and giving Lucas a rather lofty glance, as if she were engaged on important business, and not quite sure if she had the time to grant him an interview.

Putting on airs, he thought. One minute she's crying and carrying on and sucking her thumb; next thing she's acting as if she wouldn't call the Queen her cousin.

"I've come to mend your doll," he said.

"*C'est déjà fait.* The old man—Meester Towzir—he has done it." She indicated the repaired doll which lay in a small box by the fireplace, clumsily strapped together in plaster and brown paper, presumably waiting for the glue to dry.

"So you are too late," said Anna-Marie coolly. *"Merci de rien."*

Apparently dismissing Lucas from her attention, she held up the pink dress and inspected it with great care.

"Well don't strain yourself by saying thank you," he snapped, stung by her condescending manner.

"Quoi? I do not onnerstan'."

"In that case I'd better give you an English lesson."

"Ne vous dérangez pas. Monsieur Ooka—Ookapool—'e 'ave teach me some already, *c'en est assez."* She selected a length of pink silk and rethreaded her needle.

Annoyed by this evident lack of appreciation of the trouble and time he had been prepared to spend on her, he said, "Would you like me to tell you a story?"

"If you wish. *Cela m'est égal."* She bent over the pink dress again.

"I won't trouble myself if you feel like that about it," said Lucas, and he gave her a short severe lecture to the effect that she wasn't going to make herself liked at Midnight Court until she learned to behave with more politeness and gratitude to the people who did her kindnesses.

Then he left, shutting the door sharply behind him. It would be a long time, he thought, before he'd offer to do anything for *her* again.

He might have been even more exasperated if he had reopened the door. Behind it, Anna-Marie had abandoned her sewing and flung herself to the floor, pillowing her head on the pink dress. "Oh, Papa! Oh, Sidi! I don't want anyone to like me in this hateful place! I want you, only you!"

But of this Lucas knew nothing. Hearing an extraordinary sound of banging and thumping from the direction of the main staircase, he had given way to curiosity and walked in that direction. Turning a corner in the passage, he was held riveted by the scene that was taking place a little farther on.

Three men were locked together in what looked like a fight to the death. They strained and stamped, heaved and grunted and struggled, bumping against the wall and the balustrade at the stairhead. The hall was full of the sound of their gasping breath and an occasional damn.

In the dim light—the candles had not yet been lit—it was hard to make out one from another. Somebody seemed to be trying to throw somebody else over the banisters, and a third party was attempting to prevent this. Redgauntlet the hound circled round the group, hysterically barking, letting out an occasional whimper when one of the fighters knocked against or trod on him.

Lucas felt that he ought to help, and yet it was hard to know what he could do. None the less he drew nearer, and caught a glimpse of the turkey-cock red face of Sir Randolph. Now he could see that his guardian had both arms tightly wrapped round another man and seemed engaged in trying to break his ribs by sheer pressure. Sir Randolph was being hindered from his efforts by Mr. Oakapple, who was both struggling and remonstrating:

"Sir Randolph! Sir Randolph, *please!* You must leave go, sir, indeed you must! This will not do, sir, you are forgetting yourself."

"Forgetting himself, rats!" grunted the man whom Sir Randolph was trying to throw over the rail. "If *you* weren't aware that Sir Randolph is the most awkward customer for miles around, Mr. Oakapple, *I* certainly was! I knew it would be taking my life in my hands to coom along this afternoon and serve the Order. But a public servant's got his dooty to do—*agghhh!*" he gasped, as the enraged Sir Randolph managed to get a hand on his windpipe.

Then Lucas recognized the bald head and brass buttons of Mr. Gobthorpe the tax official. At the same moment

Mr. Oakapple, catching sight of Lucas for the first time, exclaimed, "Go and fetch Garridge or old Gabriel—Sir Randolph is distempered, he is not himself."

Lucas tried to edge around the group in order to get down the stairs.

"Not himself!" burst out the tax official, getting Sir Randolph's hand off his throat again, "he's exactly himself, if you were to ask me—of all the pesky, contumacious, aggravating, bellicocious tax defaulters, he's the wust I ever coom·across, or my name's not Esdras Gobthorpe."

His words increased the fury of Sir Randolph, who made another lunge at him. This had the effect of tipping the whole group over the head of the stairs, just at the moment when Lucas had squeezed by them, and they all tumbled down higgledy-piggledy, falling over one another.

Apparently, as it turned out, nobody's limbs were broken, and the sudden upset at least succeeded in disentangling the fighters. The little tax officer, Mr. Gobthorpe, with great presence of mind leapt to his feet and made for the front door, exclaiming, "I give you good day, sir! I have done my dooty. I have served the Order, which falls due in three weeks' time. After that, it's pay or go to prison. And before then you will probably receive a Summons for assault of a revenue officer in pursoot of his lawful occasions!"—with which parting shot he slammed the door behind him. Sir Randolph, eyes starting, purple with choler, might very likely have gone in pursuit, despite the restraining grasp of Mr. Oakapple, if another visitor had not just then very opportunely arrived and entered through the same door by which Mr. Gobthorpe had departed, conveniently blocking the way. He gazed in dignified surprise at Sir Randolph's face of fury.

"Ah—Mr. Throgmorton. Good afternoon," panted Mr. Oakapple. "Mr. Throgmorton, will you please represent to Sir Randolph that he must not punch a tax official, nor call him a scrimshanked blatherskite—" With caution he let go of Sir Randolph's arm, but kept a firm grasp on the tails of his velvet jacket.

"Heydey! What's all this about?" demanded the new arrival, a small, slim, sour-faced individual, very plainly and neatly dressed in a gray jacket and waistcoat, gray small-clothes and stockings, very white ruffles, and a very crisp gray wig. "What's to do, pray?"

There was a clatter of hoofs from outside as Mr. Gobthorpe the tax man made off up the drive. Sir Randolph sat down furiously on the third step of the stairway, and growled, "Fetch me a glass of brandy!"

"Ought he to have any more?" said Mr. Throgmorton, giving the baronet a sharp look.

"He has had only one bottle, this afternoon, I think," said Mr. Oakapple.

"Then he may as well have a glass—it may calm him. Boy, fetch the brandy."

After looking to Mr. Oakapple, who nodded, Lucas hurried into the huge dining room, in which no furniture now remained save for one tiny round table, a chair, and a small cupboard containing bottles and glasses. Returning with the cognac and a glass, Lucas heard Mr. Oakapple saying, "Would you not wish to return to your study, sir?"

"I don't budge from this spot until I've had a drink," growled Sir Randolph.

Taking the bottle and glass from Lucas, he poured himself a large tumblerful, spilling some, and drank it down.

No one ordered Lucas to leave, and so he remained, wondering what would happen next.

"Well? What did the tax officer say?" inquired Mr. Throgmorton, when Sir Randolph had drunk the brandy.

Lucas observed that Mr. Throgmorton, although so small and pinch-faced, did not seem to be at all in awe of Sir Randolph, but spoke very shortly, as if his patience had been tried greatly and often.

"Filthy ravening brutes! Yapping jackals! Blister them all." Sir Randolph stared furiously about, as if the hall were full of tax collectors. He made no attempt to return to his study, but poured himself a second tumblerful of spirit. "You're my lawyer, Throgmorton, why don't you pr'tect me from those vampires? Eh?"

"What did Mr. Gobthorpe say?"

"He said that either the Mill or this house would have to be sold to pay off twenty years' accumulation of unpaid taxes," Mr. Oakapple said in a low voice.

Happening to glance at Mr. Throgmorton as Mr. Oakapple said these words, Lucas observed a very sharp gleam in the lawyer's eye as if the news had some personal interest for him.

"Almost the moment for Holdernesse to make his offer," Lucas heard him mutter. "Brought so low, Grimsby will be obliged to accept. A year from now, I may be taking my ease in Monte Carlo!"

Nobody but Lucas caught this muttered remark.

"Vultures! Hyenas!" shouted Sir Randolph, thumping his brandy glass down on the stairs so violently that it shivered into fragments. "My own house, m'own place that I won in—in fair play. Give it up t'those gnawing rats? Never!"

"Then I suppose it is the Mill that must be sold," said Mr. Throgmorton calmly.

"Are you mad, man? 'Ve you taken leave 'f your wits? Mill's m'only soursh—source 'f income—almosht only source," protested Sir Randolph. He spoke complainingly, but there was a cunning gleam in his eye. "If Mill goes, what'll I live on? What'll I shup—s'port dependents on?" His eye roved about and fixed on Lucas. "Pack 'f brats in th'house—mouths t'feed. Be off, you, whelp!" he suddenly shouted at Lucas. "This's none 'f your affairs. No, stay, 'fore you go, fetch me 'nother glass."

"No more—you have had enough to drink, Sir Randolph—quite enough," interposed Mr. Throgmorton. "Come, you had best go to your study and rest. Run along, boy, there is no need for you to remain."

Mr. Oakapple also jerked his head in dismissal, and Lucas began to walk away, feeling unfairly used. None of his business, indeed! Surely, if his father had been Sir Randolph's partner, and if he was supposed to inherit a half share of the Mill when he came of age, then the sale of it should be considered his business. But apparently neither the lawyer nor Mr. Oakapple thought so.

He was halfway to the schoolroom when he recollected that he had intended to fetch in a new supply of kindling for his fire. He decided to go out to the woodshed before it was too dark, and made his way through the kitchens and the servants' quarters—now mostly empty and bare—to the stableyard.

Emerging from the woodshed with his bundle of twigs, he was accosted by Garridge, who was just dismounting from a flea-bitten gray, one of the last horses in the stables. Horse and man were caked with snow.

"Eh, Mester Lucas! The very lad! Ye can run an errand for me to Sir Randolph, if ye will."

"Why should I?" inquired Lucas rather coldly. Garridge had never shown him any particular kindness; indeed he was usually rather surly and disagreeable.

"I can hardly go into t'master's study like this, can I? An' it'll save t'poor owd nag standing in t'snow. 'Tis only to deliver a message—I'm nobbut joost coom back from town."

"What happened there? Did they go on strike at the Mill?" demanded Lucas, his dislike of Garridge overborne by curiosity.

"Nay, there'll be no strike. Not this time, leastways. The sodjers arrived an' drove 'em all out, and they've stook a coople o' th' ringleaders in the pokey. All's quiet enow."

"Scatcherd? Did they put him in jail?"

"Aye, him an' anither o' his cullies."

"Oh well, Sir Randolph will be relieved to hear that."

"Ay, an' joost as well, for my t'oother message is like to leave him flaysome enow."

"What's that?"

"Tell him the white cock lost," Garridge said, swung a leg back over the gray and kicked him into a reluctant trot.

"Is that *all?*"

Garridge made no answer, but Lucas heard him grunt to himself with satisfaction, "An' that's saved me a bang on the lug, if I knaw owt aboot t'master. I'll gan off home now."

"The white cock lost," Lucas repeated, somewhat mystified, as he carried his wood to the schoolroom.

The front hall was empty once more, when he climbed the main staircase. How strange it was, he thought, that until yesterday he had hardly set foot here above three times, and now he seemed to be continually going up and down this way. For some reason the change made him uneasy. The white cock lost. What could that mean? It had an unchancy sound, he thought. Drat old Garridge and his haste to get away—riding Sir Randolph's horse, too!

He knocked at the study door.

"What now—who is it?" a voice said sharply, and Lucas had half a mind to retreat, for the voice was that of Mr. Oakapple, not Sir Randolph, and Lucas had a guilty feeling about his unfinished composition on Industry. Also, Mr. Oakapple might be annoyed, for all he knew, at his having been a witness to the fight with Mr. Gobthorpe and Sir Randolph's drunkenness. He was still hesitating when the door was flung open.

Mr. Oakapple stood in the doorway, looking impatient.

Glancing past him, Lucas could see Sir Randolph seated at his desk, leaning forward with his head on his arms and evidently asleep, for he was snoring loudly.

"Oh, it's you," Mr. Oakapple said. "Why are you here? What do you want?"

"I have a message from Garridge, sir."

"He's no business to give you his messages. He should bring them himself. Well, what was it, then?"

"First, that the strike is off and that Scatcherd and another man have been put in jail."

"Oh. Well, I daresay Sir Randolph will be glad enough to hear that, when he wakes. What else?"

"And, sir, Garridge said to say that the white cock lost."

Mr. Oakapple had been absently looking through a leather portfolio of papers, as they spoke; Lucas had noticed that a bureau which stood against the wall was open, and that an untidy heap of documents lay on its front flap. Now, with a furious exclamation, the tutor flung the portfolio down onto Sir Randolph's desk.

"Damned old fool! Miserable old sot! I suppose that's where the fifty pounds went!"

"What fifty pounds?" Lucas asked, bewildered.

"Dear knows he gets little enough in the way of rents. Most of the farms were sold off long ago. But the Artingstalls at High Wick still pay rent faithfully, and I had reckoned that would do to give the servants their wages and buy a few provisions—no wonder I couldn't find it! He's gone and laid it on some cankered molting old rooster that probably couldn't even hop across the cockpit—"

He was so angry that the words dried in his throat; he stared down at the snoring, red-faced Sir Randolph as if he longed to wake and shake him. But then, "Oh, what's the use?" he murmured wearily, and began picking up the scattered papers, setting them straight with absent-minded precision.

Lucas, helping as best he could, asked in a subdued voice, "Do you mean that it was a wager, sir? Had Garridge put the money on a cockfight for him?"

"Yes. That's to say, if Garridge ever got as far as the cockfight and didn't pocket the stake himself," Mr. Oakapple said bitterly. "And if he did, doubtless he had some right. Lord knows when *his* wages were last paid."

"Is that why Sir Randolph is so far behind with his taxes? Because he loses all his money on bets?"

"Of course! I doubt if he has won above five bets in the last five years—to judge by the papers in there." He jerked his head toward the bureau. "Bookmakers, horse races, prizefights, moneylenders—thousands and thousands squandered on dice games, steeplechases, card games— any kind of stake—even croquet matches." Furiously Mr. Oakapple scanned a crumpled old receipt—Lucas could just see the words, Worshipful Company of Bakers' Hot Cross Bun Eating Contest—and then tore it in half. "He'll spend all that on gambling, and yet he's too mean to have a decent fire anywhere in the house, or get the roof mended—"

"I see," Lucas murmured. Many things that he had been vaguely aware of during the past months now became intelligible to him. He was surprised, not so much at these disclosures about Sir Randolph as at the revelation of Mr. Oakapple's violent feelings on the matter. The tutor had hitherto seemed such a silent, unemotional, taciturn individual that it was a shock to see him in such a passion.

"I thought you liked Sir Randolph?" Lucas ventured.

"I can't imagine why you should imagine any such thing!" snapped the tutor. "It was not very observant of you." Then, making an attempt to recover his usual rather dry manner, he added, "However, *my* feelings are of no concern. We must just make the best of things."

"But if Sir Randolph has to sell this house"—Lucas did

not love Midnight Court, but the thought of being obliged to quit was frightening—"where should we go?"

"We'd have to find somewhere else—some house without half a hundred wasted rooms. I, for one, would have little objection. . . . Run along now; it must be your suppertime. I daresay you may have it with Anna-Marie if you prefer her company."

Lucas did not prefer it. He had another question; it embarrassed him to ask it, but he felt he must. Nervous but resolute, he stammered, "Mr. Oakapple, d-does Sir Ralph pay *your* wages?"

A glance at the tutor's face gave him his answer.

"Then how do you manage?"

The tutor laughed shortly. "From hand to mouth!"

"But," Lucas persisted, more and more puzzled, "in that case, why do you stay here?"

Mr. Oakapple's continued stay at the Court, he felt, certainly could not be through fondness of the position, or of his pupil. Some expression of this thought perhaps showed in his face, for the tutor laughed again and patted him on the shoulder in a more friendly manner than he had ever shown before.

"Never mind why I stay! I have my reasons. Perhaps I'll tell you someday. Go now, before Sir Randolph wakes. Have you finished your task?"

"No, sir," Lucas replied, coming out with the truth more boldly than he might have done two days ago.

"Well, it has been a trying day. You may leave it till tomorrow morning if you make sure to do it then. In the meantime, do as you please. Amuse yourself. Perhaps you may like to go and play some game with Anna-Marie."

The tutor retired inside the study and closed the door.

Lucas walked slowly away, thinking that Mr. Oakapple could hardly have given him a more difficult order. Amuse himself! In Midnight Court! How?

Passing the open door of one of the empty bedrooms, he caught the sound of somebody singing, and looked in.

Anna-Marie was sitting on the floor with a large basket of pine cones that she had procured from somewhere; she was forming the cones into patterns on the bare boards and humming to herself in an unusually clear, true little voice. The place and occupation seemed rather cheerless.

"Hello," said Lucas. She looked up at him calmly but said nothing. "Would you like to come down to my school-room? You could bring those cones, and we could draw out a board with squares and use them to play checkers. Or we might toast bread at the fire."

"No, thank you," said Anna-Marie politely. "I am quite content with myself. Thank you," she said again with dignity, gave him a long, considering look, and turned back to her pattern.

Lucas went downstairs and finished his composition.

During the next fourteen days, nothing out of the way happened. Lucas woke every morning quite certain that bailiffs or constables must arrive that day who would turn them all out of house and home. But this did not occur. Life went on as before. A message arrived from Mr. Small-side to say that Lucas might resume his visits to the Mill. Anna-Marie displayed no further wish to accompany him, but stayed at home and occupied herself as best she could, spending a good deal of time with old Gabriel Towzer, who let her play with his tools and put up a swing for her in the stables. She also studied English with Mr. Oakapple, and Lucas was bound to admit that she made rapid progress. He was puzzled by Mr. Oakapple's manner toward Anna-Marie. The tutor showed her no especial favor and maintained his customary dry way with her, yet his eye lingered on her and followed her often; there was a new expression on his face when he watched her, as if he were

waiting for her to do or say something, as if presently his
reserve might crack and some different feeling show
through.

Relations between Lucas and Anna-Marie continued
very up and down. She took pains to make it clear that she
was not particularly anxious for his presence and could
manage quite well on her own. He, for his part, wanted it
to be clearly understood that he could derive no pleasure
from the company of a girl hardly more than half his age,
that if he spent any time with her it was purely due to his
kindness of heart.

If he did go along to the Oak Chamber and offer to tell
her a story or play cat's cradle, she was likely to say, "You
have only come here because Monsieur Towzir makes me
a better fire than you have in your room."

So he did not go very often.

With Mr. Oakapple, Lucas now felt much more comfortable and at ease. Although the tutor's manner had not
changed toward him any more than toward Anna-Marie,
Lucas, knowing more of Mr. Oakapple's difficulties, wondering more and more about his reasons for staying on at
Midnight Court, began to understand that the tutor's curt,
short way was merely an indication of his feeling that the
world was an awkward place in general, and was not intended unkindly toward Lucas in particular.

Indeed, sometimes, when Mr. Oakapple commented
with a brief smile on some improvement in his schoolwork,
Lucas felt that a kind of warmth was growing between him
and his teacher.

Anna-Marie certainly showed Mr. Oakapple a confidence and respect that she displayed toward no one else;
she would run up to him and swing on his hand if they
chanced to meet in the park, and although he did not return these demonstrations, he did not rebuff them. Lucas
was amazed to see her stop by Mr. Oakapple's chair once
and give his head an affectionate, rumpling pat, as he sat

knitting his forehead over some bills in the bare, dusty library; he nodded acknowledgment of the caress without looking up.

"Do not worry yourself so much!" she admonished him.

"Il a du fonds; he has bottom, that one," she remarked later to Lucas; this seemed to be her greatest term of praise. Bottom? Lucas wondered what she meant. But Mr. Oakapple was deep, that was certain; there was more to him than met the eye.

The weather became bitterly cold. Snow fell, and more snow. The gray clouds hung lower and thicker each morning. On their drives down into Blastburn, Lucas and Mr. Oakapple wrapped themselves in their thickest clothes; they took old sacks and the carriage blanket; they put hot bricks and a pile of straw in the bottom of the trap to keep their feet from freezing; but still they reached their destination chilled through and through, with numb feet and blue fingers. Now Lucas looked forward to the heat from the great furnaces and the steam from the glue caldrons.

But the atmosphere at the Mill remained uneasy and threatening. Outwardly, things were back to normal; the men and women went silently about their work. The troops had appeared and arrested Scatcherd and his companion so speedily that their example seemed to have deterred other would-be strikers. Protest about the wage cut had been nipped in the bud.

But under this apparent calm Lucas felt menace. He caught dark glances. The new foreman, Jobson, whose duty it now was to escort Lucas around was a dour, taciturn individual who never gave more than the bare information required of him. He seemed ill at ease, and it was plain that the hands paid him only token respect. And they were openly hostile to the manager, Mr. Smallside, whom they mockingly referred to as Smallbeer or Smallbritches.

On his fifth day at the Mill Lucas was witness to a disquieting incident.

The men, Jobson told him, had been strictly forbidden to assemble together in groups, even in twos or threes. The formation of unions, gangs, or associations would bring instant dismissal. And after Scatcherd's arrest they were particularly cautious about talking among themselves in the Mill, even to ask needful questions about work, and would spring hastily apart if Jobson or Smallside were seen approaching.

Yet there was one workman who showed no caution about talking to the others, and soon, during his visits to the Mill, Lucas began to be very much aware of him. His name was Robert Bludward.

He was remarkable, for a start, in being the only workman who was allowed to propel himself about in a wheelchair. Jobson told Lucas that both his legs had been cut off at the knee in an accident five years before, when he was an apprentice.

" 'E were too slow getting out o' t'way o' t'shuttle," Jobson explained laconically. Lucas shivered inwardly, after this, whenever he watched the great shuttle go slicing across on the steam loom that wove the more expensive carpets.

"It's a wonder he didn't die."

"He were mortal sick. Most hands would ha' been turned off, crippled like yon. But he's clever, Bob Bludward, sharp as a whittle—he'd worked out a new dye process that only cost half as mooch, an' he had an idea for a steam fan to dry the wool after it was dipped, so he were kept on. An' he made himself yon wheelchair that roons by steam."

The wheelchair was made of wicker, with a little steam engine at the back. Its driver propelled it with amazing speed—like some curious insect, it darted up ramps, through galleries, in between the lanes of pistons. The lame man had become a kind of expert in every department, apparently; he knew how to do things the best way.

No one ever knew where he might turn up next; his power of appearing like lightning whenever some difficulty arose was quite uncanny. Although the men treated him with great civility, they appeared nervous of him.

Bludward was very handsome; he had short very pale hair which curled all over his head like a ram's fleece. His face was pale too, and as sharp as if it had been cut from a block of salt, and his eyes were glass-pale; you could stare at them for minutes together, Lucas thought, and still not be sure what color they were.

As the wheelchair flitted about the Mill, the men would be galvanized into activity; Bludward seemed to have much more effect on them than Jobson, the real foreman. Lucas noticed very soon that Bludward had a kind of "shadow" or follower, who was generally to be seen not far in the rear of his chair. This was a stooped, wizened little fellow in a black-and-white cloth cap, known as Newky Shirreff. Wherever Bludward's chair rolled, Newky followed, and Lucas observed that most of the men seemed to have something to give Newky; he carried a little bag which grew heavier and heavier as the day advanced; if Lucas were close enough he sometimes caught the chink of coins. The men did not seem fond of Newky; he was greeted with sour looks and sped on his way with glum ones, but he appeared to have a remarkable power of extracting money from them.

On his fifth visit Lucas was standing alone, watching the glue-mixing process. Jobson had been called away to sign for a new intake of wool and Mr. Oakapple was in the town on one of Sir Randolph's errands.

Bludward's chair rolled past and stopped beside the glue mixer, Sam Melkinthorpe, a brawny red-headed man, who was just winching up a huge hopper of dried fishbone powder, ready to tip it into the caldron. Bludward asked some question and Lucas, drawing near, unperceived in the shadow of the hopper, was in time to hear Sam's reply,

"Nay, I can't pay thee owt at present, Bob; t'missus is poorly, so's two o' t'bairns, and I'm scraped clean wi' doctor's bills. Tha'll have to do wi'out my contribution this time."

"That won't do, you know, Sam," Bludward said calmly. "You'll have to find it somehow."

"I tell thee man, can't is can't!" Sam said shortly. "I'm drained dry, sithee." And he turned on his heel, pulled the lever to tip out the contents of the hopper, and concentrated on stirring the porridge-like mess in the caldron below.

Bludward's chair moved on. But Lucas noticed that he signaled to Newky Shirreff with a slight, negative movement of his head. Newky turned and looked back into the shadows of the "still room" where the raw materials for glues and dyes were stored in great vats. Two more men moved forward out of the gloom; they came silently but fast. Before he was aware of it, they had closed in on Sam Melkinthorpe; how it was done Lucas, half hidden behind the hopper, did not see, but suddenly Sam, with a terrified scream, had fallen into the glue caldron and was struggling to keep his head above the evil-looking mixture.

"Help! Lads, don't leave—" he began to shout, but the word *leave* came out as a choked gurgle. Meanwhile the men who had engineered his fall had vanished; the whole "accident" took place so rapidly that Lucas could hardly believe what he had seen. He did realize Melkinthorpe's dreadful danger though, and, darting forward, he snatched up the long "howk," or wooden ladle that was used for stirring, and with it managed to pull and steer the wretched man to the side of the caldron. As soon as he was within reach Lucas grabbed his hands and tried to pull him out.

But Melkinthorpe was a big man, thickset and heavy, and the weight of the glue on him made him even heavier;

Lucas began to despair of being able to get him out un-
aided, and yet he did not dare shout for help in case
Newky and the other two men returned.

Luckily at this moment Jobson reappeared. "Eh! What's
to do?" he grunted, quickly sized up the situation, and
took a firm grip on Melkinthorpe's right arm. "Now, lad,
when I say three. One—two—*three!*"

Melkinthorpe came out of the caldron with a fearful
sucking *glop!* and fell forward gasping on the sandstone
pavement. A drum of spirit and a quantity of cotton waste
were always in readiness for such accidents, and Jobson,
aided by Lucas, began swiftly soaking the cotton and wiping the man's mouth and nose clear before he should suf-
focate.

"Ey, Sam, tha had a narrow squeak then," Jobson commented briefly, when Melkinthorpe's gasps had turned to
more normal breathing. "If the lad hadn't a' been by—"

"Aye," said Sam when he could speak, "an' if I hadn't
joost tipped in a bin o' cold gurry, so the glue wasn't boiling, I'd ha' been cooked like a shrimp. I was lucky all ways,
reckon." He did not seem enthusiastic about his luck, however.

"How didst tha coom to be so shovel-footed, lad? 'Tis
not like thee to be careless."

Lucas had almost opened his mouth to speak when he
received a warning kick from Melkinthorpe, whose leg he
happened to be rubbing at that moment. He saw the man's
face distorted in a desperate grimace, as he tried to open
one of his eyes, stinging from the glue and spirit, long
enough to wink. Lucas remained silent. Fortunately Jobson
was not one to make a great deal of the incident, merely
congratulated Lucas on his promptness, and departed
soon after.

"Thanks, lad," muttered Sam when he had gone. "Now,
doan't ee breathe a word to a soul, eh, or thee'll be in

trooble, too. News travels quick, and Bludward's chaps has keen ears, sithee."

"But I don't understand," whispered Lucas. "What had you done?"

"Wouldn't pay their dues."

"What dues?"

"T'Friendly Association. If tha don't pay oop, tha gets rammed by the press, or falls in the glue, or knocked down by a troock, accidental-like. There's plenty o' 'mishaps' like that. Tha'd best be away now, lad, case one on 'em cooms back. I'll not forget what tha did."

"But will you be all right? Supose they do it again?"

"This was only a warning, likely. Reckon I'll have to find t'brass, though God knows how," said Sam, sighing.

Lucas wished he could offer to lend some money, but his allowance had not been paid for weeks; he had none on him. He rode home in the trap very thoughtful indeed, and hardly said a word to Mr. Oakapple, who had been paying another visit to the tax office and was equally silent.

That evening, unwontedly, Anna-Marie came along to Lucas's schoolroom as he was in the middle of a long letter to Greg.

There had been a great deal of banging and shouting in the neighborhood of Sir Randolph's study an hour before. Lucas had wondered if Mr. Gobthorpe had come back, or some other official; but no strangers seemed to be about, when he left the schoolroom and stole along to the great hall. Redgauntlet remained silent, and the front doors were barred. He could hear Sir Randolph shouting upstairs: "I won't see her. I tell you I will not! Let her remain in the house if she must—add one more to the army that is eating me out of house and home, what can it matter? Like rats they come to prey on a ruined man. But I will not see her, is that clear? Keep her out of my sight, or by the great Harry, there'll be trouble!"

He had appeared at the top of the stairs and started to lurch down them, swearing furiously to himself; Lucas made haste to get away.

Perhaps Anna-Marie had somehow been involved in this scene? At all events she now crept quietly into Lucas's schoolroom, with none of her usual self-possession, and curled up in silence on a cushion by the dismal fire which, by slow degrees, she proceeded to coax into a flickering blaze.

Despite the fire, the stone-floored apartment was bitterly cold. Lucas had fetched down a blanket from his bed, and kept it wrapped round him as he wrote at his desk. Outside the snow fell steadily. The room was silent, except for the tick of snowflakes against the windowpane.

Recently Lucas had redoubled his habit of *listening*—he hardly knew what for—footsteps overhead, voices, water dripping, wood creaking, the scratch of mice behind the paneling. He strained his ears now, but could catch nothing at all; the whole great empty house seemed wrapped in slumber.

"Pinhorn and Abigail have gone today, did you know?" Anna-Marie said.

"Left, do you mean?"

"*Oui.* And old Meester Towzir he say he is going—and Garridge. Who will look after the pony then?"

"I don't know." Lucas was not really paying attention to her. He wished she would stop talking, so that he could go on listening.

"*Racontez une histoire*—tell a story—*s'il vous plaît,* Lucasse?" Anna-Marie asked in a small voice.

"Oh, for goodness' sake!" he said irritably. Inventing a story was the last thing he wanted to do just then. The long cold day at the Mill, the frightening incident with Bludward and Melkinthorpe had left him exhausted but jumpy; he kept reseeing in his mind's eye the horrible spectacle of the man in the glue caldron, and his muscles would tighten again to spring forward and grab the long-handled howk. Suppose he had not been quick enough? Suppose he had missed his footing on the slippery verge and also gone into the glue?

"I'm tired just now," he told Anne-Marie. "I can't be forever thinking up tales to tell you. Sometimes my mind isn't in the right mood."

Her lip trembled. Normally she would have been prompt with some stinging retort, but this evening there was no spirit in her; she curled up, sucking her thumb, gazing at the fire, and there was another long interval of silence. Lucas, glancing over a book he was pretending to read, caught a spark of flame reflected in a tear on her cheek and felt contrite.

"I'll read aloud to you if you like," he offered awkwardly.

"Your books are not interesting to me."

"Or play checkers."

"The pine cones are in my room. It is too far to fetch them."

Lucas did not offer to go. He felt a sudden disinclination for the trip through the long dark passages.

"All right, we'll play scissors-paper-stone."

"What is that game? *'Connais pas.'*"

"Like this." He showed her how to shake her fist three times and then do different signals with her fingers. "Two fingers apart for scissors; flat hand means paper; fist clenched—*comme ça*—is a stone. And scissors can beat paper—"

"*Pourquoi?*"

"Because they can cut it, of course, silly. And paper can beat stone because you can wrap up a stone in a piece of paper; and stone can beat scissors—"

"Because they cannot cut the stone. I understand—"

"That's it, so shake your fist three times and then do one of the three things."

They shook: then Anna-Marie did a flat hand for paper; Lucas a clenched fist for stone.

"*C'est moi qui gagne!*" she said triumphantly. "Again!"

They played again. Anna-Marie was still paper, but this time Lucas had two fingers in a V for scissors and won the round. However Anna-Marie showed remarkable aptitude for guessing beforehand what Lucas was likely to do; and before long, as they played on, she was winning five games out of seven.

When she had won a hundred and thirty-two games, and Lucas ninety-nine, he declared that it must be long past her bedtime.

"Fanny will be looking for you."

"She has gone home to visit her mother."

"Mrs. Gourd then."

"She has tell me I can go to my bed when I choose."

"Well *I'm* tired if you aren't."

"Cannot I stay here with you, Luc-asse? I do not wish to go all that long journey back to my room. It is so dark in the passage. I could sleep in the basket chair."

"No you couldn't," said Lucas shortly. "It's freezing cold in here as soon as the fire goes out. Besides, there are mice."

"*Eh bien,* can I sleep also with you in your *chambre à coucher?*"

"No you can't!"

"There is another bed."

"But only blankets for one. Come along, I'll take you back to your own room. You wouldn't want to go to bed without Fifine."

"I have her here, *voilà.*" Anna-Marie fished the mended doll out from a pocket in her black stuff skirt.

"Oh. Well just the same you can't stay. You'd probably

wake up in the middle of the night in a fright, not knowing where you were. Come along."

He took her hand and pulled her, reluctant and protesting, to her feet.

"Oh! Oh! *Le pied me fourmille! Laisse-moi!*"

"It's only pins and needles. It will get better as you
walk," said Lucas unsympathetically. He lit one of his
hoard of candle stubs and led her up the east staircase and
back to her own room, which looked very unwelcoming
when they reached it. Her fire was dead, and the lamp, almost out of oil, was expiring in blue, glimmering gulps.

"I do not wish to stay here. I am afraid!"

"Rubbish. What's going to happen to you? Where's your
bird?" he said, looking around for it.

"I let it go. I did not like that it should be in a cage. It
flew out the window."

Lucas sighed. "Well, come along, get into bed," he said.
"I'll mend your fire if I can."

There were a couple of live embers under the ash, and
he managed to build a little cage with part-burned bits of
stick, and blow up a feeble flame.

"There," he said, rising from his knees. "Now you have
something to look at. Good, you're in bed. *Bonsoir,* sleep
well."

"No, wait, I am cold."

"Pile all your daytime clothes on top of you, then," he
said impatiently.

"Give them here, please, Luc-asse—if I get out my bare
feet will be so cold."

"There. Now you'll be all right."

"Oh, wait! Do not go. I am sure I hear a sound—*c'est des
voleurs, peut-être*—"

"Pish. What would robbers be doing in this house?
There is nothing left to steal. Go to sleep, Anna-Marie. I
am very tired, I want to go to bed."

At last he managed to disengage himself from her little cold clutch, and started back to his own quarters. But he too listened uneasily, with stretched ears, as he stole with even more than his usual caution along the deserted corridors. And even when he was safe in bed, it was a long, long time before he drifted off into an uneasy slumber.

LUCAS OPENED his eyes. He sat up.

He was not sure, at first, what had woken him. But he *was* awake, and very completely—tense, trembling, all his faculties stretched to their fullest extent. Something was not as it should be, he knew it; something was badly wrong. Danger was near; danger waited somewhere in the huge dark house; he was certain of that. He crouched in his bed, rigid, listening, staring at the dark, straining to catch the faintest sound. Silence. Was it complete silence, though? Or could he hear a sound—behind the loud thump of his own heart, was there not something else?

For a moment or two he half believed that it was only his own pulse that he could hear—a soft, fluttering, muttering whisper, like mice, like the scuffle of dead leaves on dry ground, like wind through brambles.

Or perhaps it was only the snow, after all?

But then stranger, more potent, more frightening than the strange sound, there came a sudden whiff that caused his nostrils to dilate—a sharp, hot, dry smell that caught in his throat, that made him bound out onto the floor as if his bed had suddenly arched its mattress and thrown him.

Fire! It was the prickling, acrid smell of fire that had made his nostrils twitch. And, in the distance, now that he was up and had pulled his door open, he could hear the crackle of flames—a snapping, scratching, savage sound that made him fling on his clothes and boots with frantic haste in the freezing dark which yet perhaps was not quite so freezing as it should be. And the dark, too, was not true dark; the black was tinged with a dark blood color that flickered, faster and faster; shadows began to slither up and down; he was aware of a light that should not be there, a glow from the corridor that led toward the great staircase.

But Anna-Marie's room lay in that direction.

He raced along the passage. The sound of his feet on the boards began to be lost in the sound that came from ahead of him, that grew louder and louder as he made his way from the east wing, where his rooms were, to the main stair and Sir Randolph's apartments.

The frightening stench of hot wood and burning paint was all around him; he heard a sudden fierce *crack!* as fire bit through some beam and a floor gave way—but where? Where was it burning? And why did no one but himself seem aware of what was happening?

"Anna!" he shouted. "Anna-Marie! Fire! Wake up! *Fire!*"

Arrived at the Oak Chamber—by now there was a leaping red glare coming from close ahead; he could see the balusters of the main staircase distinctly outlined against it—he pounded on the door. "Anna-Marie! Wake up!"

For a moment there was no answer from inside. Filled with dread, he opened the door and caught her frightened cry: *"Qu'est ce qu'il y a? Qui est-ce?"*

"Oh, you are there," he said, immeasurably relieved. "Quick, get up, get dressed, the house is on fire!"

"Ciel! Where?" She scrambled out of bed and grabbed his hand.

Smoke already filled her room, it made them both choke and gasp.

"This won't do, we can't stop here," coughed Lucas. A thicker, blinding white bolster of smoke rolled through the doorway. "Keep hold of my hand," he directed. "I'm here—that's it—hold tight!"

She needed no urging. While she clung to his wrist like a limpet he dragged together, as well as he could with one hand the blanket that covered her bed, and caught it by the four corners with her clothes inside it—at least he hoped they were inside.

"Come now, back to the door—"

"Oh, oh! I am chocking—I cannot breathe—and my eyes won't stay open. We cannot go this way!"

"We have *got* to. Keep your eyes shut. . . . I know; wait one moment," said Lucas. "Stay there and don't move—hold on to the door handle."

He knew that her basin and jug of water were kept on a stand somewhere to the left of the door. Feeling his way in that direction he found the jug, and a towel, which he plunged in the water.

Then he groped back to Anna-Marie. "Wrap this over your face," he ordered, and gathered up the corners of the blanket again. "Murder, the smoke's thick!"

"Where should we go?" whimpered Anna-Marie.

For a moment, outside her bedroom door, Lucas was overtaken by the cold, bottomless clutch of real terror. The smoke was now so completely blinding that it was not possible to see where the fire was burning, although they could hear its fierce roar and feel its heat. He was not certain which way they ought to go. Suppose they walked straight *into* the fire?

But then common sense reasserted itself. He had come from his own quarters and the fire had seemed to be ahead of him; in order to get away from it they had only to go back the way he had come.

"This way!"

"I can't, I can*not,* it is too thick!"

"You must stoop down low."

Stooping, accordingly, bent double, they ran and stumbled; Lucas, his hands occupied, one with the blanket, the other clutched by Anna-Marie, was not able to feel his way but kept one shoulder against the wall. The blanket dragged between them and tripped them.

Soon the smoke was so bad that they had to crawl. Once again Lucas was overwhelmed by terror. The fire must be all along below them—it was traveling faster than they were. Suppose the stairs in his wing were burning, suppose they could find no way down?

But he kept on doggedly, gripping Anna-Marie's wrist, hauling her after him, and somehow also managing to keep a clutch on the blanket.

The wall gave place to banisters, and then Lucas lurched forward onto his stomach as his left hand met no support when he put it down; they had reached the head of the east stairs.

"Are you all right?" called Anna-Marie in a panic. "Luc, where are you? What has happened?"

"It's all right, I fell over the head of the stairs."

He felt about with his empty hand until he found hers again. "Turn around so that you are sitting, and go down the stairs on your seat. Hold the rail."

"Oh, *j'ai peur, j'ai peur!*"

"No, you're quite all right, I'm just behind," Lucas told her with a firmness that he was far from feeling.

But when they were at last safely down the stairs and he felt solid flagstones beneath his feet, some confidence did come back to him. "It isn't many steps to my schoolroom now," he said. "I think you can put on your clothes in there. It doesn't feel so hot here; we must be farther away from the fire."

"Oh, *non!* There is just as much smoke. It is too dangerous in the house. Let us go outside."

"It's too cold. You *must* get dressed before we go outside, or you'll freeze, in your nightdress."

But when they entered Lucas's study room, they could see that it was not advisable to waste any time: already the smoke was becoming ominously thick, and the sound of the fire was increasing.

Lucas urged Anna-Marie to make all possible speed with her dressing, and he helped her to the best of his ability, tying laces and doing up buttons, thinking, as he did so, that it was no wonder girls had such awkward, complaining, timid natures; getting in and out of those clothes every day would be enough to give anyone the vapors.

"Here's an old jacket of mine—put that on, too. Now take the blanket, that's the way. Quickly—"

He had shut the door while she dressed. When he opened it, more smoke poured in, and they heard the crackle of flames in the corridor, frighteningly close at hand.

"Oh, what shall we do, what shall we do?" cried Anna-Marie.

"Out through the window," said Lucas briefly. It was only about five feet down to the ground. He slipped the catch and thrust the casement wide. A volley of snowflakes blew in, whirling wildly as they met the warm, smoke-filled air inside. "Come, quick—" he cried to Anna-Marie, outlined against the light from the doorway. He grabbed her round the waist, hoisted her up somehow, and pushed her through. A thud and a squeak told him that she had landed safely. He pushed the blanket out after her and a few of his possessions, snatched up at top speed.

"Vite, vite, quick!" Anna-Marie called, dancing up and down with impatience outside.

"All right, here I come." Lucas scrambled after her. Only just in time: beyond his door the crackle of the fire had increased to a steady roar.

The minute he was out Anna-Marie grabbed his hand once more. "Now where shall we go?"

"Round to the stableyard. Can you run?"

She nodded and followed him obediently. The snow stung on their faces; it felt like gorse prickles. They toiled in the darkness around the east end of the house, aware that great flames must be leaping to the sky overhead, because they could see dancing shadows out on the snow to their left. And above them, too, great flakes of burning material blew flaming, whirling away and vanished on the wind.

Lucas had two aims; he wanted to find the main site of the fire, and he was anxious about the welfare of Mr. Oak-apple, whose room looked out this way, onto the yard. The servants' sleeping quarters were all far away in the west wing, which perhaps was beyond the fire. But what of Sir Randolph, right in the center of the house? And where *was* Mr. Oakapple all this time?

When they reached the yard they stood aghast. Though their encounters with the fire inside the house had been frightening enough, they had had very little real notion, up to this moment, of its full power and extent. Now they saw that the whole middle part of the E-shaped mansion was completely ablaze. The fire must have spread with fearful speed, while they were making their way along the upstairs corridor to the east stairs; they had escaped not a moment too soon. The house was all hollow and illuminated with fire, like a turnip lantern; flames poured and shot from every window; as they watched, a whole section of the roof ridge crumpled and fell inward.

The scene was an extraordinary one, with the flames shooting upward, and the snow whirling down.

"Oh, mon dieu!" cried Anna-Marie. "Monsieur Oooka-pool, where is 'e?"

"Hush, it's all right—there he is," said Lucas, with huge relief. A grimed, smoke-blackened pair of figures staggered toward them across the cobbled yard, the snowy surface of which was half melted, half reddened by the reflection of the flames.

"Is that you, Lucas?" called Mr. Oakapple's voice. "Have you got Anna-Marie there? Oh, thank God. Good boy. I looked in her room but found her gone—I thought—"

"Are you all right, sir? Who is that you have there?"

Mr. Oakapple stooped and laid the figure he carried somewhat unceremoniously in the snow. It was Sir Randolph.

"I had to knock him out with a chair leg," the tutor said briefly. "He was wild—delirious—shouting a lot of gibberish about the tax men—that this was all their fault. Can you keep an eye on him for a moment while I rouse Garridge and Gabriel in the coach house—if they are not already awake. At this rate, with the wind setting as it is, the fire may spread to the servants' quarters before there is the least chance of any help coming from the town."

He hurried off in the direction of the west wing.

A swaddled female personage tottered up and revealed itself as Mrs. Gourd, strangely dressed in nightgown, nightcap, curlpapers, striped stockings, petticoat, and an old driving cape.

"Oh, mercy on us, Mester Lucas! What'll we do now? I never thought I'd get out alive—I'd be there still if Mr. Oakapple hadn't roused me. Are you all right, Missie? Dear, what a lucky thing Fanny was away, and Abby and Pinhorn left—"

"Can you stay with Anna-Marie, Mrs. Gourd?" said Lucas quickly. "I want to get the pony out of the stables in case the fire goes that way—"

He ran to the stable wing, but found that Mr. Oakapple had already had the same thought, and was leading out Noddy the mare, draped in a horse blanket.

"Garridge isn't there—but it's lucky I went, old Gabriel was fast asleep, and smelling of gin. There he comes now. Hey, Gabriel—help me pull out the governess cart, will you?"

When Lucas returned to where he had left Sir Randolph, the baronet was no longer lying in the snow. He had staggered to his feet and moved some paces away, and was swaying unsteadily, looking with a dazed expression at the golden flames leaping through the skeleton of his house.

Old Gabriel limped up and began talking to Mrs. Gourd. "My stars, what a to-do! 'Tis a mercy none on us was burned in oor beds. Eh, what a fell sight. 'Tis as well owd Sir Quincy isn't here to see it, it would surely break his heart—"

"*He* doesn't care," hissed Mrs. Gourd, looking at Sir Randolph still staring raptly at the flames. "*He* won't grieve."

The baronet seemed to catch the import of her words and turned toward her. "Quiet, woman! Still your clappering!" he growled.

The housekeeper gaped at him—he was indeed a strange spectacle, leaning on a beribboned cane, dressed in what appeared to be a kind of uniform, jacket, waistcoat, and knee breeches, all made of black-and-white striped velvet. He wore black buckled shoes and ruffled shirt—but all were grimed and smeared with soot, and wet with the snow which, as it met the heat of the blaze, hissed and turned to rain.

Sir Randolph suddenly laughed—a wild, high-pitched laugh that seemed to echo the crackle of the fire. "Care? Because this wretched heap of brick burns, that has brought me nothing *but* care since I first stepped inside its doors? Care? I tell you, I'm blithe to see it burn. Grieve? I'd sooner it were a heap of ash, any day, than let those bloodsucking revenue men get their tentacles on it—or *you*—" He suddenly swung round on Anna-Marie, who was standing between Mrs. Gourd and Gabriel.

So far as Lucas knew, it was the first time he had laid eyes on her, and the sight of her seemed to discompose him terribly. He stared and stared at her.

"Now, sir," remonstrated Mrs. Gourd. "That's downright wicked. How can you say such things? What about the bairns—what about the poor childer? Where are they to go?"

Sir Randolph made no answer. His eyes were still fixed on Anna-Marie, who stared back at him, her small pale face very clearly illuminated by the red flickering light.

"Denzil's daughter, eh?" muttered Sir Randolph harshly, weaving his head to and fro, like a fighter trying to dodge invisible blows that were being rained on him from the dark air. "M'best friend Denny's little daughter. Well, m'dear, you had a warmer welcome here than you may have reckoned. Have t'find—'nother roof f'yourself now, though. T'other brat, too—Mary's boy. No more roosting at Midnight Court, eh? And it's no use hoping that those nagging lawyers got me t'change my will; no use hoping that—" He swayed, recovered, and, leaning so close to Anna-Marie that she stepped back in alarm, he said, confidentially, "I'll tell your father, m'dear, when I see him, that I didn't much care for his slice of Clutterby Pie—"

Then, before anybody realized what he would be about and could make an attempt to stop him, he swung round on his heel and, assisting himself with his cane, made straight for the main part of the blaze, at a rapid, staggering run.

"Sir Randolph!" screamed Mrs. Gourd.

"Stop, stop, sir!" shouted Lucas, and dashed after him.

"Stay there, you young fool!" exclaimed Mr. Oakapple, and shoved Lucas back so hard that he slipped and fell in the snow. By the time Lucas had picked himself up, several other men, whom he had not seen before, had suddenly appeared, running from the direction of the stable wing.

They went after Mr. Oakapple.

"Where is he? Where has he gone?" Lucas picked himself up and started toward the house again.

"Dom fool," he heard someone say. Did they mean him, or Mr. Oakapple? A moment later he saw that the men were coming back, carrying something—a body, limp, and apparently lifeless.

"Oh, who is it?" cried Anna-Marie. "Is it that man—Sir Rrandolph?"

But it was Mr. Oakapple, who sagged in their arms with closed eyes.

"He's not *dead*?" said Lucas in horror.

"Nay, but he's badly burned—and summat fell on his head, a whole mess o' brick—t'fool would go in after t'other one—who moost 've been led on by Old Scratch himself! Ran straight into t'middle o' t'fire—did ye iver see the like?"

Mr. Oakapple was so black with soot and smoke that it was impossible to see how bad his injuries were.

"We had better get him to the infirmary," said Lucas. He had often passed the entrance, going to and from the Mill. "Why don't you lay him in the pony trap, on some straw, and I'll take him in right away.—What about Sir Randolph?" he added reluctantly.

"Nay, lad, not a hope—he met as well have joomped into a pottery kiln." Lucas shuddered. "Ony road, best get t'other one in afore he cooms to. There's nowt to be doon here—t'fire's taken too strong a hold—seems to ha' started oop i' six or siven places at oonce."

Lucas, too, had felt this must be the case. He pondered about it, as he backed the shivering Noddy between the shafts and fastened her collar. Otherwise, how could the fire have spread so very rapidly?

Had somebody lit it?

He found Anna-Marie at the rear of the trap, busy covering Mr. Oakapple with a blanket.

"I come with you," she announced.

"Yes, do," said Lucas. He certainly did not know what else to do with her.

It was a long, silent, and thoughtful drive into Blastburn. Mr. Oakapple did not recover consciousness. Neither Anna-Marie nor Lucas felt in the mood for chat. Once only was the silence broken, when she asked in a subdued voice, "Luc-asse?"

"Well?"

"What will happen to us now?"

"I don't know," said Lucas.

PART TWO
Midnight

At the infirmary a gray-robed, white-capped sister admitted them, briskly told off two porters to put Mr. Oakapple on a stretcher and carry him in; then Lucas and Anna-Marie were dismissed to a waiting room where they were left for a long, long time. Nobody came near, and the time dragged. Anna-Marie pulled the doll, Fifine, out of her pocket and sat on a bench with one foot tucked beneath her, sucking her finger. In the midst of his relief that the doll had been saved—the loss of Fifine would certainly have been the last straw for Anna-Marie—Lucas had a feeling of desolation as he remembered how very few of his own belongings he had managed to secure: a purse, which his mother had knitted him, containing a very little money which he had been trying to save for an emergency; two of his favorite pens; a miniature of his parents; and his brown leather book. Everything else would probably be burned to ashes by now, judging from the speed with which the fire had been progressing. And he was anxious for the book. When he went to harness the mare he had laid it, wrapped in a bit of sack, on top of the rain-water barrel by the stable; would it be all right there? In his anxiety to get Mr. Oakapple to hospital he had forgotten it.

They were sitting on an uncomfortable bench. The small bare room was not very warm; an iron stove at the far end had a faint glow coming from its firebox, but gave off little heat. By degrees Anna-Marie slid along until she could lean against Lucas; he thought that she sank into a half-doze, sucking away at her finger. For himself, he sat comfortlessly awake, staring at the future.

He and Anna-Marie were now doubly orphans—for

there seemed no possibility that Sir Randolph could still be alive. Would there be any part of Midnight Court left standing, the stables perhaps, in which they could continue to live? Would there be any money for them to live on? Would the Mill have to be sold? Would Mr. Oakapple be all right?

So many questions, and so few answers.

Anna-Marie stirred restlessly. Her head slipped back at an awkward angle, and Lucas put an arm round her so that she would have something more comfortable to lean against.

At last a youngish, plump-faced man in a frock coat came into the room. He walked quickly but he looked extremely tired. Lucas guessed that in a town like Blastburn, full of factories and foundries, there might be plenty doing at the infirmary all night long.

"I'm Doctor Whitaker," the man said. "Did you come in with the burn case?"

Lucas nodded, his mouth suddenly dry. "Will—will he be all right?" It was hard to speak; the words came in a croak from the back of his throat.

"He's got some bad burns," the doctor said. "Face, hands, and chest. Lucky for him we're used to burn cases here. But he'll have to stop in for at least three weeks— maybe a month or more."

"Is he awake? May I see him?" Lucas said nervously.

"No, boy. We have given him laudanum to make him sleep and kill the pain. Come back in eight hours or so. You might as well go home now."

"I see. Thank you, sir." Home? Lucas wondered. Where was home?

Anna-Marie had woken when the doctor came in. She took her finger out of her mouth and asked matter-of-factly, "Is there money to pay for Meester Ookapool? Should we bring him food here?"

Lucas was both surprised and ashamed that he had not thought of these questions.

The doctor looked kindly down at Anna-Marie. "Ask at the desk in the vestibule how much there is to pay. You can bring it next time you come. And do not bring food until the sisters tell you to. At present the patient will be taking only liquids."

"*Merci, monsieur,*" Anna-Marie said gravely.

At the desk they learned that there would be eighteen shillings to pay a week for Mr. Oakapple's care. Eighteen shillings! Lucas looked in despair at the contents of his purse. It held some twenty-nine shillings—all he had in the world. Sir Randolph had originally announced his intention of allowing Lucas ten shillings a week, but this allowance had been paid only about half a dozen times in full—sometimes Sir Randolph had handed out a portion of the sum; more often he had forgotten it completely. Since there was, in any case, little to spend money on at Midnight Court, Lucas had given up carrying cash about with him, and had never made much of a push to obtain his allowance; now he wished that he had done so.

They walked out into the hospital forecourt. A dim yellow dawn was beginning to break; the snow had stopped falling at last, but lay thick on the ground. The yard was trackless; the street beyond had already been churned into muddy ruts by the never-ending traffic of wagons taking supplies to the factories. But as the pony cart climbed the hill out of town the fields on either side of the road and the height of moorland farther off rose in curves of spotless white.

"It's very beautiful," said Lucas.

"Me, I do not find it so," remarked Anna-Marie, shivering. "And it is going to be a great nuisance to us."

"Why?"

"Well, I have been thinking, Luc-asse," she surprised

him by saying. "Sir Rrandolph is dead, and Monsieur Ook-apool is in the 'ospital, and our house is very likely burned, we shall have to find somewhere else to live."

"We certainly shall," Lucas agreed.

"Lodgings cost much money—so does food, we have also to pay for *ce pauvre* Monsieur Ookapool. We shall need a great deal of money, *ça se voit.* Have you got any?"

"Very little," he said gloomily.

"Ni moi non plus. We shall have to find work. You are a boy; you are big and strong and can do many things," she said calmly, "but for a girl like me, it is not so easy to earn money. But in Calais sometimes, when we are very poor, and Papa is ill, I am collecting often *les bouts de cigare*—"

"Cigar stubs—"

"Oui, cigar stubs—I am picking up many in the streets and from them making whole new cigars; in this way I get enough money to buy bread and *saucisson* for Papa and me."

"Did you though?" said Lucas, looking at Anna-Marie with surprise.

"But the cigar stubs are not so easy to find if the streets are snowy, *enfin.* So I may have to think of something else to do. Perhaps I can look after people's babies."

"Can you do that?"

She nodded. *"Si.* I get on well with them. *Cela m'amuse bien.* But for such tasks I think we may need to go and live in the town, not out 'ere so far away."

"Well, let's see first what has happened to our house. If we can go on living in Midnight Court, that will save us having to pay for lodgings."

"Bien, c'est vrai. It is lucky we have the horse and cart; *cela sera très utile."*

They drove on over the brow of the hill and through the lodge gate. Lucas glanced down at his companion, think-ing, Who would have imagined she had so much sense in her?

There she sat, wrapped in his old black duffel-jacket; there she sat, looking about six, she was sucking her finger again, her two skimpy little plaits hung down untidily, and she was planning away for their future as shrewdly as if she had been doing it for years.

Mrs. Gribbit, the lodgekeeper's wife, came out to say, "How is poor Mester Oakapple then?" And when Lucas had told her, she went on, "T'constables have coom oop from t'town to inspect t'ruins because foul play is soospected. They found Sir Randolph—all charred to a wisp he was, nowt left of him really—so he's been took away and put in a box."

"Oh, well, I suppose that's best," Lucas said hastily, hoping that Anna-Marie had not heard. He could not pretend grief at the death of Sir Randolph, who had not given him kindness or generosity, or even fair treatment.

"Nobody else was killed in the fire?" Anna-Marie asked.

"No, miss. Eh, it is a do. You're kindly welcome to coom back and have a soop of tea when ye've seen the constables, both of ye; I daresay ye can do with a warm-up."

They thanked her, and drove on to the ruins.

Half a dozen constables in top hats were wandering about, carefully inspecting all that was to be seen. There was not much. The destruction had been very complete. The fire must have spread even faster than Lucas had thought it might, after they had gone: everything, even the servants' quarters and the stable block had burned down to the very foundations. All that remained of the huge house with its many rooms, its tall chimneys, and its grandeur were some hundreds of yards of ashes and blackened beams, already half covered in snow. A few sad remnants lay about—a broom, a rockingchair, a washtub. The rainwater barrel on which Lucas had left his book lay on its side with one stave knocked in. Of the book there was no sign.

Lucas could not feel much sorrow about the house. Its

grandeur had had no value for him; he had been cold and lonely and unhappy and even hungry there.

But for his book he did grieve.

The superior officer of the constables, a thick-set man called Inspector Wedge, came up to Lucas and introduced himself.

"Now, Master Bell," he said, "were you aware of anybody in the town who might have borne a groodge against your grandfather?"

"Just about everybody in the town, I should think," Lucas said. "He was my guardian, not my grandfather."

"Oh," said Inspector Wedge, making a note. "Why do you say that?"

"He owed money to people and didn't pay them. He had halved the wages of the people at Midnight Mill. He had had two men sent to jail for protesting."

"Yes, that seems to tie oop with what we had heard. Now, we have observed that separate fires were kindled in half a doozen places, so as to burn the house down. It was ondoubtedly a malicious act. Did you observe any strangers at the scene of the fire last night?"

"There were some men," said Lucas. "I saw them in the stableyard. I took them for firemen."

"Did you recognize any of them?"

"No, it was snowing too hard to see clearly. And then we took my tutor off to the infirmary."

"So, for all you know, those men could have started the fire?"

"No, they could not," Anna-Marie put in composedly. Inspector Wedge was somewhat taken aback. He smiled nervously at Anna-Marie, displaying shockingly black and broken teeth.

"Why could they not, missie?" he inquired. "This would be little Miss Bell, I daresay?"

"*Non,* my name is Murgatroyd," she replied coldly. "And

the men could not have begun the fire, for I heard Sir Randolph say that he had done it himself."

"Himself, miss?" The inspector was even more startled. "Why should he do that?"

"Why, so as not to let the tax people get hold of it," Anna-Marie said simply. "Or us, of course," she added, "*Luc-asse et moi.* Imagine going to such a lot of trouble to keep other people from having his house. He was a very mean man—*quel type!*" And she thoughtfully scrunched a pile of frozen black ashes under her foot.

"But Sir Randolph had died before the stable block started to burn," the inspector persisted. "So the other men could have burned that?"

"Yes, perhaps. If it hadn't already caught." None of this seemed at all important to Lucas. The house was burned, it was destroyed. Anna-Marie and he were cold and hungry, Mr. Oakapple was hurt, they had had very little sleep and no breakfast, and they needed to find a place to live. Why bother to stand here in the freezing wind, arguing about who had set fire to the house, or why? Very likely Sir Randolph had begun it and other people, attracted by the blaze, had looted what they could and finished it off. Such a thing seemed quite possible and not interesting to him.

"I'm afraid I can't help you any more," he said politely.

Anna-Marie plainly felt as he did, but she was less polite about it.

"Why are these stupid men asking these stupid questions?" she said crossly.

At that moment Lucas noticed the bent old figure of Gabriel Towzer come out of the lodge and wave to them. "If you should want us again, Mr. Throgmorton, my guardian's man of business, will tell you where we are to be found," he told the inspector. "Come along, Anna-Marie."

They discovered, when they reached old Gabriel, that he had a suggestion to make.

"If ye've nowhere else to go, ye're kindly welcome to coom along wi' me to my widowed sister as roons a lodging house i' Blastburn. It's noon what ye'll be used to, but th'rooms is clean enough, if my sister is a bit of a mickletongue."

They thanked him, and said they would be glad to come along with him.

On the drive into Blastburn, Anna-Marie demanded of Mr. Towzer what had become of the other servants.

"Well, missie, not to put too fine a point on it, Sir Randolph was owing 'em all umpteen months o' wages, so they've e'en gone off to do as best they can for theirselves; they reckoned there was no bread and butter to be gained from loitering here."

Lucas felt rather disgusted that they had not even bothered to stay and find out what would become of little Anna-Marie, but he could see they might feel they owed scant loyalty to the household where they had received such poor treatment.

When they reached the town, old Gabriel directed them to his sister's house.

"Aye, she lets rooms to seafarers, doos my sister Kezia; she lives not far from t'docks. Her husband used to work i' Murgatroyd's, but he got killed by t'shootle five year agone, poor chap. However she doos noon so bad."

The dock area, which they had not previously visited, was in a low-lying quarter of the town, where the river ran out into the North Sea.

The roads here were neither paved nor cobbled, and they were already a mess of mud and slush. Tiny grim rows of houses were jammed tightly together on land that had probably been salt marsh before the town spread over it, and was still, Gabriel told them, liable to flood if there was an unusually high tide.

"They've built dykes all along t'edge o' t'sea—t'Mayor

had soom Dootchman coom over to show 'em how—but reckon they stinted a bit in th'height o' t'dykes. But doan't ee worrit, my sister Kezia'll put ye in oopstairs rooms where ye'll be safe enow."

"What is the river's name?" Anna-Marie asked, looking doubtfully at the tossing dirty coffee-colored water that swept past tidal mud banks covered with industrial rubbish, dead cats, broken dishes, and other oddments.

" 'Tis called the Tidey River, missie; on account o' the tides, I dessay."

"I think rather it should be called the *un*tidy river," pronounced Anna-Marie, and then, impressed by her own cleverness, she dug Lucas in the ribs and exclaimed, "Luc, Luc-asse, I have made a joke in English!"

Lucas, however, was not in a joking mood. He was dismayed by the look of this neighborhood, which seemed unutterably miserable, dirty, and unwelcoming. Rough-looking men stood idling on wharfsides; rats scuffled in garbage heaps; the houses looked damp and ruinous, although it was plain they had not long been built.

However the house of Mrs. Tetley, Gabriel's sister, seemed in good enough repair and commendably clean, with two scrubbed steps and even a knocker on the door. Lucas tied the pony to a fence while Gabriel knocked.

The door was abruptly pulled open by a hard-faced, gray-haired woman, wearing a sacking apron over a print gown. She held a broom in one hand, a rag in the other.

"Eh, Gabriel, is it thee?" she said shortly "What ill wind brings thee here?—Well, doan't stand loitering there in t'street, man, coom in if ye're cooming. I've all my grates and my stairs to do, yet."

"Nay, hadn't ye heard, Kezia? T'Court's been burned down, and I'm bahn to find another lodging."

"Well, ye needn't think ye can coom here for nowt, I can't afford to house ye free. If ye coom, ye moost pay like any other body," she said sourly. "I *have* got a coople o' rooms, as it falls, for the *Queen of Scots* joost sailed. So ye can coom for a week or two, till ye're suited. . . . So t'Court burned down, did it? Not before it was time, I daresay, if deserts are owt to go by. I've got no kind feelings toward Sir Randolph as ye know."

Lucas wondered if she had them toward anybody. He and Anna-Marie, not knowing what else to do, had followed Gabriel into the house. They found themselves in a small bleak front parlor with oilcloth on the floor and texts on the walls and a general smell of chill and damp.

"Who are *they?*" Mrs. Tetley asked Gabriel in an undertone.

"They're t'bairns from t'Court, Kezia. Sir Randolph was killed in t'fire, and they're needing a place to lodge too, sithee."

"Have ye no kin to look out for ye, then?" she asked, and when they shook their heads, "Well, I say t'same to ye as to Gabriel; ye can bide if ye pay. I take no folk as can't pay."

Lucas said they had every intention of paying and asked how much.

"One-an'-six a week each, ten shillings more if ye want breakfast or dinner. Ye can use the back kitchen to cook in afore seven or after nine. And use t'back door to go in and out. And keep out of t'house between eight and six; I cannot have lodgers sculling around oonderfoot all day long. No tobacco or alcoholic liquors are allowed on the premises." She gave Gabriel a sharp look. "Not even if it's my own kin! And no lodgers in this room, which is private. You pay on Saturdays, in advance."

Rather dispirited, Lucas agreed to these terms, and then said that he would go and call on the lawyer, Mr. Throgmorton, who would probably have arrived at his office by now, for it wanted but an hour to noon.

He asked Mrs. Tetley if Anna-Marie might break the

rules for once and go to bed, for she was pale with fatigue, and heavy-eyed. Permission was grudgingly given. Anna-Marie did not much want to be left, but since old Gabriel would be downstairs in the kitchen she at last consented. Lucas promised that he would return as soon as he had seen Mr. Throgmorton and found a place to stable the pony.

"But don't get anxious if it takes quite a long time," he added.

Mr. Throgmorton's office when he found it, after asking his way a good many times, was not calculated to raise confidence. It consisted of three small dusty rooms up six flights of steep stairs; it was plain that Sir Randolph had not wasted money on having his business handled by an expensive lawyer.

"Have you an appointment?" asked an elderly clerk in the outer office, who was endeavoring to disguise the extremely frayed condition of his sleeves with ink, presumably for want of any other occupation.

"No, but I hope Mr. Throgmorton will see me," Lucas said.

"Name?" inquired the clerk as if he personally considered this an unlikely outcome.

"Lucas Bell. Sir Randolph, who died last night, was my guardian."

The clerk nodded skeptically at that, and shrugged his shoulders; however, he put his head through the door to the inner office, which was screened off by a glass partition, held a low-voiced conversation, and came back presently to say, "He'll see you. You can go in," as if he were conferring a great and undeserved treat.

Lucas walked through the door. The small gray Mr. Throgmorton sat behind his desk, buffing his fingernails with a bit of chamois leather and peering at Lucas over his pince-nez.

"Now then, what's this, what's this, what's this?" he rattled out very quickly, giving a glance as he did so at his fob watch. "Sir Randolph, the late Sir Randolph Grimsby—you are asserting that he was your guardian?"

"Yes, sir. He was." Mr. Throgmorton had not invited Lucas to sit, so he stood.

"You have proof of this?"

"Why—why, no, sir," said Lucas, somewhat startled. "I—I suppose—that is—when my father died, he appointed Sir Randolph as my guardian in his will—so I was sent to live with him at Midnight Court—"

"You say your name is?"

"Bell, sir. Lucas Bell. My father was Edwin Bell, Sir Randolph's partner."

"Humph. Have you a copy of the will?"

"No, sir. Have you not one?"

Throgmorton's eye flashed briefly with a curious light; it recalled to Lucas the lawyer's muttered aside on the day when Sir Randolph had attacked Mr. Gobthorpe the tax officer. What had he said then? Something about taking his ease in Monte Carlo? But he made no reply now; merely shook his head and set the tips of his fingers together. Lucas wondered rather hopelessly where the will might have got to? Would it be in India? How did one look for a will?

"Have you any proof that you are Lucas Bell?"

"No, sir," said Lucas, beginning to feel as if he were walking about in a fog. What proof could he produce? The purse his mother had made him? "But I have been living at Midnight Court for a year—you have seen me there yourself, sir."

"Tush," said the lawyer, peering at Lucas through his glasses and then away again. "One boy is much the same as another. Why did you come to see me?"

"Why—" said Lucas, somewhat startled. "We have no money—nowhere to live—"

"We?"

"I and the little girl—Anna-Marie Murgatroyd—we hoped that Sir Randolph might have made some provision in his will—as my father was Sir Randolph's partner—he had told me that when I came of age I should have a half-share in Murgatroyd's Mill—"

"Now look here, boy," said Mr. Throgmorton, setting his thin lips together so tightly that they almost disappeared in his sallow face, "if this is an impudent imposture, you have come to the wrong shop! I daresay a dozen boys may turn up, claiming to be Sir Randolph's heir. We have already had six this morning—is it six, Swainby?" he called through the open door.

"Seven, sir."

"But you will not find it easy to pull the wool over *my* eyes. I can smell out an imposter, I assure you!"

"But, sir, I am no imposter. Anyone will tell you that I have been living at Midnight Court."

"In any case," said Mr. Throgmorton, suddenly switching to another tack, "it is quite useless expecting any money under Sir Randolph's will—perfectly useless—I can tell you here and now. Firstly, he never gave the least intimation of wishing to leave money to any Bells, Murgatroyds, or whatever else the pack of you choose to call yourselves. Never made any such suggestion to me. Secondly, Sir Randolph made no will of any kind, so there is in any case no question of your inheriting. Thirdly, if he had made a will, there was no money to leave—by the time he died he had not a penny in the world, in fact he owed some tens of thousands. Even if the house had not been burned, the sale of it still would not have covered his debts."

"But the Mill—"

"The Mill has already been sold, in order to pay the arrears of tax."

"Who to?" asked Lucas, with a vague notion that he might go and plead for his rights with the new owner.

"To a company—" Mr. Throgmorton slid the pince-nez down his nose and rummaged among the papers on his desk—"a company called the British Rug, Mat, and Carpet Manufacturing Corporation in Threadneedle Street, London."

"Oh," said Lucas. His heart sank. How could he possibly go to London, let alone soften the heart of something called the British Rug, Mat, and Carpet Manufacturing Corporation? "So—so what should I do, sir, do you think?"

"Do? Do?" snapped Mr. Throgmorton peevishly. "Why, stop bothering me, go away, and let me get on with my business. I do not know why I have taken such pains to give you all this information, after all! There is work to be had in the town—you look like an able-bodied boy—do not let me catch you begging here again, or I shall have you taken up for vagrancy!"

"I had not the least intention of begging, sir," said Lucas, suddenly angry. "I merely wished to know what I was entitled to." He drew himself up. "I am sorry to have troubled you." And he walked quickly away through the outer office and down the dusty stairs.

He was heavy hearted as he regained the street. His hopes of Mr. Throgmorton had not been particularly high, but this reception was even worse than he had feared.

He walked slowly and gloomily along the shabby street, with his hands in his pockets, looking vaguely about him, wondering if Mr. Throgmorton had been speaking the truth, and how he was going to break this bad news to Anna-Marie.

But then his gloom was somewhat dispersed—he did not quite know why—by the sight of a thin girl who was walking ahead of him, pushing along an untidy pair of infants in a baby carriage. They were not a particularly prepossessing pair, but the girl was talking to them and laughing, as if she enjoyed their company, and their grubby little faces wore broad smiles.

Anna-Marie would not be too discouraged, he suddenly felt sure. What a good thing it was that she turned out to have such a practical disposition: if she had been the whining, helpless kind, they would have been properly in the suds. Indeed, Lucas acknowledged to himself, he owed it to her calm discussion of their prospects on the drive home from the hospital that Mr. Throgmorton's unhelpfulness had not been more of a shock.

With some difficulty he found his way back to Haddock Street, where Mrs. Tetley's house was situated. The first thing that met his eyes was the sight of Anna-Marie, with her skirts pinned up, scrubbing the front steps and shoveling snow off the cobbled pavement.

"Eh—*te voilà!*" she said, pushing the hair off her face with the back of a dirty hand.

"Anna-Marie! You shouldn't be doing that!" said Lucas, rather upset.

"*Pourquoi pas?* Meeses Tetley ask for our money in advance. I say I have no money, me; so she say, well then, she will take it this week in work. So I have cook the dinner and done much cleaning. But now I think it is time we go back to see Monsieur Ookapool, no?"

"Yes, it is."

"Then I wash," she said, and swiftly disappeared down a path at the side of the house to the back yard, where there was a pump.

Lucas fetched the pony, which he had arranged to leave in a nearby shed at an extra cost of sixpence a week.

Anna-Marie reappeared almost at once with pink-scrubbed face and hands.

"I am thinking, Luc-asse," she began in a low voice when they were well away from the house, "that we had better stop at a *bijouterie* and sell my beads, for we have no money to pay for Monsieur Ookapool." She fingered the necklace of tiny pearls that she always wore clasped round her neck.

"It's all right. I thought of that. Don't sell your pearls," he said.

"You have some money?"

"I sold my watch."

"Then how will you know what time it is?" she said, frowning.

"Well, we are living in the town—there is always a clock somewhere. You hang on to your pearls. But I think you should hide them—it's a rough district that we are living in."

"There is nowhere safe," Anna-Marie said. "When I am cooking the dinner I have need of a *mouchoir* from my coat pocket so I go to our room. There is Madame Tetley, prying through our things—what there is to pry through. I think she is *méchante;* she looks like a scrubbing brush, and she smells like a bar of soap. I do not think we shall like living in her house."

"Nor do I," said Lucas glumly. "But perhaps presently we can find something better when I have found some work."

Rather reluctantly, he then told Anna-Marie about his disappointing interview with Mr. Throgmorton. But she only shrugged.

"*Quoi donc?* Sir Randolph has no more money, and his house is burned. To me it does not seem to make much difference if this Trog—"

"Throgmorton—"

"Trog-morton knows you or not."

Lucas decided to keep his suspicions of the lawyer to himself. What was the point in loading Anna-Marie with yet another worry?

They left the pony cart in the hospital courtyard and went to the desk, where Lucas paid over the money for

Mr. Oakapple's keep, and was told that one of them only might visit him for ten minutes, no more. Anna-Marie's face fell when she heard this, but she said, "You go see him, Luc; you know him best. Me, I wait here."

The visit proved a disappointment. The tutor was still not fully conscious, due to the laudanum he had been given, but even so he was plainly in a good deal of pain; he tossed and turned restlessly, cried out about someone called Grenvile, and then fell to incomprehensible muttering, plucking at his sheet with heavily-bandaged hands. His face, too, was all swathed in bandages.

One of the gray-robed sisters came and fed him some cooling drink through a straw.

When Lucas asked anxiously if Mr. Oakapple were going on all right, she told him that it was too early to say yet. He went back down the many flights of stone stairs in a very low and apprehensive state of mind. He had hoped that the tutor might be sensible enough to talk to—for all they knew, Mr. Oakapple might have a family who would be anxious to know about his plight and to help him—but at present getting any information from him was plainly out of the question.

Back in the downstairs lobby, he found Anna-Marie looking pale and scared. She clutched hold of Lucas's arm.

"What's the matter?" he asked.

A burly, shock-headed youth pushed by; Lucas caught a glimpse of his face and wondered where he had seen it before.

"Come away!" whispered Anna-Marie. "We talk outside." She pulled his hand, and he followed her out. The short afternoon had already darkened; the wind was rising and more snow had begun to fall.

"That *type*—" she began, when they were in the cart and moving. "You remember him, we meet him the other day in the street when we are lost—"

"Oh, yes, of course; now I remember. I knew I'd seen

him somewhere," said Lucas, frowning. "Did he bother you just now? Tease you?"

"No, no, worse than that! He ask if I have a friend in the hospital, sick. I say to him, 'What is that to you?' He say, 'Bien, if you do not pay me, I see your friend get no food, no medicine; he soon die!' "

"But how can he say so?" said Lucas, frowning. "He certainly isn't a doctor—"

"No, he is a brigand! It is a gang, who make menaces— they are assassins! The porter at the desk have told me it is best to pay them. Last week they pull a poor old man out of his bed and leave him in the yard in the rain because his sons will not pay."

"How much do they want?" asked Lucas, his heart sinking.

"Also another twenty-five shillings."

"But that's wicked—it's wicked to get money from people by such threats—"

The day began to be more than Lucas could take. Too many things were piling up against them.

"Of course it is wicked," said Anna-Marie. "But what can you do? Il faut payer ces voleurs, ces cochons! We do not want poor M. Ookapool put out in the snow. He is the one friend we have left, I think."

N EXT DAY LUCAS began doggedly looking for work. Questing back and forth, back and forth, he soon acquired a wretched familiarity with the unpleasing streets of Blastburn. Factories, shops, mills, collieries—he tried them all, and the answer was always the same: "We want no new hands, we are turning off those we have. Times are hard."

Nobody wanted an inexperienced boy. And more particularly, Lucas thought, no one wanted a boy who had any connection at all with Sir Randolph Grimsby.

The only place he had not tried—out of pride, out of a strong disinclination to show his face there, and a strong feeling that there he would be most unpopular of all—was Murgatroyd's Mill.

At the end of ten hours' hunting he was footsore, chilled to the bone, hungry, disheartened, and no nearer finding any employment.

Turning wearily from the gates of Thrupp's Furniture Manufactury—where they wanted only experienced master carpenters, inlayers, mortice men, or turners—he perceived by the great clock on the town hall that it was nearly six; and he started glumly trudging in the direction of Haddock Street. How could he face Anna-Marie with such unrelieved news of failure?

The moment of facing her came sooner than he expected. A little figure ran down the steps of the market building and came hurrying to meet him across the snowy, gaslit square.

"*Hé,* is that you, Luc-asse? I thought I recognized your walk. Listen, affairs are not too bad. Only figure to yourself, I seem to be the only person who has thought of picking up cigar ends in this foolish town, and I have collected such a quantity! Even in the snow and slush I find them, and I think it will not be too hard to dry them out. All the rich manufacturers must smoke them all the time. I have already collected three basketsful—first, I put them in my handkerchief, but it became too wet, so then I found me an old basket on the riverside—and I have sold some ends already to a man in a tobacco shop for twelve-some shillings to buy food for supper. Tomorrow I buy papers to make my own cigars; one can make more profit that way—"

She interrupted her chatter to say, "You look very tired, Luc-asse, and not at all cheerful. Come in here out of the snow and tell me what has happened to you."

At the top of the main square was a big, arcaded market building, open at each end. Inside were dozens of stalls, still doing brisk business even at this late hour, for the shift workers from the factories wanted food at all hours of the day.

There were stalls with fish and meat, stalls with big loaves of bread and shiny doughcakes, stalls where rabbits and hares dangled in their fur, stalls piled with apples and potatoes and cabbages. Clothes were sold here, too—racks of cheap cotton trousers and jackets and print dresses occupied one corner; a table was covered with wooden clogs; in another corner were blankets and household utensils, all of the simplest, coarsest kind. Another corner held second-hand goods—furniture, pots, pans, books, children's clothes, tools, farm implements. Elsewhere could be found plants in pots, birds in cages, vividly colored medicines in bottles, bales of thin gaudy cotton. Everything that humans could wish to buy—humans who did not have much money—seemed to be on sale here.

The floor of the market was stone-paved, wet and dirty from the snowy feet of the countless shoppers who had been tramping through all day long. A faint muggy warmth from all the people in it made the arcade at least more sheltered than the square outside, which was scoured by a bitter wind.

Anna-Marie pulled Lucas along to a stall with a crudely painted sign that said "Veg Soup halfpenny per Cup."

"Here," she said, "I am sure you must be hungry, and I feel *comme un meurt-de-faim!*" She bought them each a half-pennyworth from an old lady who stood behind the counter by a big iron caldron, ladling soup into brown mugs.

Lucas felt it was wrong that he should be allowing Anna-Marie to spend money on him, and made a faint protest, but she said, "*Chut!* We share all we have, you look after me; I look after you also."

The soup was thick, tasteless, made mostly from potatoes or large beans, but it was hot and comforting. Lucas cradled the coarse earthenware mug in his hands, beginning to feel just slightly more hopeful. There *must* be work somewhere that he could do.

"Now," said Anna-Marie, when the soup was drunk, "over here is the stall of Monsieur 'Obday, who is a *marchand de bric-à-brac*—I talk to him already today; he says I can have a corner of his *étalage* to sell my cigars when I have made them."

Mr. Hobday nodded in a friendly manner to Anna-Marie. He was a wizened little man with one shoulder higher than the other, very small quickly moving eyes, and two very large red ears like basket handles. At the moment he was engaged in selling a wooden mangle to a housewife. When she and her son had carried their purchase away between them, he came over to Anna-Marie and said, "Well, yoong lady, have you made enough money to buy me out yet?"

"*Non*, monsieur, but I have here my friend Luc. I think

he will find many useful things for you if you hire him."

To Lucas, Anna-Marie said, "Monsieur 'Obday is looking for a boy to find him things for his stall."

"Mind you, it's mucky work," Mr. Hobday said. "I won't pretend it ain't. No use letting on that you end the day smelling like a rose garden. Such is not the case. But if you're agreeable to that, then there's decent pickings to be made."

"I don't quite understand," Lucas said. He was very tired, and slow to realize that his luck might have turned. "Are you offering me a job?"

"That's it. I can see you're a bright-looking, well-set-up lad. I lost my last tosh boy last week—'e was a good, steady boy, too; we miss 'im crool, me and old Gudgeon; if you're interested in the job, son, and if you're prepared to level up with us and bring in the tosh *as* you find it, and not go skiving off to some other dealer—then the beat's yours."

"Thank you," said Lucas.

"You'll be working with old Gudgeon, he's a very steady cove, been with me a long time; he'll show you the ropes."

Mr. Hobday stuck out a grimy clawlike hand, which Lucas shook, feeling somewhat dazed.

"Start tomorrow, six o'clock," said Mr. Hobday. "Now you'll want clothes, which I dessay you haven't got—a long overcoat—must have big pockets—canvas trowsies and some old slops of shoes; I'll provide those; then you want a bag, and a pole seven or eight feet long: can you get those? Also there's a leather apron needful, and a dark lantern with a bull's-eye. I'll furnish those and you can pay me back out of your wages."

"What are my wages?" inquired Lucas, not yet at all clear as to the nature of this work.

"Five pun' a week, an' ten percent of the value of all you bring in. You'll find it soon mounts up. Right? Right, then. Six o'clock—better make it half five, time for you to get dressed. Good night now, I'm shutting up shop." And Mr. Hobday proceeded to pull down a set of wooden shutters and padlock them so that his stall was completely enclosed. It seemed, Lucas had noticed, to hold a most amazing hugger-mugger of different articles, some common, some possibly valuable, nearly all old and dirty.

Anna-Marie and Lucas left the market and started back toward Haddock Street.

"Where do I look for this stuff that I collect?" asked Lucas. "In the streets?"

"That I am not sure," admitted Anna-Marie. "But without doubt he or this Gudgeon will show you all you need to know. Now we must get you a bag and a pole, and then we had better take some food to poor Monsieur Ookapool, and some money to that *scélérat* at the infirmary."

The pole was cut from a dejected-looking willow, one of a pair that grew on the riverbank near to Mrs. Tetley's house; and there was an old canvas feed sack in the pony cart that would do for the bag, so Lucas was equipped for his new position.

"But, Anna-Marie," he said, "I do not like it at all that you should be alone in the streets all day long, collecting cigar ends. It is too wet and cold for you, and besides, the town is full of rough types; I am afraid that you might get teased, or hurt, or knocked down by one of those wagons that dash along so fast."

"Oh, pooh!" she said. "I can look out for myself, don't worry. And it is a great deal more amusing to be out in the market place looking for cigar ends, I can tell you, than to be at home chez Madame Tetley. She will make me work my fingers to the bone, that one, all day long, and for no pay!"

"Well, I'm sure Mr. Oakapple would not approve of your being out in the streets every day."

"*Eh, bien,* we will ask M. Ookapool what he suggests."

But poor Mr. Oakapple, when they reached his bedside, was still in no case to make constructive suggestions. He seemed to think that he was both conducting and playing the first violin in some huge invisible orchestra, and that his audience consisted of crowned heads and grand duchesses from all over Europe.

"*Lente, lente! Piano, piano!* I am so sorry, your Highness, I am sure the tuba player had no intention of hitting you on the ear. Timpani! Take your elbow off the kettledrum! *Piu maestoso!* Perhaps your Majesty would care to hold the baton for a moment while I adjust the cellist's petticoat? Madamoiselle, please empty your clarinet into the flower-pot, not into my pocket. Thank you, your Majesty, I will be glad to accept a cigar, but if you will excuse me, I shall not smoke it until after the nineteenth movement—"

"*Oh, oh, le pauvre,*" said Anna-Marie, "*il a encore un peu de fièvre—*"

"Please!" cried Mr. Oakapple, "you *must* come in exactly on the thirty-second bar. Let us start again!"

"*C'est inutile,*" said Anna-Marie with a sigh. "It is of no use expecting any helpful ideas from him." She gave the eggs and milk that they had brought for Mr. Oakapple to the sister, and they left the ward. Outside the door was the shock-headed boy, levying his protection money from the friends of patients.

"There you are then, Bright-eyes," he said to Anna-Marie, who gave him a hard look. "Got your subscription to the Friendly Boys' Club, have you?"

"Here already is eight shillings," replied Anna-Marie, handing over the last of her money. "The rest you will get tomorrow."

"All right. But you better bring it tomorrow for certain, or old Ginger Whiskers there will be out in the snow, and that would be a waste of the eight you brought today, wouldn't it?"

"Do you know," said Anna-Marie to Lucas, when they were driving back down the long hill into the heart of Blastburn, "I find this a hateful town. In my opinion everyone who lives here is wicked."

"There don't seem to be many good ones, certainly," agreed Lucas. "Except Mr. Hobday."

"About him we shall see. I think when Monsieur Ooka-pool is better, we go to live somewhere else?"

"If we can afford to move," said Lucas.

By the time they reached Mrs. Tetley's, it was nine o'clock. The eggs and milk for Mr. Oakapple, and rent in advance for a corner of Mr. Hobday's stall had used up a good deal of Anna-Marie's money, but she had also bought a pennyworth of oatmeal, which she mixed with a jugful of water and proceeded to boil over the parsimonious fire in Mrs. Tetley's back kitchen range; when it boiled she added to it a number of crusts, which she had picked up while hunting for cigars. After the whole mess was thoroughly boiled, she and Lucas each had a small potful, which was welcome enough, since the cup of soup in the market was all that either of them had eaten all day. The rest of the porridge was carefully set aside for breakfast in the tin saucepan which had been another of her purchases; then Anna-Marie lit a small tallow candle, and they went upstairs to bed. Most of Mrs. Tetley's other lodgers had already retired.

"Where do we sleep?" whispered Lucas.

"*En haut*—" Anna-Marie gestured upward. They climbed up two flights of stairs, then up a ladder, through a trapdoor. There was a small room—a loft, really, with sloping walls—a pallet on the floor, no other furniture.

"There's only one bed."

"*Soyez tranquille!* I won't disturb your sleep. Seeing that I am not large, that kind Madame Tetley has said I may sleep in here."

Anna-Marie opened a tiny door, only about two foot square, in the sloping wall, and disclosed a kind of little bunk, or closet, large enough, almost, to accommodate a big dog.

"*C'est charmant,* it fits me like a shoe."

And she curled up in it, under a heap of old rags and pieces of torn blanket.

Lucas lay awake for some time on his hard, thin mattress, wondering what the nature of his new employment could be. That it must be disagreeable, he had no doubt; otherwise it must already have been snapped up in this town where it seemed so hard to find any work at all. Five pounds a week! What would he be expected to do for such a huge sum?

But at least it would cover their expenses and pay for Mr. Oakapple's treatment.

At last he drifted into an uneasy slumber.

Lucas had been afraid that he would not be able to wake in time. His dreams were full of anxiety: he was trying to catch a runaway horse, he was late for school, he had lost something terribly precious and important—his brown book! Where was it?—he had broken some promise that he should have kept. . . .

But at least there was no difficulty about waking, or about telling the time during the hours of dark. The town of Blastburn was plentifully supplied with church clocks, and they struck all the quarters, and if they were not in agreement exactly to the minute, at least they made it plain that time was passing. And as well as the church clocks there were factory hooters, screaming their call to work, and there were the trucks and wagons, clanking over iron rails, whistling mournfully in the dark, and there was the knocker-up, running down the streets, thumping with his iron-shod stick on each door as he passed.

"Wake oop, Mrs. Kelsey, luv, it's a grand snowy morning!

"Five o' t'clock, Geordie Thompson, time tha was stirring tha stumps, man!

"Eh, are ye sleeping yet, boys, t'missus has t'bacon a-frying!"

At a quarter past five, Lucas staggered up from his pallet and put on such clothes as he had removed (not many); very little heat from the tiny kitchen fire climbed up as far as Mrs. Tetley's attic. He was stealing softly to the ladder when a soft bump told him that Anna-Marie had scrambled out of her bunk bed.

"Go back to sleep," he whispered. "There's no need for you to stir yet."

"Yes there is! If you are at work, I will be too."

Lucas tried to argue, but she had made up her mind, and there was no time to spare in arguing. So presently they were both tiptoeing down Mrs. Tetley's steep narrow stairs to the chill, stone-paved back kitchen, where Lucas stirred the ashes in the range and laid a couple of sticks on, while Anna-Marie fetched her pot of porridge out from the closet. As she picked up the pan, she let out a stifled shriek and almost dropped it again.

"What's the matter?"

"A big rat! Sitting right by my pan!"

"Lucky you put the lid on. Where is he?"

"He ran into a hole, the horrible brute!" Anna-Marie balanced the pan over the little flame that Lucas had coaxed into life. But the porridge was frozen solid, and the heat had done little more than soften it before they were obliged to gulp it down in hasty spoonfuls. However they also boiled a little water in the kettle that Mrs. Tetley allowed her lodgers to use, and each drank a hot cupful; that was their breakfast.

Lucas equipped himself with his pole and bag; Anna-

Marie took her basket, and they set out. They had expected that the town would be empty and quiet at that time of day, but it was not; many workers went on shift at six o'clock in the morning, and the dark snowy streets were full of hurrying figures: they were like iron filings being drawn toward a magnet, Lucas thought. And the sky was not dark but lit up, here and there, by great bursts of flame as one furnace or another discharged its load of clinker. Little lamplit bakeries displayed loaves and pasties which the running workers bought as they passed, to keep for their midday dinner. Horse-trams, full of factory hands, creaked along the snowy streets. Wagons loaded with produce were already jolting into the market square, and the market building itself was a scene of tremendous activity, as the stall owners carried in crates of goods and laid out their stocks.

"Ah, there you are then, my young cove," Lucas was greeted by Mr. Hobday, who looked like an industrious goblin as he darted about, taking down the shutters of his stall and disposing his extraordinary wares to the best advantage. There were strange fragments of ironmongery, rusty metal pots, pieces of china or stoneware, mostly cracked or broken, chunks of carved stone which might have come off a church, weapons, swords, pistols, even some portions of armor, and a small tray of jewelry.

"And here's Gudgeon, he's prompt to his time, too; punctuality and regular habits is what piles up the lolly. Gudgeon's your mate, boy, he's my other tosher, and he'll show you the ropes; he looks a bit simple, does old Gudgeon, but he's a staunch, cool cove in a tight corner; he's one o' the longest-working toshers in the trade. Well, old Gudgeon, what did you get for me yesterday, eh?"

Gudgeon was a big bony fellow with a leaden complexion, pale bluish eyes, and a broken nose. His hair, which was perfectly white, was cropped so short that it looked like fur, and he was so remarkably dirty that nothing more than the general outline of his person or clothes could be made out. A most extraordinary stench came from him: salty, strong, sweetish, and rank, it seemed to surround him almost visibly. Anna-Marie and Lucas each involuntarily took a pace backward. But Gudgeon did not notice this or take offense if he did; he was carefully unrolling a big canvas bag.

"Here we be, then, mester, look at this lovely little lot," he said proudly. "One candlestick—silver, or my name's not Tom Gudgeon—a velvet tablecloth—or maybe it's an altar cloth—with tassels, three shovels, some pots, a horoscope, length of iron chain, and a statue."

He spread the items out. They were dirty and damp and smelled as bad as their finder. Mr. Hobday was particularly interested in the statue, which was wooden, and seemed to be of an angel; at least it had wings. He inspected it carefully and pronounced that it was a real old 'un or *his* name was not Elias Hobday; some cove at the museum would be sure to fancy it. And the candlestick was a good one too, sterling silver with the smith's name on it.

"A very nice lot, Tom, very good indeed," he congratulated Gudgeon.

"Ah, and there's coins, too, Mester Hobday. Here we are—" Gudgeon pulled a handful of them from a kind of pouch he wore across his front: old dark coins, so thin and dirty that they looked to be of no value at all, but Mr. Hobday studied and sorted them all most carefully.

"See how honest he is, boy? Some toshers 'ud keep such stuff back, but not Tom; honest as butter, he is. I'll get this lot valued, Tom, and give you your chop tomorrow. Now you'd best be showing the boy—what did you say your name was, Luke? right—show him how to put on his rig."

Lucas went behind Mr. Hobday's stall, where he was kitted out in the canvas trousers, long coat, canvas apron, and bag, with a bull's-eye lantern strapped to his chest; a stout hoe head was nailed to his pole.

"Good hunting then, lads," said Mr. Hobday, "and I'll see you at this time tomorrow."

Lucas said a hasty good-bye to Anna-Marie who while he was getting dressed, had purchased a quantity of cigar leaves at another stall, and was now rolling new cigars filled with the teased-out tobacco extracted from yesterday's stubs, which she had left drying overnight.

"Don't wait here for me—go back to Haddock Street at six," he said. "I don't like to think of your being out alone in the dark." And then he thought how foolish this sounded, for daylight had not yet come and there was no sign that it ever would. "I'll take care to be home in time to visit Mr. Oakapple. Do be careful now," he added, still anxious at the thought of her long day alone.

"Perhaps I shall see you about the streets," said Anna-Marie hopefully.

"Perhaps."

But from all this equipment it seemed to Lucas that their destination must be somewhere more dirty and dangerous even than the streets of Blastburn. And so it proved. Tom Gudgeon led the way out of the market building, and stopped immediately, at the foot of the town cross.

" 'Tis handy they keeps this spot swept clear of snow," he said. "Saves us toshers a deal o' shoveling," and he stooped and lifted up a heavy round iron manhole cover. "In wi' you then, lad—don't loiter about."

Lucas approached and looked with horror into the round hole, which had an iron ladder bolted to one side, leading down into the blackness.

"Down *there?*"

"Where else? Tosh don't grow on trees. It ain't picked up lying about in broad daylight."

Lucas could not help shuddering as he stepped backward into the hole, and climbed down the ladder into the dark, dank place below. Gudgeon came down after him, lowering the lid above his head, which made the blackness complete.

When he arrived beside Lucas he stopped and adjusted his bull's-eye, which he had lit beforehand. "Best light yours, boy; here's a tinder."

Lucas lit the tiny bead of light and stared about, his eyes slowly becoming accustomed to the gloom. They were in an oval, brick-vaulted passage, which stank and sweated and ran with damp. Dripping swags of weed or moss hung overhead and horrible-looking gouts of thick slime trickled down the curved walls. Beside them, six inches below the pavement on which they stood, was an eight-foot-wide brick culvert through which rushed an evil-smelling torrent, foaming and gurgling.

"Where is this?" said Lucas. "Where are we?"

It was hard to make oneself heard above the noise of the water, and the loud hollow echoes which caught every word and flung it back and forth.

"Where? In the town drain, o' course. Didn't you know? We're in the sewer. Leastways this here's the main one; there's three running down to the river, an' a whole network o' smaller branches in betwixt. I don't go in those, so much; the rats is too bad. And you dassn't go too far, acos of the tide; it comes up, see, so you have to watch it, and get yourself near an entrance, time she's due to rise. Up to *there*, she can come, on a full tide."

And he pointed to a crusted mark on the wall, far above his head.

Lucas shivered. Being shut up in the dark was one of his private dreads, and he could not conceive of any place more horrible than this black, foul-smelling tunnel. At any moment he thought he might suddenly begin to scream, as the full sense of his situation pressed in on him. But

Gudgeon seemed perfectly at home here. He began to walk along at a measured pace, fishing and poking with his pole in the thick and frothy current. Occasionally he drew something out; more often than not he threw it back. Lucas followed him, doing likewise.

From time to time the liquid flowed over the footway, sometimes knee-deep. Then they were obliged to wade. Tom gestured that Lucas should keep well away from the edge of the footway. From time to time he imparted more information about his way of work.

"There's three of us working the sewers at the moment, me and Lammas and Bugle. Bugle, he has the west tunnel, Lammas has the east, and I keeps to the middle acos I've been at it the longest. The middle's the likeliest for finding tosh, but all's good. Lammas, one time, he found a orrery in the east."

"What's an orrery?"

"I dunno. But it's val'ble; he got thirty nicker for it from the museum. Old Hobday he sells my tosh for me, acos he knows best where to take it an' it saves me trouble, saves me having to get cleaned up. Looking for the things is what I like, for it's more romantical. Mind, some o' those dealers can chouse you to the bone; Hobday, he's fair enough, though.

"Now, remember: allus go where you know, otherwise you may end up in trouble. There's a many side branches where the bottom's guv way and they haven't paved it since I was a nipper; you could go in deeper than the whale hole. So keep to the main drag. Then, never stay in more than six or seven hour, acos of the tide; you got to re-member that."

"Is there anything else to remember?" said Lucas, trying to stop his teeth from chattering. He groped up a heavy thing out of the water, on his pole, but it felt very un-desirably soft and slimy, so he hurriedly flung it back.

"The rats is very dangerous—that's sartin; if you should go up a side branch, always go with another cove, for the varmints are too wide-awake to tackle you then; they know they'd git off second best.

"Then you want to watch out for the hogs, too."

"Hogs?"

Lucas tripped over an irregularity in the floor and only just saved himself from plunging into the sewer.

"Ah. There's a quantity of wild hogs got down into the sewers; don't ask me how they got there for I don't know, but they've been here since Bugle's granda's day; he can remember them. I daresay a couple found their way in some cold winter, and they've bred; they like it down here.

"Now those hogs are man-eaters; you don't want to tangle with them. You hear them coming, you climb up out o' harm's way."

"Climb up where?"

"There's manholes ivery now-and-now; where iver there's a manhole, there's a ladder; or should be, long as some thoughtless cove hasn't swiped it without considering the welfare of his mates."

"How can you tell when the hogs are coming? What kind of a noise do they make?"

"Jist a moment." Gudgeon stooped down, rummaged expertly with his pole, and fetched up a dark, square object which proved, when he wiped the slime off it, to be a box secured with a cord.

"Now a box is allus romantical, for you don't know what might be inside," he observed, feeling it all over. "Come you round here, boy, then we'll get the light from your bull's-eye too; that's the dandy; that's why we carry them this way, strapped to our chestes, so as to leave our maulers free—you need that with the rats too. You want to open a box careful, like, for if there's small things in, like as it might be pearls or di'monds, you don't want to spill 'em; there would be precious little chance of picking them up again."

This box, however, was a disappointment, for it proved to contain only papers; and they were in such a damp, sodden, and blackened condition that it was doubtful if anybody would be able to make anything of them, and certainly not Gudgeon, who, as he told Lucas, had never had the time to learn reading or scribing. However he carefully stowed it away in his bag.

"Mind you, old papers can be worth a mort; you don't want to go a-throwing of them out. Onct Bugle he found an old parchment saying as the town hall belonged to some monastery; caused a lot of trouble, that did, for the *Blastburn Post* printed a story about it, and the old prior he made a commotion and said as how his monks ought to have their hall back agin."

He moved on, swishing along up to his knees in the scummy fluid, which had again flowed over the footway.

"Did they get the hall?" Lucas asked, wanting to keep the conversation alive. The silence, with its echoing drips and splashes, was too uncomfortable.

"No, they niver did; the mayor was one too many for 'em."

"What sort of a noise do the hogs make?" Lucas presently asked again.

"You hears 'em a-squealing and a-swishing along, nine or ten at a time. One thing, they dassn't ever swim, for a hog'll cut his throat with his trotters if he attempts swimming, so, if they comes arter you and there's no ladder within running distance, take to the water."

"I see."

Lucas felt he would rather die than plunge into that disgusting stream, but no doubt if it came to a choice between the sewer and nine man-eating hogs, he might feel differently.

"Hold on a moment, I think I've got something!" he suddenly exclaimed, and pulled up his hoe, which had caught onto a heavy weight.

"Easy does it, then, boy; don't get excited and frantical."

With due care, Lucas pulled the thing to the side and eased it out.

"What a strange shape; it seems to be made of wood, but what can it be?"

It was wooden, but had ancient leather straps attached to it, most of them half rotten; among the tangle of leather was a rusty metal hoop, about six inches in diameter.

"I know what it is," said Gudgeon presently, when he had examined it, " 'tis an old saddle, that's what it be, an owd wooden saddle." He wiped it with the edge of his coat, shone his light closer, and exclaimed, "By Gar! If that baint beginner's luck for you!"

"What's so lucky about an old saddle?"

"Why, look at the edge of it, boy! 'Tis all set with sappheralds and carbuncles."

Indeed, when Gudgeon had rubbed a bit more of the slime off, Lucas could see that the saddle must once have been very grand indeed; perhaps it had belonged to the prior of the monastery that Gudgeon had mentioned—or, more likely, to some much earlier prior. It was made of wood, but had once been padded. The padding was now rotten. And traces of gilding remained here and there. Precious stones were set in the pommel and crupper; he could see them wink red and blue in the light of the bull's-eye.

"What a find, eh!" Gudgeon kept exclaiming. Lucas, however, felt that the saddle was going to be a considerable nuisance if he was going to be obliged to carry it around all day. He suggested that they should either take it back directly, or leave it in some safe spot from which they could retrieve it later.

"No, boy, no. That won't do. Fust, if we go back now, that's a waste of time; no sense in going over the same ground twice. Second, there's no place you can leave it without the tide'll come up and sweep it away. You should never park your tosh. We doesn't come back this way, see; we goes on down and out to the riverbank; that's why I doesn't take the tosh to old Hobday in the evening, but keeps it till next day. That way, we can stay in the sewer longer, and there's a chance to wash the things in the river and let 'em dry off overnight. Where did you say you was lodging?"

"In Haddock Street."

"Ah, well, that's right handy, then. No, you fetch that saddle along, boy."

So Lucas had to carry the heavy, awkward thing, and he soon heartily wished that he had not found it. Gudgeon did not offer to help with it, though Lucas gathered that the profits from the day's haul were equally split between them.

In spite of the fact that Gudgeon was due to benefit from the saddle, he did not seem altogether pleased that Lucas had found it; after referring to beginner's luck several times, he lapsed into a rather surly silence, broken by complaints that Lucas was shining his light too high, or too low, that he was keeping too close to his partner, or not close enough. And he kept a very sharp eye on all that Lucas did, as if expecting that he might pocket his finds without mentioning them to his partner.

Lucas began to wish very much that Gudgeon would find something of comparable value to cheer him, but this did not happen. He found some iron spoons in a leather bag, and a section of chain mail, a carriage wheel, and half a wooden clog; while Lucas found a lead inkwell (broken), a stone jar (broken), and a skeleton which Gudgeon identified as belonging to one of the underground hogs.

"They eats each other when they has nowt else."

Anxious to steer the conversation away from hogs, Lucas asked, "Do we stop for dinner?"

"No, it ain't convenient. We'd have to go above ground, for you can't bring vittles down here. It ain't worth stopping for all that time. Eat a big breakfuss—that's what I allus does; I has black puddings and chitterlings and bread and treacle and tea."

Lucas wished that he had done likewise, or at least that he had eaten more than a few spoonfuls of frozen porridge. He felt faint from hunger and terribly low-spirited. Would he have to spend the rest of his life in this awful place? How could he bear it?

Dear Greg, he began in his head, I am at present engaged in fishing for tosh in the sewers of Blastburn. . . .

Curiously enough, when he began hunting for suitable words to describe the awfulness of the sewer, it began to seem slightly less awful; in a way he could almost admire it, and understand how Gudgeon seemed to be quite happy to spend all his days here looking for treasure in the dark and filth.

After all, it was a whole part of the town that most people were quite unaware of, and yet it must be quite close to all the main activities going on up above.

"Where are we now?" he asked. "What's overhead?"

Gudgeon paused and reckoned in his head. "We've come about a mile—I reckons it in steps; also we've jist passed the twenty-third branch."

Some of the "branches" were merely holes in the wall, out of which gushed more liquid, sometimes very much warmer, sometimes much colder, than that through which they were wading. Other branches were almost as big as the main drain, with their own footways, and had to be crossed by little plank bridges; many of these were not in good repair.

"We'll be under the fish market now," Gudgeon said. "It

bain't far from here to the Tidey; we've come more'n half-way."

I bet there aren't so many people in the town who have been under the fish market, Lucas thought.

"What happened to your last mate?" he asked.

"Geordie? He fell into the Muckle Sump—that's a bad place in number eighteen branch, the one we call Slaughterhouse Way acos it runs down from the meat market; Geordie made sure he could see a woman's bracelet a-shining, and he leaned over too far, trying to reach it; 'tis like a bog there—not water, more slurry—an' it pulled him in fast; I heard him call and I come back, but he'd gone. He were a good boy; best I've had; it were a pity."

"Oh." Lucas digested this in silence for some time. He did not ask what had become of Gudgeon's other boys.

The long day wore on—if day it could be called in the black underground. At last a faint glimmer of light began to be visible, a mere pinhead, far, far ahead. Gradually it grew bigger until they were walking in twilight, then in gray daylight. Finally they came out under a brick arch on to the slimy mudbank of the river. The tide was very low, and a variety of objects—dead seagulls, bits of boats, bottles, broken oars, anchors, and barrel staves, were visible, stuck in the mud.

"This is where we finishes off," Gudgeon explained. "It's handier when the tide's low like this. O' course it ain't allus so. Now we got about a three-quarter-hour afore dark, so you go that way an' I'll go this, and we'll meet agin here by an' by. Give a shout if you find anything."

Lucas promised he would, but he could see that Gudgeon did not trust him, and kept a suspicious eye on him from far off. Nothing of a particularly exciting nature was found on the riverbank, however, and they presently met again to wash off their troves in the river water which, if by no means crystal clear, was at least a great deal cleaner than that of the sewer.

Then Gudgeon said he would take charge of all the findings.

"You lodging at Tetleys'? 'Tain't a bad house, but there's sailormen and all sorts there; you can't trust 'em. The tosh'll be safer at my place."

Gudgeon, apparently, lived in a derelict boat farther down the riverbank; its chief attractions seemed to be that he was undisturbed by females, need never wash, could suit himself, and had all his things about him.

" 'Tis better for a tosher to live separate. I'll take care o' the things."

There was such a sharp, mistrustful gleam in Gudgeon's eye that Lucas thought it best not to argue, though he would have liked to show the saddle to Anna-Marie, having struggled with it so far.

As they toiled up the slippery mudbank toward Haddock Street's little row of houses, now shrouded in blue dusk, a shadowy figure hailed them from farther along the bank. "Hey-o, Gudgeon, me old mate! Any good pickings?"

"So-so; very so-so, Mr. Bugle," Gudgeon replied, shaking his head. "Pickings ain't what they used to be." It was evident that he was not anxious to discuss the day's haul with the new arrival, a thin man with a pronounced squint. He kept the saddle, wrapped in a muddy bit of sailcloth, under his arm, and said, "This-yer's my new boy. Luke, he calls hisself."

Bugle walked beside them a short way, discussing current trends in sewer harvest; Lucas gathered that the sort of things which could be found varied considerably according to season; in the winter there tended to be more jewelry and dead bodies; in the summer, more household goods. Gudgeon remained silent and made it plain that he did not welcome Bugle's company.

"Well, I'll be ganning," Bugle said at length, and turned off up a narrow alley.

Gudgeon waited until he was a good distance off and then said to Lucas, "Never tell 'em what you've got, even if they should ask."

"Why not?"

"Tain't owt o' their business, the prying skivers. They'd like to know what I got, but I don't ever let 'em know. Understand?"

"All right."

"See you in the morning, then." Gudgeon gave Lucas a last long narrow-eyed scrutiny, and finally made his way off in the direction of Wharf Lane, which was where he kept his boat.

As Lucas walked along Haddock Street he was surprised to see the figure of Bugle reappear.

"Hey, boy!" Bugle called softly. "Hang on a moment!"

"What is it?" Lucas wondered if he was going to be interrogated about their day's catch.

But Bugle had a different intention.

"Here, you, what's-your-name. You're new to the town, ain't you? I wanted to give you a word o' warning. Just you watch out!"

"How do you mean?" Lucas was rather startled.

"Watch out for old Gudgeon, I mean! He uses up tosh boys uncommon fast. You're the third he's had this year. All kinds o' mishaps comes to Gudgeon's boys."

"Oh?" said Lucas.

"It's my belief he ain't pleased above half if a boy finds summat val'ble; he's a bit queer that way, Gudgeon is. Like, today, for instance, if you was to have found a gold crown or summat, 'stead o' going half shares, he might a' preferred to shove you into the Tidey and keep the whole takings. See? So, like I say, keep a watch out. I'm jist a-warning you out o' friendly motives, an' for the honor o' the profession."

"Thank you sir," said Lucas. "I'm much obliged."

Bugle nodded, and vanished up an alley called Sea Coal Lane.

Lucas walked home very thoughtfully.

Although the wind was icy and flurries of snow were once more beginning to blow down the street, Lucas went round to the pump in Mrs. Tetley's back yard, drew bucket after bucket of cold water, and scrubbed himself and his clothes until he felt very much like a burning icicle. Only when he could not bear the cold another second did he stop, wring himself dry as best he could, and go into the back kitchen.

There he found Anna-Marie, stirring away industriously at a potful of something that looked and smelled deliciously like mutton and lentil stew.

Lucas thought he had done a tolerably good job of cleaning himself up, but even before Anna-Marie had turned around and seen him, her nostrils curled up like those of a suspicious cat. As he shut the door behind him, she spun round, exclaiming, "Luc-asse! *Dieu-de-dieu-de-dieu-de-dieu!* Where *ever* have you *been?*"

LUCKILY ANNA-MARIE had again done well on the second day of her reconditioned-cigar business; during the morning she had picked up another three bags of stubs; during the afternoon she rolled and sold them in the market at sixpence apiece. She had earned twenty-eight shillings, deducting the price of papers and the rent paid to Mr. Hobday.

It was possible to pay off the Friendly Club boy entirely and buy more eggs and milk for Mr. Oakapple, and a few necessities, for Lucas and Anna-Marie had escaped from the fire with nothing but the clothes they wore.

"I am thinking, Luc-asse," Anna-Marie said thoughtfully, as they drove home from the infirmary after leaving the food for Mr. Oakapple, who was still feverish, "I am thinking it is better if you do not continue to go down into that dark dirty place, but come and help me. If one of us is picking up the stubs, and the other selling, we shall do better. I am sorry now I arrange you to meet M. 'Obday—if I had known how nasty the work was, I would not have done so."

But Lucas, greatly to her surprise, refused to come and join her in the cigar trade. And when she asked why, why he preferred to go poking about in a dark, horrible, dangerous, dirty underground place, where he did not even have the right to keep what he found, but had to pass it over to Mr. Hobday, he became quite angry.

"Oh, stop bothering on about it, Anna-Marie. It is better if one of us earns a regular wage, so we have something coming in that we can rely on. Suppose you pick up all the cigar ends in the town and there are none left, what then?"

"I do not think that will happen," she said practically.

"Or you may find that once other people notice you are

making money at it, they will start doing it, too, and then stubs will be scarcer. Or the constables might stop you. It may be against the law, to make new cigars out of old."

"Oh la la," she said, shrugging. "I don't care abou that, me! I do wish you will come and help me, Luc; besides, you smell so bad. Mrs. Tetley may grumble."

"For the seventh time, no!" he snapped. They had arrived in Haddock Street; he put the pony in the shed, with a frugal feed of hay and just a few oats. Anna-Marie stood shivering silently while he did so, with her hands in her pockets. She looked so small and thin and pale that it made him crosser still.

"Come on, it's late, and tomorrow I have to go out at half past five, let's eat quickly and go to bed."

Anna-Marie had bought a few candles, but they were expensive. After she had lit the way up to their freezing attic and they had huddled into bed with their clothes on, Lucas told her that she had better blow out the candle.

"We have got to learn to be as economical as possible." And then he lay in the dark, thinking with longing of the shabby schoolroom at Midnight Court, provided with unlimited pens, ink, writing paper, and candle ends, where he had had boundless time in which to write down his thoughts. Why had he not valued these things when he had them? Now he felt so sore, tired, scared, and depressed, that he believed his only possible comfort would be to sit peacefully alone in a room writing down a record of all that had occurred in the last few days. Much chance there was of that! He had not even his notebook.

"Are you cross because I say you smell bad?" Anna-Marie asked timidly. "I am sorry, but it is true."

"No, of course it's not that. Oh, do be quiet, Anna-Marie, and let me go to sleep."

But of course it was that, or at least partly. And it was also partly the fact that she, a girl, and so much smaller, was successfully making money and so far had supplied most of their needs and had even found him a job, while he had brought in nothing. After all, it was easy enough for *her,* he thought resentfully; anyone could pick cigar ends up in the street and roll new ones. It was quite a pleasant job really; whereas look what he had to do.

If only he need never go back into that horrible sewer again! He could still hear the tinkle and plop of drips from the vaulted roof, and the unnerving scurry and rustle as some underground creature made off up a side passage. If there were hogs and rats, what else might there be? He kept tightening his calf muscles, his feet felt as if the ground were slipping away from under them into a bottomless bog; he could still hear Bugle's voice, saying, "Gudgeon uses up tosh boys uncommon fast. You're the third he's had this year."

If Gudgeon pushed him into the Muckle Sump, what would happen to Anna-Marie, all alone in the streets of Blastburn? Who would look after her?

He heard a small sob from Anna-Marie, and the slight noise, like a soft chirp, that meant she was sucking her thumb. Impatiently he turned over on the thin pallet, pulling the blanket up over his ears.

"Go to sleep, Anna-Marie."

"I cannot," she said forlornly. "I wish I had something at all nice to think about." He was silent. After another long pause she said, "Luc? Are you still awake? I *wish* you will tell me a story. About your friend Greg, *peut-être?* Could you, do you think?"

"Are you crazy? Go to sleep."

After that, there was total silence. And it was in silence next morning that they got up, hastily ate a few bites of breakfast, and went off to their respective occupations.

When Gudgeon lifted up the big manhole cover and said, "Down you go, then, lad," Lucas had such a struggle to make himself step into the black hole that he felt almost as if it were somebody else, another shuddering reluctant person, to whom he was giving the order.

Perhaps I'm dreaming the whole thing, he thought; perhaps I'm really sitting in the schoolroom at Midnight Court; perhaps I'm not here at all.

And this mood of dreamy detachment stayed with him for quite a long spell; they walked, and sloshed, and dipped, and scooped, until, after possibly a couple of hours had passed, Gudgeon suddenly exclaimed, "Quiet! Listen!"

"What?"

"Hush!"

Then Lucas, above the swish of the sewer, began to hear a faint, shrill, distant, ear-piercing sound, like the squeal of pipes.

His fear made him quick.

"Is it hogs?"

"Ah! Reckon so. And the mischief of it is that the Causeway manhole's nearest from here, and some blaggard has made off with the ladder from that one; we'll have to foot it on to the James Street one. Step lively, boy, eh? There ain't any time to waste pronging up the tosh just now."

Lucas had no intention of doing so. He followed Gudgeon's example, and hurried along as fast as the slippery, uncertain footway would allow.

"How do you know the hogs aren't on ahead?" he panted.

"They are," Gudgeon said grimly. "Can't you hear? Leastways they're to the side of us, a-coming down Pastry Lane Passage. We got to get past afore they come out." And he splashed on through a stretch of overflow, while Lucas struggled to keep up in his noisome wake. For Lucas it was impossible to tell where the squealing—much louder now—was coming from; the echoes seemed to be all around; but Gudgeon was quite positive.

"Hogs often *do* come out o' Pastry Lane," he explained. "There's extry pickings for 'em up that way, see; all the rats that gets killed in the bakers' backyards gets chucked down there. Ah! See! What did I tell ee?"

For a brief moment, as they passed the narrow branch entrance that was called Pastry Lane Passage, he shone his bull's-eye up it, and Lucas, with a horrible closing of his throat, caught the flash of two dozen little points of red light.

"They don't *like* a light in their eyes; that'll slow 'em for a moment," said Gudgeon. "Come on, it's still a tidy way to James Street."

On, on, they pounded and slithered, panting and gulping. Lucas had lost his mood of detachment some time ago, yet even through his terror he felt a strange kind of unreality: this can't actually be happening to *me?*

From time to time Gudgeon turned momentarily and shone his bull's-eye backward; the points of red light would halt each time he did so, but they came on again each time and were getting much closer. Lucas could hear the thud and patter of sharp little galloping feet now, and a scraping sound, as some members of the herd were pushed by others against the brick walls.

A horrible thought came to him: suppose somebody else, some other inconsiderate tosh man, had removed the ladder from the James Street manhole? Suppose they had to run on for another mile? Or suppose, in their haste, they had already passed the James Street refuge?

But at last he heard Gudgeon, ahead of him, give a grunt of satisfaction, and the shadows from his bull's-eye flowed suddenly downward instead of swinging from side to side.

" 'Ere we are, then, boy; look slippy," he called back, now suspended somewhere overhead.

Lucas wanted no urging; the hogs were only a few yards behind him, thrusting each other forward; he could see their small black hairy shapes as he turned to climb and smell a rank, warm piggy odor, even above the reek of the drain.

He slipped, fumbling for the ladder, which began at waist height—pushed himself up with his pole—felt a sudden sharp pain in his left leg—kicked out in a frenzy of fright—and then he was up, and safe. The little red eyes flashed for a moment below, and then were gone; the impetus of the herd, with the hogs at the back pushing on the ones in front, was too rapid for them to stop. In a couple of minutes, furiously squealing and champing, they had disappeared again into the blackness of the tunnel.

"That's all right then," said Gudgeon, calmly, descending several rungs of the ladder. "—Well, stir your stumps, boy, down you go; don't dangle there like an apple on a codlin tree."

"But aren't we going out?"

"Out?"

"Through the manhole?"

"Lord love you, no! And waste a whole morning? Not on your peggy! Why, if we was to leave the sewer every time we met a handful o' hogs, we'd not collect a farden's worth o' tosh in a fortnight. Any road, that lot won't come back—they never do, jist run on and on. No, the only danger is once they get you down and tromple on you; *then* they stop all right. *Then* you're done for. Long's you whip up a ladder, smartish, when they catch up with you, you 'ont take no hurt from 'em. Like now."

"One of them bit my leg," said Lucas.

"Well, you should'a been nippier! You will next time, I'll lay. Now we'll have to go back a half mile to Sinkhole Reach; that's where I first heard 'em, and we missed all that section; that's one of the best stretches for tosh in the whole neighborhood."

That evening, after Lucas had handed over his findings—no jeweled saddle today, only a dirty and uninteresting collection of broken metal and wooden objects—to Mr. Gudgeon, and washed himself under the pump until his feet and hands felt ready to fall off from cold and his teeth would not stop chattering, he screwed himself up to apologize to Anna-Marie.

"I am sorry I was bad-tempered last night, Anna-Marie. The sewers are so horrible that I can't stop thinking about them, and it makes me edgy." But still he did not tell Anna-Marie about the hogs, or Gudgeon's peculiar nature; let her think that filth and dark were all he had to worry about.

"It is of no consequence," she said haughtily. She handed him a lump of pease porridge. "I simply do not see why, if it is so horrible, you are *imbécile* enough to go on working there."

Lucas did not try to explain that it was a matter of pride; that he had to. He felt sure that Anna-Marie would be completely blank to such an explanation. "You wouldn't understand," he said tiredly.

"Because I am just a stupid girl! Only good for picking up cigar ends. If someone offered *me* a nicer way to make a living, I would take it."

"Your job isn't so bad."

She turned away, her lip quivering, and said, "I do not tell you *all* about it. Some girls say to me I have not the right to pick up cigar ends in Blastburn because I do not come from here."

"Well, tell them to go to blazes! You aren't taking away their living."

Changing the subject, Anna-Marie said, "You can go by yourself to see M. Ookapool this evening. There is no use for two of us to go while, anyway, he cannot speak. I will stay here, me, and make more cigars. There are the eggs and milk for him on the shelf."

"Oh, very well," said Lucas irritably, swilling down the

last stodgy mouthful of pease pudding with a drink of water. He ached all over with exhaustion, his leg hurt, and he was still hungry; he would not have minded staying at home and making cigars himself. But somebody had to take Mr. Oakapple his food.

Anna-Marie began washing out the pease-porridge pot, in a tin basin.

"How did you get that bruise on your arm?" he asked.

"I fell. It was slippery."

"Well, take care. I'll see you later," he said, and went out. The snow had changed to a bitterly cold rain which froze as it fell and turned the streets to an icy, slippery swamp. Well, he thought, backing out the pony and turning her, there's at least one advantage of the sewers: no snow down there.

He was getting into the cart when old Gabriel passed him, apparently without recognizing him.

"Good evening, Mr. Towzer," Lucas said.

The old man turned, and Lucas caught a strong reek of Geneva spirit.

Gabriel looked at Lucas vaguely and laid a hand on his arm.

"Hush!" he whispered. "What the eye don't see, the Bible don't gnash its teeth at." He started waveringly toward the house, then paused to say, "I *said* she were a mickle-mouth!"

Up at the infirmary, matters had not greatly changed. Mr. Oakapple was still unable to recognize anybody or to talk sense, but one of the sisters said that he had made a little progress and was taking nourishment. Lucas hoped she was telling the truth, that the eggs and milk they brought with so much trouble were not going elsewhere. How could he be sure? Whom could one trust in this town?

He did not stay long; there was no point.

On the way out, he thought he recognized a familiar back leaving the out-patients' surgery, where minor injuries, generally received in the factories, were treated and bandaged.

In the courtyard, Lucas overtook this person and saw that it was, as he had thought, Mr. Smallside from the Mill, with a bandage covering half his forehead.

"Mr. Smallside!" Lucas exclaimed, eagerly, running forward to catch him by the arm. Here was somebody who could prove his identity to Mr. Throgmorton.

The manager started; his eye fell on Lucas, then swiftly left him; he shook off Lucas's hand, as if he had been accosted by mistake, and walked on.

Lucas again ran to catch up with him. "Mr. Smallside! Don't you remember me? From the Court? Lucas Bell!"

Smallside glanced rapidly all around. Nobody was within earshot.

"Quiet, boy!" he said urgently in an undertone. "Have you no sense? The very name of Randolph Grimsby, or of Midnight Court, is so unpopular in the town that the words are enough to get you stoned; even strung up from a lamppost. How do you think I came by this black eye? For having been Sir Randolph's manager—appointed by him. I've had to quit Murgatroyd's—I'm getting the night coach to Manchester. If you are wise you'll do likewise. Don't tell anybody you saw me!"

And he disappeared into a shadowed passageway.

As he drove home, Lucas tried to decide whether he should pass on this warning to Anna-Marie. It was not easy to give advice to her, he thought; unless she happened to agree with it, she was just as likely to do the opposite. And she was very proud of her name; she would not wish to conceal that.

She was sitting cross-legged in her bunk, rolling cigars,

when Lucas went up. Poor little thing, he thought; what a life for her.

"I am working, so it is proper for me to use the candle," she said defensively.

"You had better have gone to sleep; you look tired."

"I am all right," she said stiffly.

"Would—would you like to play a game of scissors-paper-stone?" Lucas offered. He was aware that it would have been a better peace offering if he had suggested telling a story, but he was too tired; he simply could not set his mind to the task of invention.

"No, thank you," Anna-Marie said politely. "You need not be bothered playing child's games with me. If you wish to sleep, I will put out the candle."

"Very well."

Again they went to sleep in silence.

It seemed strange that days should pass swiftly in the sewers, yet, on the whole, they did. Perhaps it was because of the dark, and the monotony. The black, wet hours went by; sometimes the toshers were chased by hogs and had to run for it; once or twice Lucas felt his heart come into his mouth when great rats, big as terriers, darted or snapped at him and had to be beaten off with his pole. On Saturday he received his wages of five pounds from Mr. Hobday plus a bonus of seven shillings, which was his percentage on the various things he had found. He had an uneasy feeling that this was probably much less than he should have received—what about that saddle, after all?—but really there seemed no means of checking.

"What did Mr. Hobday do with the saddle?" he asked Gudgeon.

"That bain't none of your concern, boy. You tend to the toshing, let Mester Hobday tend to the dealing," Gudgeon replied, leaving Lucas still full of doubts.

However it was satisfactory to have more than five pounds; it seemed like a huge sum. Lucas was able to pay Mrs. Tetley, and the next week's infirmary fee for Mr. Oakapple, and the bribe money to Joe Bludward the Friendly Club boy, who never failed to turn up, taking his collection, as the patients' relatives left the wards. That didn't leave much change from the week's money. But at least it meant that what Anna-Marie earned could be kept for food and their daily needs.

Two paydays later, before taking the plunge down the manhole, Lucas went to a secondhand-clothes stall in the market and bought a red coat with a hood, which he had been considering for several days. It was worn but still thick, and he liked the color.

He went across to Mr. Hobday's stall, where Anna-Marie was setting out her cigars in a tray of plaited straw that she had made.

"Here," he said. "Put this on. It ought to fit you quite well. And it's warmer than that worn-out old black thing. It's a nicer color, too."

She looked very surprised; her mouth fell open. Before she could say anything, Lucas hurriedly ended, "I must be off, I'm late. See you this evening," and ran after Gudgeon, who was impatiently gesturing to him. But all day, in the blackness of the sewer, he was a little cheered by the thought of Anna-Marie wearing the red coat; it seemed to sit in one corner of his mind like a small red beacon.

She needed something to cheer her, he thought; she had been very silent and withdrawn for the last few evenings.

Mr. Oakapple had spoken a few words on the previous night; that evening Anna-Marie volunteered to come up to the infirmary with Lucas.

"Perhaps he will like some soup now, or a cake—not just egg and milk," she said, and made up a packet of food.

The rain had given way to snow again and there was fog too; icicles hung from the roof of the shed; it was a bitter-cold night. But Anna-Marie, when she came out to the cart, had only her old black coat on, with a handkerchief tied round her head.

"Why don't you put on your red coat?" Lucas said. "Hurry! I'll wait for you."

"I do not have it."

"Why not?" His voice sounded sharp, merely because he was puzzled.

"I sold it," said Anna-Marie.

"*Sold* it?" Automatically Lucas flicked the reins, and the pony started. But his attention was all concentrated on Anna-Marie, who sat staring straight ahead, with her small pale face so tightly controlled that it looked like the face on a shilling.

Lucas had to control himself too. He was seized by a violent inclination to storm at her, shake her, push her off the cart and tell her to walk home. What a childish, silly, spiteful thing to have done! Well, it would be a long time before he gave her another present, she needn't think he was going to fling away any more of his hard-earned money on buying things for her to sell again.

For the first time in many days a letter to Greg formed in his mind.

"Dear Greg, I am driving through the main street of Blastburn, up Milestone Hill. Snow is falling out of the fog, like white leaves coming down from the ghosts of trees. (He was not satisfied with that, though; he would have to change it later.) Anna-Marie is with me, but she is in one of her peculiar, awkward, contrary moods. Today she sold the red coat I had given her—just to be rude and saucy, just to show me that she doesn't need the things I can buy with my wages. If I weren't older and bigger and a boy, I'd smack her ungrateful little head. . . ." Forming the words in his mind cooled down his bad temper, and he looked about him more calmly as they drove up the hill, thinking that the vague foggy shapes of two pottery kilns looked like a picture of a Russian town that Mr. Oakapple had once shown him in a geography book.

Then he heard a stifled sound beside him and saw out of the corner of his eye that Anna-Marie was wiping her cheek, trying to do it inconspicuously.

"What's the matter now?" Lucas demanded. "Are you crying?"

She took a great breath. "I—I am sorry, Luc-asse. It is nothing."

"Of course it's something," he said angrily. "First you sell the coat I bought for you, then you cry. *Nothing* you do has any sense in it, if you ask me."

At this Anna-Marie broke down entirely. "Oh," she wept, "I hoped that perhaps you would not ask about the coat—or that you would understand. I was so sorry to sell it. But the color showed up too much. It made me too noticeable."

"Noticeable? How do you mean?" A new anxiety took hold of Lucas. "How can I understand if you don't explain what all this is about? Are the constables after you? Is it what I thought? That making cigars out of stubs is against the law?"

"No," she sobbed, "not that. At least I don't think so. But it is some boys. The girls tell them about my cigar collecting and now they come and say that I must not do it, because only they have the right. I am sure it is not true, but they say it. And sometimes they upset my stall and spoil my cigars, treading on them. And if they see me in the street they chase me and throw stones, so I can go only in the small streets where there are no pieces of cigar. That is why for the last few days I have made very little money, and I am very much afraid it will be the same tomorrow—"

"So that was why you didn't want to wear the red coat?"

"And I sell it because I make so little money today I do not have enough to buy things for Monsieur Ookapool—"

Lucas felt quite numb with rage. This is too much, he thought; just *too much*. Whatever providence is doing this to us ought to see that we have had as much as we can stand.

"Was it they who bruised your arm?"

"It was a stone. Usually I am quick to duck, but that time not so quick."

"Just wait till I catch some of them—"

"*No*, Luc! It is not only that they are big, but they are many. What could one person, two people, do against a whole crowd?"

"We'll talk about it after we see Mr. Oakapple," he said.

They had arrived at the infirmary. Lucas strode in, absent-minded with rage, and Anna-Marie, loaded with the basket, had difficulty keeping up with him. Suddenly he remembered and took it from her, then walked on, his forehead creased with furious concentration. They ought to go, they ought to leave the town, this was no place for Anna-Marie to be. But where could they go? And what about Mr. Oakapple? There seemed no limit to the number of problems that faced them.

Mr. Oakapple, however, was visibly on the mend this evening. He lay propped up on pillows, instead of flat, and the bandages had been removed from his face, which was still red and painful-looking but not scarred or mutilated.

When he saw Lucas and Anna-Marie, he gave a small difficult smile; evidently it still hurt him to move his cheek muscles. "Well! I had wondered who were the kind brownies who kept bringing me eggs and milk. I had thought it could hardly be Sir Randolph or Mrs. Gourd. So it was you two! I am very much obliged to you."

"It was no trouble," said Lucas gruffly, and Anna-Marie,

a pink flush suffusing her pallor, cried, "Oh, we are so please to see you better, Monsieur Ookapool!"

"How are things up at the Court?" inquired the tutor. "Was very much damage done? My recollections of that night are all confused—nothing is clear—"

Lucas hesitated. His instinct was not to upset Mr. Oakapple by telling him all the truth. But Anna-Marie burst out impetuously, "Why, monsieur, nothing is left at all—*du tout, du tout!* And Madame Gourd and Fanny and all the *domestiques* are gone away, and Sir Randolph, 'e is dead, and Lucas and me are living in the town. All is different since you have been ill."

"Good heavens!" said the tutor feebly. "All Midnight burned? And Sir Randolph dead?"

He seemed so shocked at the news that Lucas felt anxious and glanced about for a sister. One was passing through the ward. She came over and gave Mr. Oakapple a drink.

"Is he all right?" Lucas asked.

"Yes—yes—going on well. You can fetch him home in a week, I should think. But he will need to take life very quietly for several months after that; probably till spring."

Home! Lucas and Anna-Marie looked at one another in consternation.

Then Lucas said, "Sir, I'm glad to see you better, for we wondered if you had any friends or family who ought to have been told that you were ill?"

Again the tutor smiled his small difficult smile. "No, you can set your minds easy on that head! Like yourselves, I have no one. My father died ten years ago, and my mother, two. There is nobody that you need have worried with the fact that I'm stuck here with my head in a bag."

"Except us," said Anna-Marie gently. "*We* have been worried about you, monsieur."

He moved one of his bandaged hands from under the covers and patted her awkwardly on the head. "Thank you, little one. You are a very kind girl. But you should not have troubled your small head about me."

"Have you no friends at all, sir? Somebody that you might go to stay with when you come out?"

"I can think of none," said the tutor. "Except my old master at the choir school, and he is *very* old by now; I would not wish to be a trouble to him. Perhaps I could get a room at your lodgings in the town. Who looks after you? Does Mr. Throgmorton see to the expenses for you?"

"Well, no—" said Lucas.

"Then how do you manage?"

At this moment the sister returned to say that visiting hours were over, and they were able to escape without the need for going into long and difficult explanations.

"Phew!" said Lucas, when they were outside. "It seems that his being better is going to make things more difficult for us, not easier—"

"When he *really* is better it will be easier," said Anna-Marie.

"But that's a long way away."

"In the spring." She kicked a lump of snow and said, "If spring ever does come in this hateful town!"

"It's only December now," said Lucas. "And we must certainly find a better place than Mrs. Tetley's to take Mr. Oakapple to; he'd never get well there."

"Luc," Anna-Marie said suddenly. "I have an idea."

"What is it?" he asked, with caution. He was so tired that even his mind felt stiff; he was not sure if he would be able to deal sensibly with any of Anna-Marie's ingenious ideas.

"Well—all the big Midnight House was burn down—nothing is left there to live in—"

"I know. You don't need to tell me."

"But there is *one* place that doesn't burn, and I have only just thought of it."

"*I* can't think of anywhere that didn't burn."

"Do you not remember that first time we go driving with

Mr. Ookapool and I ask, What is that mound, and he say, That is the old icehouse? Far, far away, in the corner of the park?"

"Why, yes," said Lucas slowly. "Now you mention it, I do remember—"

"Luc!" She grabbed his hand, really excited now, as the idea expanded in both their minds. "Why do we not go and look at it? Now?"

"But it's miles away, and late at night!"

"But the snow have stopped snowing, and the moon shines. And also I do not believe it is so very far."

"But it's two miles to the lodge—"

"I know—if we go up, all the way up the long hill and in at the big gate, is a long way. But I have seen, when I was in the park, there is a big tree shaped like a *point d'interrogation*, over by a little wood near the park wall—and, look, I can see that very same tree from here, against the snowy hill!"

It was true. They had come out of the infirmary court-yard and were standing in the road. The infirmary was the last building on the edge of the town; up above it, the road ran beside snow-covered fields, which presently turned to moorland. And on the other side ran the high wall which encircled Midnight Park. And beyond the wall was the tree shaped like a question mark.

"If we could get over the wall," said Anna-Marie, "then the icehouse is quite near that tree, so it would be not far at all from here."

"Yes. But how do we get over the wall? Still it's worth looking, I agree."

"People from the town used to go into the park to catch rabbits," said Anna-Marie. "I have often heard that poor old Gabriel say so, before he is always so drunk. There must be a way through somewhere."

There was a long narrow copse, a kind of overgrown

hedge—fir and holly mixed with little ash trees—growing beside the park wall. Without saying anything further, Lucas led the pony and trap off the road, and tied the pony under a good-sized fir tree, where she would be in shelter.

"Come on then," he said. Across his mind flitted the memory of the old woman he had seen—the witch? But Mr. Oakapple had said that was a lot of nonsense. She might have been some poor old vagabond who had chosen to pass a night or so there. . . .

Anna-Marie gave a little skip. "Oh, I did so hope you would think this is a good idea!" she said. "If only there is a way through!"

Luckily the moon, now the snow had stopped, was bright enough so that there was no difficulty in seeing what was to be seen. They walked straight through the copse until they came up against the twenty-foot-high wall.

"Now which way should we go?" said Anna-Marie.

"Let's try downhill toward the town first. It's most likely, if there is an entrance, that it would be as close to the town as possible."

So they turned left and made their way downhill.

When they came to the edge of the copse—

"Good heavens," said Lucas, pausing. "That's Murga-troyd's Mill right down below. I didn't realize how much road must curve around. Why, the mill is absolutely next door to the park."

"I suppose when my *grandpère* build the Mill, there is no town. Monsieur Ookapool tell me that the houses and the other factories come later. So he put his mill by his park."

"I suppose so," said Lucas, brought up short by the fact, which he tended to forget, that it had been Anna-Marie's grandfather who had been the founder of this whole huge black clutter of factories and houses, wealth and poverty and employers and workpeople. And here was his granddaughter skipping through the snow under the midnight moon without a penny to her pocket!

They had crossed a bare expanse of snow and entered another bit of the little wood.

"Ah, ah!" cried Anna-Marie triumphantly. "Look! Look! Didn't I guess right?"

If the moon had not been shining and the ground covered with snow, they might have missed the gap in the wall. For it was extremely narrow, and cunningly concealed beside the trunk and under the branches of a big old yew tree whose dark snow-laden boughs hung down all round, making a kind of evergreen cave. But because the moon was shining so brightly on the snowy grass of the park beyond the wall, the narrow crack showed up like a keyhole in a dark door with a light on the other side.

"I can just get through—I think—perhaps it will be too small for you, Luc!"

But when they had ducked under the yew and made their way to the gap, they found that it was about two feet wide and four feet high—quite big enough to get through comfortably. Someone had gone to considerable trouble to make the hole where it would not be seen; a thick growth of ivy on the other side obscured it from any but a close observer. Lucas noticed also that the stones at the top had been carefully mortared and a kind of rude arch contrived, so that falling stonework would not make the entrance bigger or more conspicuous.

"And there is the icehouse!" whispered Anna-Marie.

Somehow, now they were inside the park, they felt the need to proceed with caution. They moved silently over the snow toward the circular mound, which looked like a giant-sized molehill.

"Hush!" breathed Lucas, when Anna-Marie's feet scrunched in the untrodden snow. Then he gripped her tightly by the wrist and stood still, cocking his head sideways, exercising his ears with the acute concentration that he employed when listening for hogs in the sewer.

"*C'est bien singulier,*" whispered Anna-Marie, "*mais je crois que j'entends un bébé qui pleure!*"

Lucas, too, could have sworn that he heard a baby. But what would one be doing out in the middle of snowy Midnight Park at this time of night? They must, both of them, be imagining it. Perhaps it was an owl.

They reached the icehouse and stole round it, looking for the entrance.

"There are two doors, I remember—a big door and a little door—"

"There!" Anna-Marie ran on ahead. A kind of cleft showed in the smooth, turfed-over side of the mound. When they reached it, there was a heavy wooden door, set in a stone arch.

"It's sure to be locked," whispered Lucas. "And the key was probably burned in the fire; I daresay it was one of those big ones that always hung on the rack of keys in the kitchen."

But when he gently tried the door's handle, it turned, and the door came smoothly back toward him.

"Oh, *quel bonheur!* We can go in. See, Luc, all is coming out *just* as I told you."

Anna-Marie was so pleased with herself that Lucas was sorely tempted to say something snubbing. Still it was true, she *had* suggested the place, and it *was* all turning out as she had predicted. And, if the icehouse wasn't too cold—or rat-infested—or dripping with damp—there didn't seem to be any reason why they shouldn't consider living there. At least it was free.

"I wish I'd brought my bull's-eye," Lucas murmured.

A narrow dark passage led inward from the door. Anna-Marie's eagerness to lead the way suddenly left her, and she politely stood back to let Lucas move ahead. Although he had not got the lantern with him, he did have flint and steel and tinder.

"We could do with a dry twig," he whispered. "See if you can find a bit of brush—"

The words came to a stop in his mouth. For an inner door had suddenly opened ahead of them, letting out a mild glow of light into the rough stone passage where they stood.

"Is that somebody come to call on me?" inquired a gentle voice, a voice that neither of them had ever heard before.

PART THREE
Daybreak

LUCAS FELT Anna-Marie's fingers clench around his left wrist so tightly that his fingers, cold already, began to go numb.

He too was greatly startled. A light, and a voice, in this dark, out of the way spot, were the last things to be expected. But, he realized, he did not feel very much frightened; whoever it was behind that half-open door could not possibly be as bad as the hogs or the rats in the sewers of Blastburn. So he went forward, blinking slightly, into the light.

After all, it was not so very bright—hardly more dazzling than the moon on the snow outside. Three or four rush dips, set in pottery holders, burned smokily and gave a shadowy, flickering radiance. The remains of a log fire smoldered gently upon an open hearth, contributing little more than a dull red glow.

Anna-Marie moved after Lucas and stood close beside him, still clutching his hand, while they took stock of the person who lived in the place they had hoped to inhabit.

She was an old lady. The word lady immediately came into Lucas's mind, although her dress was extremely rough, made of woolen material, and covered with a sacking apron. She wore battered old boots as well, and her snowy hair was skewered up on top of her head in a large untidy knot by what looked like a twig of yew. She was tall—rather taller than Lucas—and thin as a scarecrow. In the dim light it was hard to make out the color of her cheeks, but they looked wrinkled and weatherbeaten, like the skin of an old apple that has been left in the grass all winter long. Her hands were thin as gulls' claws. But her face! Lucas thought he had never seen a face combining such authority and such goodness. The nose was so straight, and the sockets of the eyes so deep, that the old lady's face reminded Lucas of a yoke—the kind of yoke used for carrying two milk pails with a bar across the top—it had that firmness and strength. And her eyes, deepset in triangular caverns, were bright—bright—but what color in that hazy light, neither Lucas nor Anna-Marie could determine.

"Well! This is an unexpected pleasure," said the old lady, smiling, when she, on her side, had taken a survey of Lucas and Anna-Marie. Her voice, clear and deep, rang like a bell in the stone-built place. "You made me a little anxious when I first heard you; there are some rough types in the town these days who occasionally come into the park for a bit of poaching, but I do not think that you are like that."

"No—no," stammered Lucas, finding his tongue. "I am sorry we disturbed you, ma'am. We did not think there was anybody here."

At this moment Lucas felt the tight grip on his arm relax. He rubbed the place absently with his other hand while he watched Anna-Marie, who now did a thing he had never seen her do before: she moved forward and gravely curtsied to the old lady.

"*Bonsoir, madame,*" she said. "*On ne veut pas vous déranger.*"

The old lady inclined her head with equal gravity. "*Bonsoir, ma petite,*" she said. "You do not disturb me at all. On the contrary. I am enchanted to be visited. Won't you sit down?"

There were two or three sawed-off sections of tree trunk, which did duty as stools; also, Lucas noticed, the rocking chair which he had last seen among the snowy ruins of the Court. The old lady gestured toward the seats, and went to put a handful of sticks on the fire, which immediately burst into a cheerful flame.

Anna-Marie, however, chose to sit on the floor, which was stone-paved, and covered by loosely woven rugs. In the brighter light it was possible to see that a dog and cat also lay by the hearth, stretched out asleep in attitudes of utter comfort.

"Why, that's Redgauntlet," Lucas suddenly said. He had thought the hound must have died in the fire.

"Is that his name? Poor thing, I found him wandering, very sorrowful. And you two," the old lady said, looking at them attentively, "you must be the children from the Court. I have seen you from a distance; never close to. What are your names, my dears?"

"Lucas Bell, ma'am," said Lucas; and simultaneously Anna-Marie, with her usual dignity, said, "*Je m'appelle Anna-Marie Eulalie Murgatroyd, madame.*"

The old lady had been moving toward a heavy wooden chest. But at Anna-Marie's words she turned round—not hastily or jerkily but quite fast all the same. "Murgatroyd," she repeated, in a tone of deep interest, studying Anna-Marie more attentively than ever. "Then who is your father, my little one?"

"He was called Sirr Denzil Murgatroyd, miladi. He is dead since last year."

"Since last year. . . . And you come from France?"

"*Oui, madame.*"

"Then, my dear," said the old lady, suddenly breaking into a smile that made Lucas feel warm, all the way down to his thawing toes, "then you are my granddaughter and I am your grandmother. Isn't that delightful!"

And she reached down her hand to take that of Anna-Marie, who jumped up and gave the old lady a hug.

"You are my grandmother? I do not at all understand. But it is very nice. *Very* nice! I did not know that I had a grandmother. Papa told me that *grand'mère* and *grandpère* had died."

"Then," said Lucas, working it out slowly, "then you must be Lady Murgatroyd, the wife of Sir Quincy?"

"Yes, quite right, my boy."

"But why are you living here? In the icehouse?"

"Well," said the old lady briskly, "I don't know if you are familiar with the story of how Sir Randolph Grimsby came to be in possession of Midnight Court?"

"He won it by a bet. From your son. And then your husband died?"

Lucas felt uncomfortable at saying these things, but the old lady took them calmly enough.

"Just so. That was a sad time," she said, looking back as if through a telescope at a far-distant prospect. "Well, I am extremely fond of my home, and I very much disliked leaving it. When I was obliged to go, I didn't go very *far*. I went to live in the village of Clutterby with an old nurse of mine, who had retired to her family cottage. I lived with her till she died. And I kept an eye on things there—I wanted to be sure that my old servants were not ill used—that kind of thing. Sir Randolph had never met me—Quincy would never receive him at the Court—he didn't know me, so I could call in from time to time—leave a parish magazine— see how things were going on. Most of the old servants left, fairly soon—except for old Gabriel. They couldn't stand Sir Randolph. And I soon saw that no use whatsoever was being made of the icehouse, so in the course of time I decided to come and live here. Old Gabriel gave me a bit of help, building a fireplace—he promised not to tell anybody who I was. Very few people noticed that I was living here; I believe those who did thought I was an old beggar woman. Nobody has ever disturbed me. Really," she said with satisfaction, looking around, "it makes a very comfortable home."

Lucas glanced around the room too, his eyes now being accustomed to the light. One corner of the largish place, he saw, was occupied by a hand loom, with a half-woven length of material on it.

"Oh," cried Anna-Marie, "*voilà mon canari*—the one I set free!"

"He didn't like it out in that cold park, my child. He is passing the winter with me."

Lady Murgatroyd gave a soft whistle and the canary, who had been asleep on the loom, took his head out from under his wing and came whirring across the room, with a loud cheerful chirrup, to sit on her shoulder.

Lady Murgatroyd's sitting room was shaped like two fifths of a round tart. So there must, Lucas thought, be two or three more rooms occupying the rest of the round ice-house. This deduction was borne out by a sleepy wail which they now heard coming from a door set back in a shadowy corner.

"She's wakeful tonight," said Lady Murgatroyd and disappeared through the door.

When she returned, she carried a wicker cradle, which she put down near one of the rush lights, saying, "She's always good as long as she has a light to look at."

"You have a *baby, Grand'mère?*" exclaimed Anna-Marie, looking into the cradle.

"Not mine, my dear! Just a loan. A poor woman who was going to Australia and afraid that her baby might die on the ship. Those transports are *not* hygienic. So the baby stays with me until she is old enough to travel."

"But, *Grand'mère,* isn't it hard work for you to look after a baby, so old as you are? And supposing you were to die?"

"I can see you have a practical nature, my child; just like me. Well," the old lady's forehead was creased by two lines into a thoughtful frown, "I felt some responsibility. If I had been given any say in the matter, that mill would be a *very* different place. So it was up to me to look after the baby of someone who didn't want to work there, wasn't it?

And I shall simply have to stay alive until the baby is grown up. Though, now I come to think of it, if I should die, now, you can look after the baby, can't you?"

"Of course," Anna-Marie said. "I am very good at looking after babies, me."

"She has a bad habit of eating earth, poor dear; I think that sometimes it was all they had to give her."

Lady Murgatroyd remembered that she had been on her way to the chest, before she discovered Anna-Marie's identity. She went back, and brought out a stone crock, which proved to contain gingersnaps.

"I don't bake very often nowadays," she apologized "They may be past their best."

To the hungry Lucas and Anna-Marie, the gingersnaps seemed perfect: hard, chewy, sweet, and dark. They had three apiece before remembering that it was bad manners to gobble.

"I can give you some tea, if you like," said Lady Murgatroyd, setting a kettle to hang over the fire, "but I'm afraid I've no milk till tomorrow. The baby had the last of it."

"*Grand'mère*," said Anna-Marie curiously, "please do not think it impertinent if I ask, but have you any money? Do you go to shops? How do you make your *ménage* here?"

"I have a very little money, my dear," Lady Murgatroyd said. "Well, you know how my house and all was lost. But I need little, so I manage quite well. I give lessons in music and singing."

"*Here?*"

The old lady smiled at Anna-Marie's expression of astonishment. "No, not here. I go to people's houses in the town. And I do not use my own name; Murgatroyd is such a well-known name here that it might cause embarrassment. So I call myself Madame Minetti. And by my lessons I make enough money to buy luxuries like books."

Indeed, apart from the chest, the rugs and the tree trunks, the principal furniture in the place seemed to be books; there were certainly plenty of these, lying in piles round the sides of the room, stacked in boxes, ranged on planks, many of them left open with a twig to mark the place.

"Well, now," said Lady Murgatroyd, "you know all about me. So let me hear your histories. You first." She nodded to Lucas— "You haven't said much yet. By your name you should be a son of that Edwin Bell who had come to be manager of the mill not long before my husband died."

"That's right, ma'am."

"He was a good man. What became of him?"

"He stayed on and put money into the mill and became Sir Randolph's partner. And he married my mother—her name was Mary Dunnithorne—"

"I remember her," said Lady Murgatroyd, nodding. "She was a distant cousin of mine."

"—and he went to India, to look after the cotton buying. . . . And he died out there, with my mother; and he'd named Sir Randolph as my guardian in his will, so I was sent back here."

"Poor boy." Lady Murgatroyd's voice was full of compassion. "And you, *petite?*"

"We lived in Calais. . . . *Maman* died before I can remember. We were very poor. Papa never was able to make much money. He used to teach, but he liked better to stay at home and make up songs. All the ladies used to give me clothes and they never fitted. And then Papa died," Anna-Marie said forlornly.

So that is why her clothes were such an odd lot when she arrived, Lucas thought. He felt impatient with himself for never having bothered to ask Anna-Marie about her life in Calais.

"And so you are both orphans. And where do you live, now that Midnight Court is burned down? And Sir Randolph has died, has he not?"

"*Si, Grand'mère.* We live with old Mr. Towzer's sister in

Haddock Street. But it is not at all nice. And there is no money, so I make cigars, and Luc—he collects things for a *bric-à-brac* seller."

"In the sewers," Lucas said firmly.

"So you are very hard-working," said Lady Murgatroyd. "And that is good. Well, I can't support you with money, for I haven't much, but as we are all in some sense related, would you like to come and live with me here? You would have to go on earning your livings, but it might be nicer here than in Haddock Street. And we would all be company for one another."

"To tell you the truth, ma'am," said Lucas, "that was the idea we had in our minds when we came to look at this place."

"I had it first!" said Anna-Marie. "But is there room for all of us, *Grand'mère?*"

"Yes, there are three more rooms, *petite*. I think we may manage famously."

Lucas hesitated. "There is one thing—" he began.

"What is the trouble, my boy?"

"There is my tutor. He is in hospital—he was badly burned, in the fire, trying to rescue Sir Randolph. When he comes out, we shall have to look after him, for he has nowhere to go—"

"Ah, *oui*," broke in Anna-Marie. "*Ce pauvre* Monsieur Ookapool, but he is very *gentil*. I am sure you will like him, *Grand'mère*."

"What is his name? Ooka—?"

"Oakapple—Mr. Julian Oakapple, ma'am."

"*Julian Oakapple?* Oh," said Lady Murgatroyd, "I do not have to see him to like him. I think he may be somebody that I have wanted to meet for a long, long time."

It was agreed that, since the pony must anyway be put in shelter, Lucas should return to Haddock Street for the night. He would then give notice to Mrs. Tetley, collect their few possessions, and return in the morning. As it was Sunday he would not be working in the sewer, and could spend the day settling in to the icehouse and building some kind of accommodation for the pony.

As it happened, Mrs. Tetley herself pounced on Lucas next morning while he was boiling water for his breakfast in the little back kitchen. It was almost the first time he had seen her since moving in, for on weekdays he went off long before she was up, and she always spent the evenings handing out tracts against drunkenness in the local ale-houses.

Mrs. Tetley, as usual, was dressed in a print apron with a kerchief round her head, but just the same, one hand supported by a mop, the other on her hip, she contrived to look as dignified and affronted as Britannia with her trident.

"Yoong man! I moost ask you to leave my house! If I'd had any notion, when I let ye lodge here, that ye were going in for that nasty toshing, I'd niver have let ye set foot in t'place. This is a respectable house, I'll have ye know. All t'lodgers have been objecting, and neighbours for three houses along. I'm sorry," she said, though plainly she was not, "but there it is. I moost ask you to leave today."

"Why, that's quite all right, Mrs. Tetley," Lucas said blithely. "for I was just going to give you notice myself. So there's no bones broken. I believe Anna-Marie paid the rent yesterday, so perhaps you'd be good enough to give me six days' money back, in lieu of a week's notice."

But this Mrs. Tetley had not the least intention of doing, and Lucas could not be bothered to press for it; he was so pleased to be getting out of her dismal little house. In the middle of the conversation, old Gabriel came into the back kitchen. Lucas had seen very little of the old man since they moved; when seen he was either going out in search of gin or coming back drunk. He looked very subdued and low-spirited.

When Mrs. Tetley left the kitchen for a moment, "Here, lad," whispered old Gabriel, pulling a very dirty pound note from his pocket, "I'll split the differ wi' you a bit. It fair sickens me to see my own flesh and blood acting so."

"Oh, no, no, Mr. Towzer, I wouldn't dream of taking your money," said Lucas, greatly touched by the old man's gesture.

Somewhat relieved, Gabriel put the note back. "I'm leaving too," he confided. "I towd ye my sister Kezia were a mickletongue, but I'd forgot she were a teetotal termagant too. 'Tis more than a body can stand. I'm off to my other sister, over to Keighley. But, Mester Lucas, ye'll be careful, won't ee? There's terrible bad feeling in t'town against a'body connected wi' Sir Randolph, acos it were decided at t'Crowner's Quest as he'd set fire to t'house hisself, to spite t'tax folk. If t'Court could ha' been sold, there'd ha' been cash enow to pay t'taxes and settle up all t'wages owing, and like enow, too, soom rich lord might ha' coom to live there an' given employment to plenty o' folk from t'town."

"Yes, I see," said Lucas.

"So I'd not mention ye come from t'Court, ye and the little lass."

"What'll happen to the park now, do you think?"

"There's talk o' some chap called Lord Holdernesse buying it, as owns a lot o' coal mines, an' he met dig a mine there; that'd give employment to folk."

"Oh," said Lucas. His spirits fell horribly. Dig up Midnight Park? What would happen to Lady Murgatroyd, who had lived there for so long?

"Mr. Towzer—" he began.

But at this moment Mrs. Tetley returned, and stood

watching with a lynx eye while Lucas carried out his few belongings and piled them on the cart. Old Gabriel wandered off, muttering, probably to the nearest alehouse, and Lucas drove back to Midnight Park.

Lady Murgatroyd and Anna-Marie, meanwhile, had been collecting brushwood and getting to know one another.

"Do you know what I enjoyed most about losing all my money?" said Lady Murgatroyd, expertly lopping away with a billhook. "It was learning how easy it is to do a great many things like this. When I was a real lady and rode around in a carriage, I though that chimneysweeping and bricklaying and carpentry and weaving cloth and making bowls and plates could only be done by chimneysweeps and bricklayers and carpenters and weavers and potters. Now I know that anybody can do these things, for I am not at all clever, and if I can do them, it is certain that anyone else can."

Nevertheless, Anna-Marie thought, her grandmother did look clever: her face was so lively, and had so much shape to it. Like a carving in a church, Anna-Marie thought. And her eyes, set in the deep triangular hollows, turned out, when seen by daylight, to be a strange and beautiful gray-green, the color of weathered stone.

"*Grand'mère*," said Anna-Marie, dumping an armful of brushwood in Lady Murgatroyd's wooden wheelbarrow, "why is everybody in Blastburn so horrible? Truly I think we have met only one kind person, *ce monsieur* 'Obday, and even of him I am not sure, for I think he may not be paying Luc as much as he should."

Lady Murgatroyd passed a dirt-stained hand over her high forehead.

"I am afraid it is partly your grandfather's fault," she said thoughtfully. "For it was he who started the town, with Midnight Mill. When he first built the mill, it was to be a good place for people to work in, with fair wages and everything made as well as it could be. And so it was, for a long time. But then your grandfather was so disappointed when your father would not learn to look after the Mill but wanted to write music instead—"

"Oh, and he did! He wrote beautiful music! I can remember many, many of the tunes—"

"Yes, but as well he was rather wild, and did some things that upset your grandfather."

"Did they upset you, *Grand'mère?*"

"Not so much," said Lady Murgatroyd, with a private smile. "He was a wild boy, Denny, but we understood one another very well, he and I. . . . But so, instead of making sure that the Mill was carefully run and in a good order to hand on to his son, your grandfather began to take less and less interest in it. He had it looked after by a manager instead of going there every day himself. Well, then Sir Randolph won it—you have heard about that?"

"Yes, Luc told me, *Grand'mère*—"

"And Sir Randolph looked after it still worse. All *he* wanted, I am afraid, was to get as much money as possible for his gambling, so things were done in a poor way, and the people were paid less, and the machinery has been allowed to get old and dangerous. And the other factories in the town are run in the same way, because the other owners have discovered that is the way to make a lot of money quickly, if you don't care what happens to the people who come after you."

"But why is everybody in the town so mean and *méchant*—the boys who throw stones at me for picking up cigar ends, and the ones who take money not to hurt people in hospital, and mock at strangers in the street, and seem to hate everybody?"

"It is because they are so poor. When you have only just

enough to keep alive, you are frightened of anybody who might take it from you, so you hate them. And you get your money in any way you can."

"But you are poor, *Grand'mère,* and yet you don't seem to hate people?"

"Well," said Lady Murgatroyd cheerfully, "I've *had* everything taken away from me, and I found it wasn't so bad after all. It was a big relief not to have to look after Midnight Court, I can tell you! There was always a broken window or a smoking chimney that needed attention; I never had a minute. Whereas now I can do just what I like—read or weave or paint pictures, or just sit and remember old times."

"So perhaps," said Anna-Marie, "it might be better for the people in the town to have everything taken from them?"

"But they have never had much at all, poor things! It would be better, much better, if they could have *enough,* so they could stop worrying and be kinder to each other."

"But *Grand'mère,*" said Anna-Marie thoughtfully, "how do people *know* when they have enough? For I think Sir Randolph was quite rich and yet he was *avare.*"

"Stingy."

"Stingy; thank you."

"Yes; well," said Lady Murgatroyd, taking up the handles of the loaded barrow and wheeling it over the snow as quickly and easily as if she were twenty, not seventy, "I suppose he was worried all the time about losing his money."

"So how can you teach people not to worry?"

"You ask some large-sized questions, *petite-fille!* I suppose you can do it in two ways, and neither is easy."

"*Et quoi?*"

"Either you make their lives so much better that they don't have to worry—"

"Or?"

"You somehow teach them that worrying doesn't help, but is only a waste of time."

"I think both ways together would be best," said Anna-Marie. "For some people will always be worrying—if only about whether the soup is going to be thick enough or if the milk will go sour. So you make them comfortable *and* you tell them not to unquiet themselves."

"*Eh bien, ma petite!* If anyone is going to do that to the people of Blastburn, it will have to be you, not me!"

"Why, *Grand'mère?*"

"I am too old."

"*Oh, quelle blague, Grand'mère!*" Anna-Marie said, laughing. "You are droll! If you can chimneysweep and lay bricks and make *poterie,* I think you can also tell the people of Blastburn to cheer up. . . . Aha, there comes Luc!" Her sharp eye had spotted him slipping through the gap in the wall with their basket. She bolted over the snow to help him.

Luckily it was a dim, foggy day. Although no snow fell, the yellow-gray clouds hung low, full of smoke; a dull red sun climbed a little way above the horizon, crept into a cloud, and sank again quite soon. Even the keenest eyes could not have seen more than thirty yards through the gloom, and nobody was about to see Lucas, Anna-Marie, and Lady Murgatroyd building a lean-to stable of stakes and brushwood against the park wall, in the little copse.

"In the summer," said Lady Murgatroyd, "we may as well enlarge the gap in the wall, so as to let the pony come through and graze in the park."

"But *Grand'mère,* suppose the park is sold to someone who does not want us here?"

"Now you are worrying needlessly," said Lady Murgatroyd. "If that happens, then we will make other plans."

Lucas told them what old Gabriel had said about the

park being sold for coal-mining land. Lady Murgatroyd sighed at the thought, but she said, "Well, it would certainly give employment to a lot of people. And if they put a mine here, we'd have plenty of warning beforehand, so that we could find somewhere else to live. There! I call that a really luxurious stable."

"*Un palais de cheval*," agreed Anna-Marie. The stable was walled and thatched with tightly bound bundles of brushwood; they had even constructed a brushwood door which hung on hinges made from leather straps; and the floor was snugly lined with dry bracken, which they had scratched out from under the snow.

"I would not mind sleeping in here myself," said Anna-Marie.

"Oh, in that case, you can have it, and we'll keep Noddy in the icehouse," Lucas said gravely.

"*Tais-toi, imbécile!* But still," said Anna-Marie, "when it is springtime and Monsieur Ookapool is here, maybe we build another *petite cabane, n'est-ce pas?* It would be nice to sleep here under the trees, I think."

"There are still bluebells in spring here," said Lady Murgatroyd. "Even though the town has grown so big and smoky."

For a moment they were all thinking of spring; it seemed almost as if the bluebells were there already.

Then Lady Murgatroyd said, "It's nearly dark; come along in."

Anna-Marie had already made herself familiar with the interior of the icehouse. Now she had a very enjoyable time showing it to Lucas. There was the big room with the fireplace where Lady Murgatroyd lived and slept, comfortably furnished with rugs and books and tree trunks. Then there were three smaller rooms, one of which Lady Murgatroyd had used as a larder, because it had slate shelves all up one wall. One was her washroom, because it contained a very large stone basin, which in Sir Quincy's day had been used for making ice cream. And the third was empty. Bet the baby at present occupied this room in her wicker cradle. It had been decided that Anna-Marie should share it with her, and that Lucas should have the larder. His room had a small door leading out, and all three rooms, as well as the big one, had little grating-windows cunningly sunk in the turf so that they were almost invisible from outside, unless you stood very close, and yet they let in some light.

"Isn't it a nice house, Luc," Anna-Marie kept saying.

"No, it's an icehouse!"

"Ah, bah! *Tu es vraiement stupide!*"

"Children! Suppertime!" Lady Murgatroyd called.

At supper—which consisted of a very delicious cheese-and-apple pie—Lady Murgatroyd explained that if they liked to bring back meat from Blastburn, she would not have the slightest objection to cooking it, but she herself ate only eggs, cheese, fruit, and vegetables.

"I have always found that best for my voice," she explained.

"Do you sing songs, *Grand'mère?*"

"I used to, *petite-fille;* now I only teach."

"I wish you will sing to me; Papa used to."

"Yes, he had a beautiful tenor voice. And you, my child, can you sing?"

"Oh yes. And I make up tunes."

"Then, after supper, I will show you my tuning fork."

"Papa had one of those."

"I'm sure he did. But mine is a special one."

After the meal, true to her word, Lady Murgatroyd produced the tuning fork from a wooden case. It looked ordinary enough: a bluish metal prong which, when banged on the stone wall, gave out a sweet tingling note.

"Why is it special?" Anna-Marie wanted to know.

"You have heard of a composer called Georges Frédéric Handel?"

"Oh, *si!* He has written some music about water." She hummed a bit of it.

"Quite right. He was born over a hundred years ago, and died in seventeen fifty-nine, as you may know. This tuning fork belonged to him."

"Truly?" said Anna-Marie, very amazed.

"True as I stand her here. When Handel died, he left his tuning fork to a friend of his, an English musician and singer called Henry Metcalfe, who made up some beautiful songs. And Henry Metcalfe gave it, when he grew old, to a German composer called Diefenmacher, who wrote organ music. He died in eighteen hundred, and left the tuning fork to a French singer called Hector Boismachère. And *he* was my father and left it to me."

"Oh, *Grand'mère!* So you are French?"

"Half French, half English; like you. So, you see, the tuning fork has always been passed on from one musician to another. And I hope it always will be."

"So you, grandmother, when you grow older, will have to find a musician to give it to."

"Yes, I shall," said Lady Murgatroyd.

Anna-Marie begged her grandmother to sing a song. And before long they were singing together, half in French, half in English, nursery songs, ballads, whatever came into their heads.

Lucas, who could not tell one note from another, listened politely. But his eyes, ever since he came into the icehouse, had been straying more and more eagerly toward the books. Lady Murgatroyd said, laughing, "Do read whichever of them you would like. I am afraid they are mostly poetry and plays, but there is some travel and biography. And a bit of philosophy."

Lucas was across the room before she had finished

speaking. He opened one book and then another. He was lost.

A couple of hours later, Lady Murgatroyd said gently, "I don't want to be a killjoy but you did say, didn't you, that you had to get up at half past five so as to get to your sewer at six o'clock?"

Lucas dragged himself out of a play called *The White Devil*. It was like pulling himself out of the Muckle Sump. "Yes, of course," he said dazedly. "What time is it, my lady?"

"Oh, why not call me grandmother? You and Anna-Marie might just as well count yourselves as cousins. It's ten o'clock." She pointed to an old silver-gilt clock which sat in a hole in the wall where one stone had been removed. "And you needn't worry about waking in the morning. Listen."

She pressed a button at the back of the clock and it immediately played a sweet silvery tune: "London Bridge Is Falling Down."

"You see," said Lady Murgatroyd, "it is an *alarm clock;* set this little hand to the time at which you want to get up, and the clock will wake you by playing its tune. Put it on the shelf by your bed."

Lucas and Anna-Marie had piled themselves beds out of more bracken, which had been drying in front of the fire all evening, giving off a leafy, earthy smell. Lady Murgatroyd luckily had two spare blankets, and Lucas said that he would buy some more in the market; cotton blankets cost only five shillings there. Meanwhile they also piled sacks, and what clothes they had, on top of the blankets, for the stone rooms were cold.

"But this bed is much, much more comfortable than the one at Mrs. Tetley's," Anna-Marie said.

After they had gone to bed Lucas came out of his room again—his own room—to ask, "Ma'am—Grandmother—do you have any spare paper that you aren't using?"

"To write on, do you mean?"

He nodded.

"I have some blank account books of my husband's that you are welcome to use. Over there in that corner, see? I brought them, thinking I might keep a diary in them, but then I found more interesting things to do. You are welcome to them, my dear boy." She paused, looked at him thoughtfully, and then said, "Now, I ask myself, does this belong to you? I found it, and have been keeping it, somehow expecting that the owner might come back looking for it."

From the wooden chest she produced a brown leather book—the book that he had believed burned.

Lucas found that he was unable to speak. He gave Lady Murgatroyd a throttling hug, and went back to bed, from where he could see a star, just one, stuck in the middle of his tiny grating window.

He slept.

WHILE THEY WERE building the stable, Lucas had—rather cautiously—suggested to Anna-Marie that there was not much use in her trying to keep on her cigar trade if the boys of the town were determined to stop her. He had been afraid that her hot temper might make her wish to go on battling against their unfair persecution, but luckily the practical side of her nature came uppermost.

"No: I do not see any point, if they are going to take away all my work and spoil it; I do not wish to work for nothing. *C'est de la folie, cela!* In the morning I shall ask the advice of *Grand'mère;* she knows so much; I am sure she will think of some good plan."

This was such a relief to Lucas that he did not even consider discussing Anna-Marie's occupation with Lady Murgatroyd, but went off to bed easier in his mind than he had been for weeks, and slept dreamlessly until the gentle silvery notes of "London Bridge Is Falling Down" woke him at half-past five.

From here, it was no farther to the Market Square than it had been from Haddock Street, so he need start no earlier. He had persuaded Anna-Marie that there was no purpose in her getting up so early, as she was not coming with him. Lady Murgatroyd had made him some chestnut porridge the previous evening, cooking the chestnuts over the fire in a little water until they were boiling, then placing the pot, which was made of heavy earthenware with a lid, inside a padded box, thickly stuffed with hay. To his amazement, for though she had told him the porridge would be ready for breakfast, he had not really believed her, he found it still hot in the morning, and perfectly cooked. It made a delicious breakfast, completed by three more gingersnaps.

He had on his outer clothes and was on the point of leaving quietly through his own little door when Anna-Marie darted silently into his room.

"Good-bye, dear Luc! I could not let you go off without saying *bonjour*," she said, and gave him a hug. "Take care! And find something nice in that nasty place."

He went off feeling warm, well fed, and cheerful, in spite of being bound for the sewers; how different from leaving Haddock Street with its smell of boiled dirty potato peelings and atmosphere of grudging dislike. Now his mind had so much to occupy it that he hardly knew where to begin.

In fact he did not notice that Gudgeon greeted him with a scowl and seemed—even for Gudgeon—unusually surly.

Anna-Marie had returned to bed after saying good-bye to Lucas, and even gone back to sleep for a short time, but the baby woke at seven and wanted to play; so after that there was no more sleep. Bet was just old enough to scramble out of her cradle and crawl about the floor, strong enough to overturn anything that could be upset and to break anything breakable if it were left within her reach.

She did, too, seem to be passionately fond of stuffing anything into her mouth: sand, ashes, moss, earth, charcoal, the bracken lining of Anna-Marie's bed—the more unsuitable it was, the better she liked it.

"*Grand Dieu!*" panted Anna-Marie at the end of an exhausting hour. "How, *Grand'mère*, an old lady, ever kept up with you, I cannot imagine. *Je n'ai aucune idée.*"

"Day, day," repeated the baby, happily thumping a wooden spoon against the copper can in which Lady Murgatroyd fetched water from the spring in the park.

"*Grand'mère*," said Anna-Marie, when they had fed the baby her bread and milk and were eating their own (the bread made by Lady Murgatroyd twice a week, the milk fetched from a farm on the moor), "*Grand'mère,* what can I do? As work, I mean?"

"You are sure that you would not rather stay here and help me? Others of your age would still be going to school. You are quite young."

"No," said Anna-Marie positively. "We have not enough money that I stay at home. And if Luc works it is fair that I work also. And others of my age also work. Certainly I wish to help you, *Grand'mère,* but it shall be after I get home or before I go. I would like also to learn singing from you and how to make that *potage de marrons* and many other things, but first we must have enough money so that we are not a burden on you, *Grand'mère.* After all, you did not even know that you had a grandchild."

"No indeed. It was the nicest surprise in the world. I had heard that the *Sea-Witch,* that was the boat on which your father went to France, had been sunk and all the people on her drowned, so I thought that he was dead."

"He swam to shore; he has told me about it many times. And *he* thought that you were dead, *Grand'maman;* he told me once that he read a piece in a newspaper about how Grandpère died just after Papa left home, and it said that you had died too."

"Pieces in newspapers are generally wrong," said Lady Murgatroyd sadly. "And look what a lot of harm they do. If it had not been for that, your father might have written a letter to me years ago."

"And come to visit you, *peut-être.*"

"I am not sure that he could have done that. But I could have gone to see him in France."

"Why could he not come to England? He would never tell me that."

"Well—you know about how Sir Randolph won Midnight Court."

Anna-Marie nodded. "Yes. And I think he was a *rrrogue* to do it so," she said vehemently. "If I had known when he was still alive, I would have told him so, to his face."

"And he wanted to fight a duel with your father, because people were saying Sir Randolph had cheated. But your father would not fight; he said he was not interested in whether Sir Randolph had cheated or not, and fighting would not prove anything, either way."

"I would have fought him, me," said Anna-Marie.

"Well—it is possible that he did have to fight him in the end. It is all quite a mystery. Your father was planning to sail to France in this little fishing boat, the *Sea-Witch,* leaving from the port of Shoreham. Two people went with him as far as the coast. Tom Grenvile, a college friend of his who had lent him a horse and some money, was one. Ah, poor Tom," Lady Murgatroyd sighed.

"And who was the other?"

"The other was a young boy, no more than fifteen years old, who was very greatly devoted to your father. He had run away from his home and his school, and he begged to be allowed to go to France. Your father said no, but he might come as far as the coast; he kept trying to persuade the boy to turn back, but he would not; your father did not know what to do about him."

"I should have been like that too. *Naturally* he wanted to go with Papa. And so, what happened?"

"When they came to the seashore—it was at night—there was an ambush."

"An *ambush?* But this is an adventure you are telling me, *Grand'mère.*"

"It certainly was. A whole party of men, five or six, were there, in masks, with swords, and they attacked your papa, and his friend, and the boy."

"They were sent by Sir Randolph. Maybe he was there too," stated Anna-Marie.

"It is possible. Certainly your father had no other enemies. But why, just the same? Sir Randolph had the house and everything else already; there was nothing to be gained by killing your papa."

"If he had cheated there was. In case anyone found out. But also I think it made him feel bad—horrible—whenever he thought of my papa. The only way *not* to feel bad—he believed—would be to kill my papa altogether."

Lady Murgatroyd looked at her thoughtfully. "You may be right."

"I *am* right," said Anna-Marie with certainty. "For he went on feeling horrible all the rest of his life; everybody knows that. And when he saw me—just before he jumped himself into the fire—he said to me, 'I shall tell your papa that I didn't much care for his slice of Clutterby Pie.' "

"Poor stupid man," murmured Lady Murgatroyd. "What a lot of harm he caused."

"But what about the ambush, *Grand'maman?* What happened?"

"Well, your father was a good fighter, when he was obliged to be. Two men of the attackers were killed. Your father's friend was very badly injured. And the boy was hurt too. Then the boat arrived, and the sailors came ashore, and the other men ran away.

"The sailors sailed the *Sea-Witch* along the coast to the town of Brighton, where there was a good doctor, and they carried the hurt boy and man ashore. What could your father do? He could not take them to France, hurt like that. He left all his money with the doctor and begged him to write to their families, telling them where they were.

"Then he went to France."

"It must have been *dreadful* for the boy," said Anna-

Marie broodingly. "Wanting to go so badly, and then hurt and not able to, and sent back home like a child. Was he *much* hurt?"

"Not fatally. His parents came and fetched him. I never saw him."

"But you saw the other one? That was how you heard about the ambush?"

"Yes. Tom had been very seriously hurt—stabbed through the lung—and he did not get better but died at the doctor's house. His parents went to be with him, and they were friends of mine and sent for me, so that I could hear about my poor Denny's last journey. By then, you see, we had heard that the *Sea-Witch* had been wrecked in a gale, and it was said that no one swam ashore."

Lady Murgatroyd's steady eyes moved to the fire and stayed there for a moment or two.

"And this friend, Tom Grenvile, he told how your father, when he was bidding them good-bye, said, 'I'm dished, now, Tommy, for I've killed two men'—and it was true, he had—'I'll have to stay out of the Isle of Albion.' "

"But he hadn't killed them on purpose!" cried Anna-Marie indignantly. "They attacked first."

"Yes, but Sir Randolph was a very powerful man at that time, even a friend of the king. And rich, too, of course, because he had won all that property. He might have been able to hire clever lawyers and tell some story that made it look as if your father had attacked first."

"On his way to France? That is not likely."

"Well," said Lady Murgatroyd, "it is all over now. And a long time ago."

"I wonder what happened to the boy?"

"Haven't you guessed?"

"No, why?"

"It was your Mr. Oakapple."

"Monsieur Ookapool? Oh!" exclaimed Anna-Marie, "I

always *knew* he was very good, and now I am sure of it. When I see him, what a hug I shall give him for loving my papa so much."

Then she pondered in silence for a while, and said, "But I wonder why—why *ever*—he should go to work as a tutor in the house of Sir Randolph. For he must have hated him worse than anyone in the world."

"Yes, I have been wondering that too," said Lady Murgatroyd. "But perhaps if we ask him he will tell us."

"Now, *Grand'mère,*" said Anna-Marie. "About my work. What can I do?"

"Well, you could do piecework at home."

"What is piecework?"

"Sewing—making shirts, trousers, that kind of thing."

"*Non,*" said Anna-Marie with finality. "I detest sewing. I would rather chop trees."

"I do not think they are using girls to chop trees. Well, I suppose you could go to work on the dust hill."

"What is that?"

"Have you seen the dustcarts that go through the streets? They collect the rubbish, and it is all taken to a big yard on the east side of the town, where it is sorted, and anything valuable in it is taken out and sold, and the farmers buy the street sweepings to manure their fields. They have a number of women and girls working there, sifting the dust."

"Well, I would certainly prefer that to making shirts," said Anna-Marie. "And I suppose one might always find something valuable—like Luc in the drains."

"It would not be very comfortable, though, in this cold weather. Piecework would be better. It is not very well paid, unfortunately."

"What about *Grandpère*'s mill? Could I not work there? Luc says they take quite young girls, of my age."

"I suppose you could work there," Lady Murgatroyd

said rather doubtfully. "It may be better since Sir Randolph died."

"Well, I will try the Mill," Anna-Marie decided. "For one thing, it is close, not far to walk. And if after all I do not like it, then I will work in the dust yard."

Lady Murgatroyd did not seem entirely happy about Anna-Marie's choice, but there were not a great many alternatives, for Murgatroyd's Mill was the only factory that took children of Anna-Marie's age.

"At all events, you may learn some things that may be useful to you later on, about how such places work. In case you ever come to run one yourself!"

"I shall never run such a place, me."

Anna-Marie gave her grandmother a kiss, and said, "I shall go now, directly. *Au revoir, Grand'mère*. It will not be so bad, for Luc has told me a little about it, so I shall not feel too ignorant."

Just the same, when she had crossed the snowy park, slipped through the gap in the wall, rejoined the main road, and run down the hill, Anna-Marie did feel somewhat daunted as she approached the high, black, forbidding fence and gates of the mill yard. However, dodging the loaded trucks that went rumbling along on rails right through the gate, she sidled in, and crossed to the little office where Lucas had conversed with Mr. Smallside. A sharp-looking man with red hair like a fox was now the manager, it seemed; he looked Anna-Marie up and down, and snapped, "What do you want?"

"I wish to work here," said Anna-Marie in her best English.

"You're too little."

"Others are smaller," said Anna-Marie, who had noticed a couple of girls busy sweeping up wool waste in the yard with brushes and dustpans. "I have eight years. And I am clever."

"Cool, too," said the manager, looking at her with slightly more favor. "Oh, well, I daresay we can use you. Got your mother's consent?"

"*Je n'ai pas*—I have not a mother."

"Father, then?"

"My father is dead also."

"Nobody to make a fuss if you fall under a truck, eh?" said the manager agreeably. "All right, we'll try you. Start as a claw-cleaner." He lifted his voice and bawled, "Rose Sproggs!"

A woman came hurriedly across the yard, threading her way between the wagons loaded with bales of wool. She was thin and anxious-looking, somewhat hard-featured, with her hair done up in a kerchief; it was hard to guess her age, but she might have been somewhere between eighteen and twenty-five.

"Here's a new cleaner for you," said the manager. "What's your name?" to Anna-Marie.

"*Je m'appelle*—I am call Anna-Marie Minetti."

"Too long. We'll call you Anna. Take her and show her what to do, Rose."

"Reet, Mester Gravestone."

"How much do you pay me?" said Anna-Marie, ignoring the impatient beckoning of Rose.

"Shilling a day."

"Is not much."

"Take it or leave it. That's all kids get."

"Coom on," said Rose. "I haven't all day to listen to thee argue."

Anna-Marie followed, shrugging.

Rose looked her up and down and said, "Pigtails'll 'ave to coom off."

"*Quoi?*"

Rose led the way to a small workshop at the yard end where crates were made and minor repairs carried out.

"Loan us thy shears, Jim," she called to a man in a carpenter's apron and, without more ado, cut off Anna-Marie's braids.

"They might get caught oop in t'machinery, ye see, luv," she explained, not unkindly. "Better lose thy pigtails than thy head. Onyway it's a rule. Want to keep them?" She handed the two small black braids to Anna-Marie, who silently put them in her pocket. "Now tha'll need an overall; well, tha can have Janey Herdman's; she got roon down by a troock. It's in the combing shed—this way. Follow me, and look sharp; the troocks runs all over, and they doosn't wait for thee to step aside."

Although Lucas had talked to her a little about the factory and given her a vague idea of its workings, Anna-Marie soon became confused as she followed Rose among the dirty black buildings, sometimes through narrow passages, sometimes across wide yards, or through workshops filled with clanging machinery.

"Right," said Rose as, having equipped Anna-Marie with a short calico overall that tied at the back, she led the way down a long narrow gallery.

"Now, this 'ere's one o' the combing sheds. These things are called claws, see, an' they comb the wool. An' it's your job to keep cleaning them out, for they soon gets chocked oop wi' all the dirt and scrubble that's in the raw wool."

All the way along the wall facing them were a series of curved heavy metal claws, something like those of a claw hammer, but about three feet long. They were rising and falling the whole time in continuous succession, giving the effect of a giant piano having scales played on it by an invisible performer. The claws fell onto a mass of wool, which was stretched over a rotating drum underneath a grating.

"Now, this is what tha does," said Rose. She climbed on to the grating, which was a couple of feet above floor level, and walked along it, expertly pulling the wool waste out of each pair of claws as it rose up, with the action of somebody pulling hair out of a comb. "Do that, see?—walk all along the shed—it's twenty yards—then coom back an' start agen."

"Nothing else?"

"Nay, there's nowt else to a claw-cleaner's job. Claws gets chocked oop reet quick. I'll pop back from time to time to see how th'art getting on—I'm the overseer, sithee. Dinner break's at noon, has tha brought soom crib?"

"Pardon?" said Anna-Marie, who found it hard to follow; Rose had a very broad accent, and many of the words she used were unfamiliar.

"Has tha brought owt to eat? Oh, well, tha can have a morsel o' mine; anoother day, best bring a bite o' bread an' cheese. You can eat it down on the floor there. Now, the Friendly Lads'll be sure to be roond soon enow, pay them, or they'll be making trooble for thee."

"Who are the Friendly Lads?" asked Anna-Marie, though she had a fair guess.

" 'Tis the Friendly Society. They look after you if you're sick, an' they argues about higher wages wi' the chaps as roons th'mill, but mostly what they doos is collect money from the folk as doos the work. Tha cannot argue wi' them, or they'll shoov you into the mincer."

"Are they the same ones who collect up at the infirmary?"

"Aye, it's different collectors but the same society. Now I must be away to the other combing sheds. Don't let the claws get clogged, or the machine'll stick, and Mester Gravestone'll give us the rough side o' his toongue; besides, it's dangerous."

And Rose jumped nimbly off the grating and departed.

Faced with the endlessly rising and falling row of claws, Anna-Marie had a moment of panic—if only they would stop for a moment, just so that she could look at them calmly. But they did not stop, and so she climbed up on to the grating and began to move along it, as Rose had done, snatching the waste from each pair of claws as it came up.

She soon discovered that unless she nipped out the waste matter with great speed and judgment, her fingers were pinched against the next pair of claws coming up—the snatch had to be made at exactly the right moment. It took her some time to gauge the proper speed and sequence of movements; before she had got it right, her fingers had become stiff and black with bruises. Even after she had learned the motion, it did not do to let her attention slip for a second. Rose had walked along the row quite casually, with her eyes on the door or the floor, talking over her shoulder while she pulled out the waste, but if Anna-Marie took her eyes off her hands for a moment, she was in trouble. Moreover the waste that was picked out by the claws tended to be full of prickles and splinters, which also jabbed into her fingers and made them very sore.

By the time a whistle blew, presumably for dinner, Anna-Marie had decided that it would be hard to find a more stupid or disagreeable way of earning one's living. Picking up cigar ends was far preferable. The cleaning could easily be done better some other way, she thought; if one could devise a pair of wooden tongs, say, held together by a pin, perhaps with leather tips—

"Hey, oop, lass!" called Rose. "Tha can knock off, now. Twenty minutes for crib."

Anna-Marie was glad to stop. As well as her aching fingers, she was having trouble with her eyes, and was obliged to shut them for a couple of minutes. They were so dazzled by the endlessly flowing rise and fall of the claws that she felt quite giddy; it was a relief to sit down on the floor. Another girl called Biddy hopped up onto the grating and continued cleaning out the claws; Biddy, it seemed, had already eaten.

Rose kindly offered Anna-Marie a share of her coarse Yorkshire cheese and brown bread; but Anna-Marie felt shy about taking someone else's food, and in any case did not feel very hungry. She preferred to lean back against the wall, sucking the splinters out of her fingers.

"Ey, hey," said Rose in a low tone, looking along the shed. "I knew Mester Moneygrubber'd not be long smelling thee oot."

A man in a wicker wheelchair was approaching them down the narrow gangway. "New helper, then?" he said to Rose.

"Ah," she replied without enthusiasm, and, to Anna-Marie, "This 'ere's Mester Bludward, as roons the Friendly Society, an' that's Newky Shirreff, as collects th'dues. 'Appen tha'll not have any brass on thee as yet?"

"Brass?" Anna-Marie was puzzled.

"Dibs, mint sauce, cash."

"No I have not."

"Then I'll lend it thee."

"Twopence a week if tha's oonder twelve," put in the little man, Newky Shirreff, sidling forward with his collecting bag.

"But I do not at all wish to join your *société*," said Anna-Marie crossly. "Why should I be obliged to pay you twopence a week when I am only paid a shilling a day?"

"Sharp little tyke, bain't she?" said Newky Shirreff, looking at Anna-Marie with disfavor.

"Ah, she knaws nowt as yet." Rose dropped two pennies into his bag and contrived to give Anna-Marie a fierce pinch as she did so. "She'll soon learn oor ways."

"What's thy name, lass?" Bludward studied Anna-Marie coldly.

"She's called Anna," said Rose. "An' she's farin' oop to be a reet handy little claw-cleaner."

The two men moved off along the gangway, and Rose, waiting till they were out of sight, hissed, "Niver get on t'wrong side o' that pair, luv! Tha wants to watch thy tongue wi' them worse nor wi' the bosses!"

"But why?"

"I telled thee! Cross Bob Bludward, an', like as not, tha'll finish oop oonder t'carpet press, or sliced in two by t'shoottle. Bludward's got more say-so in t'mill than t'manager hisself, ony day."

"Well I think he is not at all a nice man and I do not think this place is well arranged," said Anna-Marie with a frown. But at that moment the whistle blew for the end of the dinner break, and she had to go back to her claw-cleaning.

Anna-Marie arrived home at the icehouse that evening considerably before Lucas, for he had stopped to spend twopence of his earnings at the public bathhouse, a large draughty stone building in one corner of the Market Square which offered a halfpenny wash, penny shower, twopenny cold bath, or threepenny hot. Lucas had also arranged to leave his sewer clothes in a chest behind Mr. Hobday's stall, and keep a spare set there for home wear; he did not wish to fill Lady Murgatroyd's refuge with a smell of drains.

He had stopped in the market, as well, to buy eggs, cheese, and other groceries. By the time he arrived home, the baby had been fed and put to bed. Lady Murgatroyd and her granddaughter were busy experimenting with some pieces of wood and leather, out of which they seemed to be constructing a giant pair of sugar tongs.

"What's that for?" inquired Lucas, and then he exclaimed, "Why, Anna-Marie—what's happened to your hair? And what did you do to your fingers? Did you burn them in the fire?"

"Oh, it is nothing," said Anna-Marie. "Only the claw

hammers at the Mill. When I shall be more *habile*, it will not happen. Especially if I can use these *pincettes* that *Grand'mère* is making."

"At the *Mill?*"

Lucas was most upset to hear that Anna-Marie had taken employment as a claw-cleaner at the Mill. No argument would change his opinion that this was an extremely undesirable arrangement, and that Anna-Marie would be better doing almost anything else.

"It's a bad place," he kept saying. "It's dangerous. You don't know the half of it yet!"

Secretly Anna-Marie was much inclined to agree with him but she was certainly not going to let him have the final say. "Ah, bah, it is not so bad! Besides, what else can I do? Nobody else employs persons of my age, *Grand'mère* says so."

"You could take in sewing. You could work as a servant in someone's house."

"*Merci de rien!* If I worked as a servant I should have to live with the people—who might be very disagreeable—and I should never see you or *Grand'mère*. And I do not like to sew."

"You sewed your pink dress."

"Only because it had to be done."

"Eat, and stop arguing, the two of you," said Lady Murgatroyd. "As soon as the weather improves, Anna-Marie may prefer to work on the dust heap. And in the evenings I will teach her to sing and play the flute; I am sure that in time she will be able to help me give my music lessons. And you, Lucas, should perhaps think of trying presently for a job on the *Blastburn Post,* if writing is what you like to do best. Nobody would wish to work either in Murgatroyd's Mill or in the sewers for longer than they had to. Only, while you are there, learn all you can!"

"But some people will always have to work there," objected Anna-Marie, taking a bite of onion tart. "There will always be mills and sewers."

"Well! Then you must think of how to make them more enjoyable for the people who work there."

Anna-Marie burst out laughing. "There will have to be a law that *tout le monde* must pour a bottle of perfume down the drain holes every day! As for the Mill, I think it would be better if there is not one. I do not see the need for it, me. People could make their own carpets, like *Grand'mère*."

"But it gives work to many," said Lucas.

"Well, they must earn their money somewhere else, *figure-toi*."

"Isn't it time you went to the infirmary?" said Lady Murgatroyd. "I have made a custard and a cheesecake for you to take to Mr. Oakapple."

Anna-Marie was dying to see Mr. Oakapple. After the story about her father and the ambush, she felt that she would look at the tutor with new eyes. On the short drive down the hill she related to Lucas all that her grandmother had told her. He seemed to listen intently enough, but he was very silent; in fact he had been rather silent ever since he came home. Anna-Marie had the feeling that there was something weighing on his mind which, for reasons of his own, he had decided not to tell her. On the way back I will ask him what is the matter, she decided. It is not right that he should not share his worry.

When they reached the hospital, they were somewhat disconcerted to be told by one of the white-capped Sisters that Mr. Oakapple's bed was required for another patient.

"We should be obliged if you could take him home today," the Sister said.

The request was politely phrased, but it was plain that they really had no choice in the matter. When they reached the ward they found that in fact Mr. Oakapple was already up and dressed in a suit of somewhat ill-fitting secondhand clothes that had been provided for him. He was sitting in a chair and looked deathly tired and shaky, as if he ought to be back in bed.

"But I thought you said he should stay for another two weeks?" Lucas protested to the Sister.

"I know I did, my boy, but there has been a bad roof fall in one of the collieries, and we have a great many urgent cases coming in; we need all the beds we can spare."

Lucas saw the force of this, but he felt extremely worried as to whether they would be able to give Mr. Oakapple the proper kind of care.

Anna-Marie, however, was simply pleased at the news. "*Grand'mère* will know what to do for him!" she whispered to Lucas. "And it will be much, much nicer to have him at home. Besides, then we need not pay those *cochons* of Friendly Boys!"

Slowly, with many pauses, they assisted Mr. Oakapple downstairs, and out to the cart. He was painfully weak and breathless; getting him up and on to a seat was a long and difficult process.

"Where are you taking me?" he inquired, as Lucas turned the pony's head uphill.

"We have left our lodgings in the town and gone to live in the old icehouse," Lucas explained.

"The icehouse?" Mr. Oakapple said weakly. "Is that comfortable?" He sounded rather dismayed at the prospect. No doubt, Lucas thought, if he had been well, he might have regarded the move to the icehouse as a practical notion, but in his present frail condition it was plain that he did not relish the idea of living in a kind of cave.

"It is all right, monsieur," said Anna-Marie reassuringly. "Truly, you will find it *quite* comfortable when you get there."

"I can't imagine how you are managing to live at all," said Mr. Oakapple in a troubled voice, gingerly touching one hand to his newly healed cheek. "If I were only a little stronger. . . . How are you managing about money, the pair of you? Did Throgmorton give you no help at all?"

"No, sir. He said Sir Randolph left no will, and that anyway there was no money to leave. And the Mill was sold to pay the taxes."

"Yes, I see. . . . I suppose all your father's money was sunk in the Mill—"

"But we are doing very well, monsieur," broke in Anna-Marie. "I work in the Mill, and Luc, he is a tosher in the sewers, and we make enough money—plenty! You do not have to worry about us at all. We can look after you till you are well, do not disquiet yourself! Besides, we have such a surprise for you—"

"Wait, Anna-Marie!" warned Lucas.

He could see that Mr. Oakapple was not fit for the move, that he was really very near to collapse. Although the mare plodded along slowly, Lucas could not steer her away from all the bumps in the snow, which jarred the tutor's hurts. And the night was bitterly cold. Besides, Lucas thought, just being out of hospital, obliged to face the difficulties of the world again, was very tiring.

"I don't think Mr. Oakapple is ready for more news until we have him sitting by the fire," he told Anna-Marie. "And we've got the walk to worry about now."

Lucas had in fact wondered whether it might be better to go the long way round, through the lodge gates, and drive the cart across the snow to the icehouse. But he was not at all sure if the poor old mare would be able to pull the trap through the deep snow; it would be dreadful to get stuck. And it was much farther; Mr. Oakapple was shivering badly already, and if he were to catch cold his recovery might be set back even more. So, having considered the alternative and decided against it, Lucas drove the cart as close as he could get to the hole in the wall.

"This part is going to be troublesome, sir. Can you walk a couple of hundred yards, do you think?"

"I must, mustn't I?" remarked the tutor, with a return to his former dry manner. "We'll just have to take it slowly. Perhaps you could find me a walking-stick."

Lucas found him a stick, and he and Anna-Marie each took one of the tutor's arms to help him over the rough ground. Getting through the thickety little wood was extremely difficult and harassing; Lucas crept along by Mr. Oakapple, supporting him as well as he could; Anna-Marie went backwards ahead of them, pulling aside the branches and brambles. Luckily the moon shone overhead. Then there was a painful and tiring struggle while they assisted the tutor to get through the gap in the wall.

"Really, what an awkward, useless lump I am," he said, impatient with his own weakness. "I begin to wonder if, when you have got me into this hidey-hole of yours, I shall ever get out again!"

He meant to make a joke, but he did not sound hopeful about his own prospects.

"I have a good idea, monsieur," said Anna-Marie when he was through the wall. "Wait there just a moment—lean against the wall, so—and I will run and get you *Grand'mère*'s chair, so that you can sit and rest as we go."

She darted off across the snow.

"Did you save some furniture from the Court, then?" asked Mr. Oakapple in weak bewilderment. "She said *Grand'mère*' s chair?" Then he stopped speaking, as two figures appeared outside the icehouse, carrying the chair between them.

"Who is that?"

Mr. Oakapple put the question so quietly that Lucas could only just hear his voice. And before Lucas could answer Lady Murgatroyd was beside him, taking his arm to support him.

"There, monsieur!" Anna-Marie proudly thumped the

chair down beside him. "Now, sit quickly, and rest yourself. *Grand'mère* has brought you some cordial, too."

"It is made from herbs and honey," said Lady Murgatroyd. "Swallow it down as fast as you can. If I had known you were coming out of the hospital today we could have prepared a litter to carry you in. It is too bad that they turned you out when you are still so weak. Never mind, once we get you indoors, we shall look after you famously!"

"Ma'am," said Mr. Oakapple, looking up into her face.

"Drink first," she said firmly, steadying the little stone flask which she held with his hand round it.

He drank and rested a moment longer; then he struggled up and they helped him over half the distance to the icehouse; Anna-Marie brought up the chair and he sat in it again, always looking at Lady Murgatroyd's face; then he walked the rest of the way, and was helped inside the house.

Anna-Marie had again darted on ahead and, consulting Lady Murgatroyd with a look, had pulled her grandmother's sleeping-cot over until it stood near the fireplace. Mr. Oakapple was steered straight to it, and they made a pile of folded rugs to support his back.

"There," said Anna-Marie, covering him with a fluffy sheepskin. "Now you are as snug, monsieur, as a bumblebee in a rose. All you have to do is to go to sleep. And when you wake you will feel so much better."

"Perhaps he should take a little soup first, though," said Lady Murgatroyd, and she set a potful on the hearth. "I had made this ready for the children when they came back from visiting, but there is plenty for all."

"Ma'am," Mr. Oakapple began again, but she said, "I can see plainly that you are so tired you are almost fainting. Truly you must rest. Wait until you have had some soup."

It was true that the tutor was ashy pale, except for the

patches of scarlet on his face and hands where the burn scars were fading. He lay back weakly, and gazed around the big shadowy place with a strange look of astonishment and acceptance on his face.

Anna-Marie bustled about, fetching more covers, and a wedge of wood to put behind Mr. Oakapple under the rugs, which would support him more comfortably, she fancied; then she brought a wooden tray with a plate, bread, salt, a mug of water, and a spoon for him to eat his soup with; then she curled up on the floor beside her grandmother and sat sucking her thumb, waiting till the soup should be hot. Lady Murgatroyd meanwhile sat calmly and silently on one of the stump stools, gazing at the flames. And Lucas, having seen that there was nothing he could usefully do at present, had withdrawn to a book-filled corner and taken up a book. But he was not reading.

At last Anna-Marie pronounced the soup to be ready, and served it out to everybody in mugs.

"You, *Grand'mère?*"

"Yes, I will take a little, thank you, my child. You see what a useful helper I have acquired," Lady Murgatroyd said, smiling at Mr. Oakapple.

The soup had given him back a little color. He said, "Ma'am, how long have you been here? In Midnight Park?"

"Longer than you," she said cheerfully. "I suppose it may be ten years now. I can remember when you came; I have seen quite a lot from my hermitage! But one thing I did not know, and that was, that the tutor who came to look after Sir Randolph's ward was the Julian Oakapple who had been such a devoted friend to my poor Denny."

She stood up and, walking over, took his injured hand in both of hers. "I know what you did for him," she said simply. "I know you hurt your hand protecting him from a sword thrust. Tom Grenvile told me that, before he died."

She looked at the gloved hand. "You were a violinist, were you not? I remember Denny talking of your great promise. It must have been a hard thing to get over. And you were so young."

"Yes," he said. "It was hard. But not so hard as believing that he had died when the ship sank."

"What did you do, after you got better?" she asked.

"Oh—my parents sent me back to school, as soon as my hand was healed. They were not harsh to me; they told me the injury to my hand was a judgment. I could still sing. I learned all they could teach me at the school, and then I taught. I did not want to quit this part of the country because, somehow, I always had a faint hope that perhaps Sir Denzil was not really dead, and that possibly some day matters might be righted—by some miracle—so that he could come back. . . . Was that why you stayed here, Lady Murgatroyd?"

"Partly," she said. "Also, when people are gone, if you are old, you cling to a place. . . . So then, what did you do?"

"Then," he said slowly, "a strange thing happened. That was about five years ago. I was in Blastburn, and I heard a sailor singing down by the docks. It was a song I knew very well—one that Sir Denzil had made up for me to sing. I thought nobody knew it but me. So I asked the man where he had learned it, and he said from an Englishman who had taught him in school, in Dieppe."

"Dieppe!" said Anna-Marie, who had been listening intently to this conversation. "Yes, we lived in Dieppe for a while, before we moved to Calais. Papa would always live as near to England as possible."

"Oh, my poor son," said Lady Murgatroyd softly to herself.

"So I traveled to Dieppe," said Mr. Oakapple. "And I asked. And people said, Yes, an Englishman had lived there, but he had married and moved away. No one knew where. So then I traveled about, searching. I could not find out where he had gone. I stayed in France three years, teaching English, always moving about—"

"*That* is why you speak French so well, monsieur—"

"And then my mother was ill, and lonely, and wrote, saying, Come back. So I came back. And then, not long after she died, I read in the *Blastburn Post* that the orphan son of Sir Randolph's partner had come to live at the Court. I had no employment just then, for I had been looking after my mother, so I offered myself for the position of tutor."

"Why did you do that?" Lady Murgatroyd asked.

Mr. Oakapple looked at the fire. "One reason was that I wanted to come here again," he said. "This was where I first saw your son—Sir Denzil. There was a midsummer fete in the grounds—I was nine, I came with my choir school and played my fiddle; there were strawberries and cream," he said smiling, "and you gave away the prizes in a white dress, Lady Murgatroyd. And Sir Denzil was there, home from college, and he said I played like an angel and must come and play for him whenever he gave a party, and that when he left college and had a house of his own, I should come and be his musical director and play for him always."

"I remember those fetes," Lady Murgatroyd said. "We had two or three every summer—before Denny quarreled with his father. We used to have archery competitions and roast an ox. But I do not remember that one especially. What were your other reasons for wanting to come back here?"

"Oh," said Mr. Oakapple, still staring at the fire. "At first I had some wild notion of killing Sir Randolph. I could not see why a person who had done such harm should be allowed to stay alive. But then when I saw what a poor, sick creature he was, I thought only that perhaps I might be able to persuade him to confess that he had cheated over the wager when he won the place. Or that I might persuade him to leave the Court to your son when he made his will. But I succeeded in doing neither of those things. . . . And then came a letter from a woman in Calais to say that Sir Denzil had died, and she had charge of his little daughter. So, I thought, This was why I came here. And, without telling Sir Randolph, I wrote to the woman and told her to send Anna-Marie."

"Oh, I am so glad that you did so, Meester Ookapool," said Anna-Marie. "Just think, if you had not I should never have met *Grand'mère,* or Luc, or you. For that I am going to give you a kiss," and she came and did so, but carefully, on his ear, where it would not hurt him. "But it is so sad that you went to Dieppe and not to Calais, where we were all the time."

"Yes. It is sad," said Mr. Oakapple.

"Tell me, monsieur, what was the song you heard the sailor sing?"

"It was called 'Meet Me at Midnight.' "

"Oh yes, I know it. Papa would sometimes sing it to me. It went,

> Meet me, meet me at Midnight,
> Among the Queen Anne's lace
> Midnight is not a moment,
> Midnight is a place—"

She sang the words. Mr. Oakapple looked up sharply at the sound of her voice. Lady Murgatroyd met his eye over the top of Anna-Marie's head, and nodded. But she said, "It is late, Mr. Oakapple—or perhaps I may be allowed to call you Julian? After all you were my son's friend. I think you should go to sleep now. And these children have to go to their work early. There will be plenty of time for all we want to do."

They went to bed.

Lady Murgatroyd arranged herself a bed in Anna-Marie's room and left her bed for Mr. Oakapple. "Tomorrow we will clear out the empty room for Julian," she said. "Really, we are getting to be quite a household!"

"People, a dog, a cat, a bird, and a baby," said Anna-Marie. "All we need is a fish."

When she was in bed she said sleepily, "You must show Meester Ookapool your tuning fork tomorrow, *Grand'mère*. I think he will like to see it."

Lucas who had been very silent all evening, went to bed without saying more than a bare good night to anybody.

He was terribly unhappy.

First, he found the story of Sir Denzil Murgatroyd almost too sad to be borne. Secondly—although he was ashamed of it—he could not help feeling that there was a kind of tie, knitting together the other three—Lady Murgatroyd, Anna-Marie, Mr. Oakapple—and that it did not include him. He was outside their circle. And, third, he had a private worry of his own, related to the increasingly strange behavior of Mr. Gudgeon. But there was no point in mentioning this to the others. It had nothing to do with them.

MR. OAKAPPLE took several weeks to recover from the setback occasioned by his suddenly being obliged to get up, and the exhausting trip from hospital. He was feverish, and in some pain, and slept a good deal of the time.

"It was to be expected," said Lady Murgatroyd. "But there is no need to worry. He has a strong constitution, and the tansy tea is helping him. And I have some oil of almonds that we will rub on him presently which will reduce the inflammation and help his skin to heal quickly. All he needs at present is good nourishing broth, milk, and eggs; really there is very little difference between feeding him and feeding Bet."

"You are a great comfort, *Grand'mère*," said Anna-Marie. "Really I not think that I and Luc could have managed to look after Monsieur Ookapool very well on our own."

Anna-Marie had settled into life at the combing shed without too much trouble. Her occupation was somewhat solitary, but she had made friends with several of the other claw-cleaners whom she met during meal breaks; she had taught them a couple of songs she had made up to enliven the rhythmic monotonous task. One, which began,

> Claws a-rising, claws a-falling,
> All the livelong day
> Time a-creeping, time a-crawling,
> All to make a length of shawling
> For some lady gay,
> Or some granny gray,
> Who will only say,
> Tut! This color's quite appalling—
> Take the stuff away,

went to a very catchy tune and was soon to be heard all over the mill.

The wooden tongs that Anna-Marie and her grandmother had constructed between them proved highly satisfactory. Using them, Anna-Marie found she was able to avoid getting her fingers nipped, and furthermore she was able to clean out the line of claws very much faster, so that she could snatch a couple of minutes' rest when she reached the end of the line, instead of being always in a hurry and slightly behind.

"Eh, yon's a champion notion!" exclaimed Rose when she came round and saw it. "But tha'd be best to hide it when Bob Bludward's aboot."

"Why?" said Anna-Marie crossly. "What concern is it of his how I do my work, so it gets done properly? He is not the foreman."

"Because th'art doing it better and quicker nor onyone else—tha can get the row clean in five minutes, 'stead o' eight—if the manager finds out, likely he'll set all the rows o' claws moving at a faster rate, an' that'll be hard on t'other cleaners."

"Then they had better make tongs for everybody else," said Anna-Marie.

"More like they'll say as th'hands must make their own, as tha've doon. Onless Bob Bludward might persuade t'manager as how he invented the claws; then he gets paid for the notion, an' they might adopt it."

"But he did not invent them," said Anna-Marie.

"Tha hasn't got the idea yet, luv," said Rose. "Bob Bludward's the only chap as is allowed to invent new notions round here!"

During the next few weeks Lucas became more and more silent and withdrawn. Anna-Marie noticed this, worried about it, and asked him what troubled him, but he merely said it was nothing that could be helped.

"What do you think is the matter with him, *Grand'mère?*"
Anna-Marie asked her grandmother.

"I think it is something connected with his work," said
Lady Murgatroyd. "But there is no use trying to make him
talk about it until he opens the matter himself."

Anna-Marie went on worrying about it.

One evening Lucas was unusually late home.

Mr. Oakapple had been a good deal better that day and,
toward evening, was allowed up to sit in the rocking chair,
looking much more like his old self. He and Lady Murgatroyd had been having a long and happy conversation
about Sir Denzil.

How strange it was, thought Anna-Marie, putting the
baby into her cradle with a wooden toy that Lucas had
carved for her—he had not written much in his book
lately—how strange that *Grand'mère* and Monsieur Ookapool were both separately so fond of the same person, in
such different ways, and yet they did not know each other.
And I was fond of him too, she thought; he was my papa;
I was fondest of all! But it is sad that they grieved for him
all that time and did not know he was alive; it is very sad.
Papa could not have known that poor Monsieur Ookapool
was so badly hurt, or he would have been sure to try to
find out *somehow* if he was getting better. I know Papa was
fond of him; I remember his telling me about a boy he
knew who sang his songs so well; that must have been
Monsieur Ookapool. I must tell him that sometime; perhaps he will like to hear it.

Now they were talking about Sir Randolph.

"I always made certain that he must have cheated in that
wager somehow," said Lady Murgatroyd. "I was away from
home at the time, visiting my cousin Gus Holdernesse in
London. But my husband had a favorite retriever called
True, who always slept in his bedroom. Gabriel Towzer,
who was our butler then, told me that True never barked
until Denzil arrived; I'm sure that if a stranger had come

into Quincy's room he would certainly have barked."

"How do you think Sir Randolph could have cheated, then, ma'am? And if you did think so, why did you take no action to have the matter investigated?"

"Why should I bother?" said Lady Murgatroyd simply. "My husband was dead, my son was dead—so I thought. And there was a lot of boredom and unnecessary formality about the old life that I was glad enough to escape. I have been quite contented—much more so than Sir Randolph, I am sure. His life was wasted from first to last. The only person who could have made anything of him was Mary Dunnithorne—and she, not surprisingly, refused to marry him when he asked her. She married Lucas's father instead!"

Anna-Marie was not interested in Sir Randolph. She felt that he was better forgotten. "Have you told Monsieur Ookapool about Handel's tuning fork, *Grand'mère?*" she asked.

Lady Murgatroyd had not, and the tuning fork was fetched. Mr. Oakapple was fascinated by it, and held it in his hands for a long time, turning it over and over.

Lady Murgatroyd also brought out her flute and a couple of recorders. They passed a pleasant hour in singing and playing; Anna-Marie was discovered to have a natural aptitude for finding her way through a tune by ear on either instrument. Bet was enchanted at all this musical activity and remained absolutely motionless, gazing and beaming, for a whole hour.

But presently Anna-Marie began to play a good many wrong notes.

"You are becoming tired, *ma petite,*" said her grandmother. "We had better stop."

"It is not that," said Anna-Marie. "But, *Grand'mère,* I am so anxious about Luc. He has *never* been so late as this before. What can be the matter?"

"I expect he will turn up by and by," said Lady Murgatroyd. "I asked him to buy me some oil of camphor; perhaps he has gone round by the market and been delayed."

But more time passed, and still Lucas did not come. Anna-Marie became so worried that she could not sit still, but wandered about the big untidy room, into Lucas's room and out again; several times she went to the front door and looked out, to see if there was any sign of him coming across the park, but it was snowing again, and there was nothing to be seen.

"Lucas is so sensible," Lady Murgatroyd said. "It seems unlikely that he would have got into any kind of trouble."

"But, *Grand'mère,* that sewer is such an awful place! I know he hates it, although he insists on continuing to work there. And I do not at all like the sound of that Gudgeon who works with him. Oh, how I wish he would come!"

Another half hour went by. At last Anna-Marie could stand the inactivity of waiting no longer. "I am going to go and search for him," she announced.

"But where will you go, child? It is certainly strange that he has not come home by this time," agreed Lady Murgatroyd, now rather troubled herself. "But you cannot go down into the sewers to look for him, if he is still there—"

"No but I could tell the other men. I must do *something,*" Anna-Marie said, clenching her hands together in the urgency of her anxiety. "I feel that some bad thing has happened to Luc—I feel it here"—and she pressed a fist against her ribs.

"It is very singular that he is so late," Mr. Oakapple agreed. "In general, Lucas is a very reliable, punctual boy; I have never known him play truant or get into scrapes; in fact it is just the other way round; instead of going out he is always writing away in that brown book of his."

"The hour is rather late for Anna-Marie to be wandering about the town by herself," Lady Murgatroyd said. "Julian, if I go with her, do you think that you can contrive to keep an eye on the baby?"

Mr. Oakapple did seem a little daunted by this suggestion, but he agreed that it was the least he could do in exchange for the care and hospitality that he was receiving.

"I daresay she will go to sleep very soon," Lady Murgatroyd assured him. "And all you have to do to keep her amused is to sing to her, after all!"

"Well, I will do my best, ma'am. If only I had a fiddle and could still play it," he murmured, sighing.

Lady Murgatroyd paused in the act of wrapping herself up in a thick blue cape made from her own handwoven material.

"Have you ever considered learning to play the violin left-handed?" she said. "People have done it, you know. I daresay we could find you an old instrument to practice on. Of course, it might be rather awkward playing in an orchestra, but then that isn't your first wish, is it?"

Mr. Oakapple stared at her. His mouth opened, but he did not speak.

"After all, it is time you got back to playing," Lady Murgatroyd went on calmly. "Are you ready, *petite-fille*? Right, let us go."

And leaving Mr. Oakapple silent and preoccupied, staring at his two hands, they went out into the snowy night.

"Where do you intend going first?" Lady Murgatroyd asked her granddaughter as they walked down the hill into Blastburn.

"First I shall go to the market place, and see if Monsieur 'Obday is still at his stall. He might know whether Luc and that Gudgeon had come out from the sewer at the end of the day."

"A good plan," approved Lady Murgatroyd. So they went to the market and made their way to Mr. Hobday's stall. Anna-Marie was interested to observe that quite a number of people appeared to know her grandmother; either she had given them music lessons, or helped them in other ways. She was greeted with much goodwill and civility as Madame Minetti. An old man limped up to thank her for writing a letter for him to his son in Wales; the boy had written back and all was well. A woman came to say that the medicine had stopped her baby's fits; and another man thanked her for her help in connection with some character called Old Nye.

"He's a changed creetur, ma'am; I dunno what you done, you mun ha' bewitched him! He's peaceful as a babby an' works twelve hours a day."

"What a lot of people you know, *Grand'mère!*"

"Yes; it is queer," Lady Murgatroyd remarked. "Living in the icehouse, I have many more friends than ever I did when we lived at the Court and used to give so many parties."

"Who was old Nye, *Grand'maman?*"

"He was a donkey—a most intractable, obstinate character," Lady Murgatroyd said, laughing.

"What did you do to him?"

"Blew up his nostrils; that is a good way of becoming friendly with animals."

"I wonder if it would work with people? Did you do that with Redgauntlet also? He is much nicer than he used to be; he always would snap and snarl at me whenever he saw me."

"Well, poor thing, he seems to have had a very disagreeable master. I expect he finds his life much more enjoyable now that he has to go out and catch his own dinner in the park."

Mr. Hobday, luckily, was still at his stall, tidying up and pulling down the shutters for the night.

"Monsieur 'Obday, Monsieur 'Obday," cried Anna-

Marie, running up to him. "Have you seen my friend Luc *ou ce vieux* Gudgeon? Luc has not come home to supper yet, and we are so anxious about him!"

Mr. Hobday paused in what he was doing. A somewhat shifty expression came over his face. But he spoke with exaggerated heartiness. "Halloo, 'tis the yoong lady! Haven't seen you about for a two-three weeks. Cigar business not so good lately?"

"No—I am working at Murgatroyd's Mill now," Anna-Marie said shortly. "But, monsieur, about Luc—have you seen him?"

"Why, he were here 'smornin' at his reg'lar time. But then, I doan't see him evenings, ye know—he gives the tosh to old Gudgeon an' goes straight home."

"Well, have you seen Gudgeon then?"

"Nay, *he* goes straight home too. I'll see him in the morning, sithee."

"I am not interested in the morning," Anna-Marie said impatiently. "Where does he live, this Gudgeon? We will go to his house and ask him when he has last seen Luc."

A deeper shade of uneasiness passed over Mr. Hobday's face. He began fiddling with his stock, picking things up and putting them down. "Oh, I wouldn't do that, missie," he said without looking at Anna-Marie. "He's a foonny old cove, is old Gudgeon. He might act a bit okkard if you was to go a-bothering of him. He don't care for folks going to his house; might scare you a bit."

"Just the same I think we had better go to see him," Lady Murgatroyd said.

Mr. Hobday had not noticed that Anna-Marie had a companion, for Lady Murgatroyd had been standing somewhat behind her, in the shadow. He started violently and dropped a china jar which he had been holding. It broke.

"I think you had better give us this Gudgeon's address," Lady Murgatroyd said calmly.

"Y-y-yes, ma'am. He lives in an owd boat doon by th' Tidey River, in Wharf Lane. 'Tis the only one there; ye can't mistake."

"Thank you; we will go there directly," said Lady Murgatroyd, and walked away, leaving Mr. Hobday staring after them with drops of sweat rolling down his wizened cheeks, although it was a cold night.

"I am thinking, *Grand'mère,*" said Anna-Marie as they walked away. "Wharf Lane is a dark, dirty place, down by the river—it would be good if we buy two torches to take with us. We can get them here."

She turned aside to a lamp-oil and candle stall, which also sold articles known as "rats"—bundles of rushes or rags, tied to sticks and soaked in tar. Anna-Marie bought a couple of these for twopence apiece, and they hurried in the direction of Wharf Lane, through streets that became progressively darker and narrower and dirtier, until they were making their way down a tiny narrow passageway that would have been dark as pitch if they had not begged a light for their torches from a night watchman who was keeping guard over a load of hides on Tanner's Wharf.

"You seem to know this part of the town quite well?" said Lady Murgatroyd.

"Oh yes; when I am hunting for my cigar ends, you see, and the boys would not let me search the big streets, I went everywhere, *partout.* I do not find many here though," said Anna-Marie.

"Well, it is lucky for us you came here; otherwise we would certainly have lost our way a dozen times over."

The old boat occupied by Mr. Gudgeon was visible merely as a darkish bump on the riverbank when they first saw it.

"What if he is not at home?" Lady Murgatroyd said, but when they came closer to the boat they could see that a dim smoky light showed through one of the portholes. And there was a strong greasy smell of frying fish.

Anna-Marie banged on the side of the boat. When this produced no response, she picked up a stone and banged harder and louder. Still there was no answer from inside the boat, though it was plain that somebody was in there, for movements and footsteps could be heard.

"Well, we had better go in," said Anna-Marie, and climbed up onto the boat. "*Mon Dieu,* this boat smells even worse than Luc when he comes home before he has washed himself."

Indeed it was evident that a good many of the articles retrieved from the sewer were stacked and stored on Mr. Gudgeon's boat; there was hardly any deck space left. Lady Murgatroyd followed Anna-Marie, and they found a pair of doors, leading to a cabin, and knocked again.

This time that there was no doubt that they had been heard, for the movements inside ceased completely, and there was a long, suspicious silence.

Anna-Marie rapped again, imperatively, with her stone.

"Who be there?" growled a surly voice.

"Open!" called Anna-Marie.

"We want to speak to you," added Lady Murgatroyd.

Anna-Marie rattled the door. It was finally unbolted and slowly pushed open. Anna-Marie could just recognize the figure that stood there, outlined against the light, as Gudgeon, by his white hair and tosher's costume, but he was so dirty that his features were hardly visible, even when they stepped closer with their flaring torches.

"Mr. Gudgeon!" said Anna-Marie. "We are anxious about Luc. Where is he? Did he leave the sewer with you this evening?"

For several minutes Gudgeon did not reply. At last, looking sideways at them in a curious manner, he muttered, "Woe to him that increaseth that is not his."

"Mr. Gudgeon!" said Lady Murgatroyd. "Where is the boy, Lucas, who works with you?"

"Hypocrites die in youth, and their life is unclean."

"Mr. Gudgeon—*Where is Lucas?*"

"I have gathered the peculiar treasure of kings. But two hundred pennyworth is not sufficient."

"*Please,* Monsieur Gudgeon!" cried Anna-Marie desperately. "Will you not tell us what has happened to Luc? We are so anxious about him."

Mr. Gudgeon became angry. He banged his fist furiously against the doorjamb and thundered at them: "Woe to them that draw iniquity with cords! Woe unto you that are rich, to you that are full, to you that laugh. Leave the cities and dwell in the rock! Hear this, thou that art given to pleasures!"

"Do you think he is mad?" Anna-Marie whispered doubtfully to Lady Murgatroyd.

"Perhaps—Mr. Gudgeon!" said Lady Murgatroyd loudly. "Will you please give us a clear answer? We want to know about the boy who works with you. Is he here?"

"I was left alone and saw this great vision. The weaned child put his hand in the cockatrice den. And the whole herd ran violently down! Behold he drinketh up the river and hasteth not."

"Oh, *mon Dieu!*" exclaimed Anna-Marie. She was half crying. "How can we find out what he means? He talks nothing but rubbish!"

Mr. Gudgeon retired inside his cabin for a moment, and then suddenly reappeared, looking extremely menacing, waving a rusty saw. "Trouble me not, the door is shut!" he shouted at them.

They backed away from him, warily.

"Do you suppose he might have Luc inside there?" Anna-Marie whispered.

"I think we should try to see."

However, Mr. Gudgeon waving the saw was a fairly alarming sight, as he advanced toward them with the whites of his eyes gleaming in the torchlight.

"D-do you think we should call the constables?" asked

Anna-Marie with her teeth chattering. *"J'ai peur, moi!"*

"I think we shall have to. His manner is certainly very strange. And the things he says do seem as if they might have something to do with Lucas."

They clambered quickly but cautiously off the boat. Then Mr. Gudgeon suddenly surprised them by leaping off the boat himself, and bounding away from them along the riverbank, shouting at the top of his lungs, "Hast thou entered into the treasure of the snow? Or hast thou seen the treasure of the hail? I wash myself in snow water and make my hands clean, for I slew a lion in a pit on a snowy day!"

Shouting and flourishing the saw, he disappeared into the darkness.

"I must confess," said Lady Murgatroyd, "that I do not like the look of this at all. However, now seems a good moment to inspect the inside of his boat. Do you take a quick look, my child, while I keep watch in case he decides to come back again."

Accordingly Anna-Marie scrambled back on board and, trembling but resolute, edged her way into the smoky cabin, which was lit only by a fire burning in a brazier. She held her torch high and looked around. The stench in here was so thick that it was like being surrounded by frightful fur; quite plainly, Mr. Gudgeon never cleaned either himself or his dwelling. Bones, old crusts, half-eaten carrots, lay scattered among muddy and unappetizing-looking treasures which had either been rejected by Mr. Hobday or never shown to him. The inside of the cabin was so squalid that, quite apart from her fear of Gudgeon returning, about fifty seconds of it was all Anna-Marie could endure.

There was no sign of Lucas.

"Il n'est pas là," she reported, jumping off the boat.

"Well that's a relief, at all events," said Lady Murgatroyd. "For really I began to believe that poor madman might have Lucas tied up in there, or be intending to slice him up for his breakfast."

"What do you think we should do now?"

"I think we should follow him a little way, if we can, and see where he goes."

"Good," said Anna-Marie. "I think so too. And Luc has told me that the way into the sewer lies somewhere along this bank. If—if we must," she said, jamming her teeth together to stop them from chattering, "I think we should go in there and hunt for Luc. It is good we have our torches."

They made their way with caution along the slippery bank, on which the fast-falling snow did not lie for long, but continually formed a thin melting crust over the soft mud; it was hard to walk on top without sinking through. The tide was coming in; small crescent-shaped waves nibbled along the mud below them. The wind blew strongly and carried the smoke and flame from their torches ahead of them; it seemed to carry the light as well.

"Where do you suppose Gudgeon has gone?" Anna-Marie said in a low voice.

"He may be anywhere," said Lady Murgatroyd rather hopelessly. "It is so hard to see through the snow. . . . No wonder poor Lucas has been rather despondent lately. He can hardly have enjoyed patroling the sewers with Gudgeon. Has he been like this all along?"

"No, no, I think at first he was quite sensible—oh, what is that?"

The light from their torches had flickered on something moving rapidly through the snowflakes ahead of them: bounding along, stooping, rising up, and continuing on an erratic, zigzag progress.

"I think it is Gudgeon again," Lady Murgatroyd said, screening her eyes with her hand to keep out the snow. "I am sure nobody else would be dancing about on the river-bank in such weather. Perhaps we had now better go up into the town and call the constables—"

"He seems to be searching for something. I do not think he has seen us," said Anna-Marie, biting her lip. "Let us just wait to see if he goes into the sewer; I am sure the entrance must be close to here. If we had a weapon—something to fight with, in case he looks back and sees us and becomes *méchant*—"

"A stone is better than nothing. There are plenty of those."

Providing themselves with suitable stones, they moved on carefully toward Gudgeon. All they could see of him at present was his head. Where he stood, the riverbank was divided by a deep gully. He had descended into it, and now bent down, so that he was completely concealed from view.

"That must be the sewer entrance—Luc has said there is a little river running out. Wait here, *Grand'mère,* one moment, while I tiptoe up and see what he is doing—"

Stooping low, Anna-Marie stole along to the edge of the gully and looked over.

"Be very careful!" Lady Murgatroyd called in a whisper. But in the driving snow there was not a very great chance of her being seen.

Anna-Marie knelt on the verge and peered, screwing up her eyes. Then suddenly she let out a shriek:

"Oh, *coquin, assassin, monstre!* Stop what you are doing, leave him!"

"What is it?" demanded Lady Murgatroyd.

Anna-Marie had lifted her arm and flung the stone she held as hard as she was able; there followed a thud from below, and a shout. She picked up another stone and scrambled over the edge. Lady Murgatroyd followed her with all speed and found her crouched over something resembling a pile of old rags that lay at the water's edge.

Gudgeon, who had evidently lost his balance and fallen when the stone hit him, was clambering to his feet, muttering something about a jewel of gold in a swine's snout. The light from Lady Murgatroyd's torch picked out a gleam in the snow halfway up the slope. It was the saw, which Gudgeon had dropped when he fell. Very prudently, Lady Murgatroyd grasped the handle before he could recover it, and flung it out into the river.

Gudgeon began to wail. "My hope is lost, I am cut off. I will go to a cave and lodge there."

Waving his arms in a frantic manner he ran up the side of the stinking rivulet and disappeared under a black archway.

Anna-Marie was frenziedly pulling and lifting the crumpled heap of garments down by the water.

"Oh," she sobbed, "if he has hurt him—if he has killed him!"

"Is it Lucas?"

"Yes! And he is so cold! And all covered in slime and mud! I cannot see if he is cut, even, or if he breathes—"

"Well, let us get him away from the water's edge," said Lady Murgatroyd. "What a mercy that we came along when we did, for in another fifteen minutes the tide would have carried him away."

"I think that Gudgeon—that pig, that brute!—was just going to push him into the water when I saw him."

Between them they lifted and pulled the inert body of Lucas up to a safer point on the bank. Then Lady Murgatroyd felt carefully for his heartbeat and pronounced him to be alive.

"He is breathing, but very slowly. And he is dreadfully cold. I think we shall need to get help; we cannot carry him far between us. I had best stay here with him, my child, while you run fast and fetch assistance; there are houses not too far away."

"Yes, you are right. I will be quick as lightning," promised Anna-Marie. Then she bounded away up the slope.

She was as good as her word. Within seven minutes Lady Murgatroyd heard her call, "Here we are, *Grand'mère!* Is he all right still?"

She came climbing back down the bank with a youngish and active-looking man close behind her. "I was lucky to meet this monsieur not far away in Haddock Street and he is good enough to come and assist us—"

"Eh, poor lad! 'Twere loocky for him you happened along this way. He looks like one o' the tosh boys," said the man, expertly sliding an arm under Lucas's shoulders, while Anna-Marie and Lady Murgatroyd took a leg apiece. "He wouldn't ha' lasted the night through if ye hadn't found him, reckon."

"Where shall we carry him?" panted Anna-Marie. "There is the house of Madame Tetley at this end of the street—but I daresay she would not be pleased—"

"Nay, t'best thing'll be to take him to my mam's house— she lives nobbut a dumpling's throw away," the man said, and guided them to a house at the opposite end of the street from Mrs. Tetley's. There he deposited Lucas, gently enough, on the cobbled footway, while he knocked on the door.

"Hey, oop, moother! Art tha home?"

"A'reet, a'reet, no need to raise the dead, lad!" cried a voice from within, and the door was flung open by a plump, goodnatured-looking woman with whitish-fair hair in curlpapers, and a soiled apron, and felt slippers. "What's to do, then Davey?"

" 'Tis a poor lad half drownded—can tha take him in an' give him a bit of a roob-down an' a warm-oop?"

"Eh, for sure—t'poor yoong chap. Fetch him in, there's a kettle a-boiling this minute!"

They hoisted Lucas up once more and carried him into a tiny hot kitchen which seemed to be full of firelight and people. As there was nowhere else to put him, they laid him by the hearth—the man's mother first prudently unrolled a large piece of sailcloth over her rag hearth rug. There were shocked and sympathetic exclamations from all over the room—a family party seemed to be in progress. Anna-Marie and her grandmother were instantly offered cups of hot tea and wedges of dough cake, while the man who had assisted them was commanded by his mother to fetch down the paigle cordial from her bedroom.

"We'd do best to put the poor thing straight in a bath in t'back kitchen, wi' a bit of mustard in—"

"The very thing," agreed Lady Murgatroyd. "We are very much obliged to you."

"Eh," cried the plump woman, looking at her closely. "If it baint Madam Minetti! Do ye mind, ma'am, ye helped Jock, my eldest, to win t'Cup for t'best all-round choirboy—eh, he were all-round an' all! There it stands to this day." She pointed to a huge brass cup on the mantel.

The son who had gone to fetch the cordial returned and knelt to pour a dose of it between Lucas's pale and muddy lips. Anna-Marie now noticed for the first time that he had only one eye. The other was covered by a black patch. His face was faintly familiar; where had she seen it before?

" 'Tis Madam Minetti, Davey, as helped oor Jock win t'cup!"

"Jock Scatcherd, of course; I remember. A very good treble, he had. Where is he now?" Lady Murgatroyd inquired.

"He would go as a sailor, ma'am—ah, look, t'lad's stirring. Granma's cordial 'ud fetch back a dead snail that had been frozen a fortnit. Hold him oop a bit, Davey, an' you, Cathy, fetch soom towels, an' Lucy, pour t'watter in t'toob, an' Percy, lay a bit o' mat oot there, an' Auntie, put a screen across t'back door, an' Polly, fetch t'scrobbing broosh—"

Amid a general scurry and hubbub Lucas was carried into the back kitchen, where about half the family fell on him and peeled off his muddy clothes and put him into the wooden washtub of steaming water and rubbed him and scrubbed him.

"Eh! T'poor thing! He's all scraped an' scratted an' haggled—reckon t'hogs has been at him—"

"Is he badly hurt?" inquired Lady Murgatroyd. It was quite impossible to see Lucas for the throng of willing helpers.

"Nay, but he were loocky. He must ha' scaped away from t'hogs joost in time. Most folk as they nibbles niver gets to eat anoother dinner."

"Will he be all right?" demanded Anna-Marie.

"Aye, lass, he'll be champion by an' by. He'll be stiff an' sore, happen, for a week or so. 'Twas a good thing for him ye came by. Do ye know him?"

"Yes, he is my friend, he works with this Gudgeon, who I think is *un assassin*—"

"Eh, aye, yon Gudgeon," said an old man in the corner who had not spoken yet. " 'Tis a reet scandal the noomber o' lads he an' yon Hobday ha' finished off between 'em."

"Is he mad, then, this Gudgeon?" asked Lady Murgatroyd.

"Not to say clean daft—a bit tootched, like. Times he's sensible enow, oother times he goes cuckoo-wild—and can ye woonder, considering the onnatural life he has doon there i' the dark, day in, day out?"

"Yes, but that's not to say he should be allowed—You mean everybody knows about him and nobody stops him?"

"Nay, I reckon folks thinks as it's noon o' their business." Then the old man took his pipe out of his mouth and said, "What did ye say the lady's name was, Marthy?"

"Madam Minetti."

"Nay, that bain't no Madam Minetti. 'Tis owd Lady Murgatroyd, as put a splint on my foot, time I got trompled by a bull."

"Why so I did," said Lady Murgatroyd. "And you're Willum Scatcherd, who used to work in the dairy up at the Court and left to be a baker's apprentice."

"I thowt ye were dead, ma'am, when owd Sir Quincy died."

"No, I'm not dead yet," said Lady Murgatroyd, and she and the old man, who seemed delighted to see her, instantly fell into a long talk about old times when Sir Quincy was alive. "Arr, things was better then, ma'am, afore that Sir Randolph coom, what stoock my granson i' the pokey."

Scatcherd, said Anna-Marie to herself. Of course he was the one-eyed man who was making a speech and the soldiers went galloping by to arrest him.

"Did you get out prison, then?" she asked, as he happened to come and sit beside her, after putting away the cowslip cordial.

"Aye, there were no witnesses against me, once yon Smallside had left t'Mill. None other would speak. We has oor fights among oorselves, but they divvn't go outside. And wi' old Randy Grimsby dead, they could find no reason to keep me."

"Will you go back to the mill, then?"

"Reckon so, lass; I've got mates there, see. What's *thy* name, then?

"She's my granddaughter," put in Lady Murgatroyd, looking across the hearth.

At this moment Lucas was brought from the back kitchen in a half-reviving condition, and set in a chair, wrapped in a blanket.

"Luc! Are you feeling better? Can you tell us what happened? Was it *le vieux Gudgeon*? Did he attack you?"

"I—I can't remember much," Lucas murmured dazedly. He was confused by the warmth and the strange room and the number of unfamiliar faces all around him.

The Scatcherds were a black-eyed, red-cheeked, tousle-headed clan; he felt as if he had fallen into a Punch-and-Judy show. "Yes, yes—it was Gudgeon—for two weeks he had become stranger and stranger—he seemed as if he disliked me and then as if he *hated* me—he kept talking in a very odd way—I think it was bits out of the Bible—and he watched me all the time and made me walk in front of him because he said I was hiding things from him—though I wasn't. I asked Mr. Hobday about him and he said it was nothing, he'd get over it in a day or two, he always did—"

"Ah, that's Gudgeon all over," remarked Mrs. Scatcherd. "When he gets taken this road he gets *that* soospicious he wouldna troost his own broother—if he had woon—"

"Then today—was it today?—there were some hogs coming—I remember that—and something hit me hard on the head and I fell—I suppose Gudgeon hit me—and the hogs all came rushing at me, I remember *that*—"

He shuddered at the memory. "And then I think I managed to roll into the sewer. And then I found myself here. I'm very grateful to you, ma'am," he said to Mrs. Scatcherd, who was handing him a large mug of tea laced with cowslip cordial.

"Ee, think nowt of it, ye poor thing—I'm reet glad that *woon* o' Gudgeon's boys got away at least—maybe ye can lay an information against him now. An' that Hobday—he moost 'a had a fair notion o' what was going on."

"Nay," said Davey Scatcherd, who had been studying Lucas. "I know *thee!* Tha'rt the lad from t'Court as I was set to show over t'mill afore I got roon in. I' mercy's name, what wast tha doing doon in t'sewer wi' owd Gudgeon?"

"That's a long story. I don't think Lucas is quite strong enough for storytelling yet," said Lady Murgatroyd in her deep voice. "Other people have their livings to earn as well as you, Davey Scatcherd!"

Davey grinned and said, "Aye, ma'am!"

"Should we take Luc home now?" said Anna-Marie. "Is he strong enough to walk? I am thinking that Monsieur Ookapool will be making himself anxious about us."

"He will indeed," said Lady Murgatroyd. "*Are* you strong enough to walk, my dear boy?"

Lucas thought he was, but he had no clothes; the savage little teeth of the hogs had chewed everything he had on to ragged scraps. However the Scatcherd family were easily able to provide a set of garments from among their various members. Lucas stood up, presently, but he was still rather weak on his legs.

"I'll step along wi' thee a bit o' the way," said Davey Scatcherd. "For I was on my way up toon to a meeting o' t'pressers', glue boilers', an' claw operators' union when a' this gallimafry took place."

"I thought they weren't allowed to have unions?" Anna-Marie said incautiously.

"Whisht! Nowt said breaks no head."

They started off, Davey and Lady Murgatroyd supporting Lucas on either side.

"Excercise'll be the best thing for thee, sithee," Davey said.

Lucas thought how amazingly different Davey seemed now from the rather unfriendly, sarcastic person who had shown him over the works. And yet what had made the difference? Davey had no more cause to be friendly now than then. He had just come out of prison, too; he might have been expected to feel bitter.

"I'm sorry you were sent to prison," Lucas said awkwardly.

"Nay, it weren't so bad. Not mooch groob, but tha gets a bit o' time to think. 'Tweren't *thy* fault, ony road. 'Twere on account o' Stingy Randy cutting the wages. I daresay he kept thee short too."

"He did that," said Lucas with feeling.

"Mr. Scatcherd," said Anna-Marie.

"Eh, call me Davey, lass; a'body doos."

"*Eh bien,* Davey, then; is your union the same as the Friendly Lads?"

Davey halted long enough to utter a terrible oath and spit into the gutter. "Nay, it isn't, then," he said, more moderately, when he had recovered himself. " 'T Friendly Boys is now but a set o'raskills lining their pockets by squeezin' poor decent folk. Bob Bludward's the head an' front of it, an' woon o' these days him an' me's due for a rare randy-dandy."

"So," pursued Anna-Marie, "what does *your* union want?"

"Why, better wages, that folk could live on, an' better working conditions. Fewer folk falling into t'glue or getting scroonched by t'press. Ye'll pardon me, I'm sure, ma'am, but things has gone all to Habbakuk since owd Sir Quincy built t'place."

"Yes, I'm sadly aware of that," said Lady Murgatroyd. "And I hope you achieve your aims. Now I'm sure we can manage from here and need take you no farther out of your way. We are greatly obliged to you for all your trouble—"

They had paused outside Murgatroyd's Mill itself.

"Why," said Davey, puzzled, scratching his head, "where i' Mickle's name do you live, then? There's no hooses oot yonder."

"Up in the park," said Lady Murgatroyd, "in the old icehouse. Till somebody turns us out! I understand the park has been sold."

"In the icehouse? Well I'll be dommed. Haven't ye—pardon my asking—haven't ye any brass, then, ma'am?"

"No more than you, Davey—only what I earn. Thank you for all your help. We'll bring back the clothes tomorrow," Lady Murgatroyd said.

They started up the hill. Anna-Marie took Lucas's arm, but he was moving more easily now; the exercise had done him good.

Davey stood looking after them, scratching his head, until they were around the bend in the road. Then he said,

"Well, by gar!" and turned to walk back into the town.

Lucas had intended to start straight off next morning hunting for a new job.

"*Now,* I hope," Anna-Marie had said to him on the last, slow stretch of the walk home, "Now you will not any more insist on working in this sewer, perhaps?"

"No," he said. "No, I'm not going back there. But—you know—it is just as *Grand'mère* said; when something has once happened to you, then you know it isn't quite as bad as you expected. Now I've been trampled on by hogs and fallen into the sewer, it will never seem quite so awful again. Just the same," he added, "I don't care if I never see another hog for the rest of my life."

"And what about *ce Gudgeon affreux?*" demanded Anna-Marie. "You will go and lay an information about him, I hope?"

"I'm not sure," said Lucas. "He can't help it."

" 'Obday can help it, *enfin!*"

"Well, I'll think about it. But in the morning I'll try to get a job in the Mill. I think Davey Scatcherd might put in a good word for me."

In the morning, though, he was so stiff that he could hardly move, and had such a sore throat that Lady Murgatroyd dosed him with rose-hip syrup, rubbed him all over with balsam oil, and told him not to stir hand or foot until she gave him leave.

"For all we know you may have caught typhus fever by falling into that place—let alone the infection you may have picked up from hog-bites."

"You may as well do as she says," Mr. Oakapple observed drily. "Look how meek and biddable she has made *me.*" He was sitting with the canary perched on top of his head, entertaining the baby by handing her back the various pine cones, pebbles, and lumps of knotted wood that she chose to throw out of her cradle. Lucas could not help laughing, though it hurt his throat to do so.

Lady Murgatroyd was going off to give a music lesson. "You can all amuse each other while I am gone. It still snows, so you are not even to think of going out."

"Except me, *Grand'mère,*" said Anna-Marie, who was just setting off for her shift at the Mill.

Lucas felt unhappy that he had to stay at home while Anna-Marie was out working.

"I am not bringing in any money," he fretted.

"Nor am I," Mr. Oakapple pointed out. "But complaining won't help. The only answer is to behave in a rational manner and get better as fast as you can."

Toward the end of the week, however, they had an unexpected caller who relieved Lucas's anxieties about money.

This was Mr. Hobday, who came tapping at the door in the snowy dusk, looking evasive and guilty and ingratiating and apologetic all at the same time.

"Very sorry to see you poorly, lad," he said nervously rubbing his little clawlike hands together, his ears redder than ever with the cold and with embarrassment. "Very sorry to see that."

"So you should be," said Mr. Oakapple severely, Lucas having told him who Mr. Hobday was. "You should be thoroughly ashamed of yourself for allowing boys into the sewer in the company of that dangerous lunatic. You deserve to be thrown into jail."

"All right, all right, all right, guvnor, don't lay it on any more!" cried Mr. Hobday, tearing his hair and pulling his own ears. "It's been one arter another at me all week—fust that little lass was a-bawling at me—an' gor, *she's* got a tongue like a haddock knife—then the owd lady, Madam Minetti, *she* pitched into me; 'Very sorry, ma'am, very sorry, if I'd a knowed the young lad were a connection o' yourn I'd never a' taken him on,' I says, 'but he needed the money an' how was I to know he were your great-grand-cousin?' 'Whose cousin he be, that bain't the point,' says she, 'the point be you shouldn't a done it to *anyone's* cousin, an' he's sore an' bruised, 'sides being frit to death, an' you should pay him summat handsome in compensation.' 'Very well, ma'am,' says I. An' last of all young Firebrand Scatcherd, *he* come up and lays into me about poor old Gudgeon—but what's a cove to do? If I doesn't send a boy down wi' Gudgeon, he gets more and more coveticious an' niggurious, the old muckworm, he keeps all the tosh himself and brings me *nothing,* an' I have all the expense of the stall an' his wages, so I has to have a boy to keep an eye on him, see? How can I help it if he goes a bit March-mad now an' now, an' turns on the boys spiteful-like? Boys should be able to look arter themselves, that's what *I* says. Now you, my young cove, *you're* a active, coriaceous lad, gristly enough to stand up to old Gudgeon, just the right sort for a tosh boy, an' I hope you'll come back to the profession when you're over this little setback."

"No he certainly won't," said Lady Murgatroyd, who had returned from giving a music lesson in the middle of Hobday's speech, "and what about that compensation?"

"Yes, yes, marm, o' course I were coming to that," Mr. Hobday said injuredly. "I were just explaining that by rights *I* oughta be compensated, acos if I haven't a boy to send down to keep an eye on old Gudgeon I'm going to lose oughty-hundred per cent o' my takings an' how am I going to live, answer me that? Gudgeon's no use on his own."

"Don't send him down, then."

"But he *loves* to go down in the sewer. 'Tis the only thing he do love. You can't keep him outa there."

"Let him go then, if he prefers it. But you'll have to find some other way to live," Lady Murgatroyd said dispassionately. "Or go down yourself, of course."

"Find some—go down—" Mr. Hobday stared at her aghast. Then he pulled himself together and said, "Well, now, about this here compensation. I fund a thing I thowt mit be of use to ye, so I brung that, an' hope to oblige. Ye mind, maybe, ol' Gudgeon dredged up a little owd wooden box wi' some papers in it, fust day you was out wi' him, Luke, boy. I was a-looking through 'em, lately, for you allus has to look through papers, an' I seen on wi' the name BELL on't, an', thinks I, that mit have summat to do wi' young Luke Bell, so I fetched it along, an' hope that'll compensate ye for any slight discombobulation you bin put to along of old Gudgeon."

With an elaborate flourish he handed Lucas a small packet of very dirty papers.

"Why, thank you, Mr. Hobday," said Lucas, somewhat surprised. "It was thoughtful of you to—to think of me. I'll read through them, and if they don't seem to have anything to do with me, I'll return them to you. But I hope you were thinking of some *cash* compensation too?"

Mr. Hobday looked very much dashed, not to say martyred. "*Cash?* Well—I hadn't—" he began.

"How about that jeweled saddle, for instance?" pursued Lucas. "How much did that fetch? Did you give me my ten per cent?"

"Oh, 'er didn't goo for much," Mr. Hobday said shiftily.

"Did you sell it to the museum?"

"Ah, but they museum coves are a set o' flinthearts," protested Mr. Hobday.

"Come, come," said Lady Murgatroyd, "you know we can very well ask them what they paid for it."

Mr. Hobday was very cast down by this, and in the end the information was extracted from him that the saddle, set with rubies and sapphires, had sold for six hundred pounds, of which thirty pounds was properly Lucas's. Sighing heavily, he paid over thirty grubby pound notes and took his departure.

"And do not let us hear of your subjecting any more boys to that shocking risk," Lady Murgatroyd remarked mildly as he went out, "or you will find yourself in trouble."

"Thirty pounds!" said Lucas joyfully when he had gone. "Why, we can live on that for weeks. Anna-Marie can leave the Mill."

"She may not wish to," pointed out Lady Murgatroyd. "She may feel about it as you did about the sewer. But let us look at these papers. What are they?"

Whatever they were, they were so extremely dirty that it was a task of great difficulty and delicacy to get them separated one from another. Lady Murgatroyd, whose fingers were practiced at the intricacies of weaving, settled down to the operation, passing each one as she prized it free to Lucas, who carefully swabbed the dirt off the surface with a spirit made from fermented chestnuts which Lady Murgatroyd used for cleaning her clavichord.

"Why," Lucas exclaimed, when he had the first document clean enough to read. "This is a note to Mr. Throgmorton—a receipt for five pounds from Bertram Smallside. It does not seem to have anything to do with me—nothing at all."

"Go on—there are plenty more. You may come to something yet."

As Lucas continued cleaning the papers, he discovered that all of them appeared to relate to Mr. Throgmorton—there were a number of other receipts from different persons and some of Mr. Throgmorton's receipted bills, including one from Lucas's own father—a bill of ten pounds for legal work. And at the bottom of the heap were two documents that caused Lucas to give a cry of astonishment.

"Why, this is my father's will! And his deed of partnership with Sir Randolph. And they were both drawn up by Mr. Throgmorton. So it is very singular that he did not remember anything about them."

"Singular indeed," said Mr. Oakapple, limping across to read the papers over Lucas's shoulder. "Yes—Deed of partnership between Sir Randolph Grimsby, Bart., and Edwin Lucas Bell, Esquire. And Last Will and Testament of Edwin Lucas Bell. And I see that your father *did* leave a little money besides the funds that were sunk in the Mill—I shall be interested to hear how Throgmorton can account for that. I think we must go and call on the gentleman as soon as I am a little stronger on my legs. I wonder how these papers came to be in the sewer? Perhaps Throgmorton thought that was the safest way to get rid of them."

Lady Murgatroyd had been studying the receipts.

"Now here is a curious thing," she murmured to herself. "Receipts going back twenty years, for payments made by Throgmorton on behalf of Sir Randolph to Bertram Smallside, Gabriel Towzer, Amos Garridge, and Wm. Scatcherd—Five pounds a week each."

"*Five pounds a week each?*" exclaimed Mr. Oakapple in tones of amazement. "Why, I never imagined that Sir Randolph had kept up a regular payment to anyone for twenty *weeks*—let alone twenty years."

"Very likely he would not have if Mr. Throgmorton had not had charge of the business. They ceased at his death."

"I do not wonder."

"Smallside—Garridge—Towzer—and Scatcherd. What can he have been paying them for, all that time?"

"What a pity we did not know about this while I was lodging at Gabriel's sister's house," Lucas said. "I could easily have asked him. Now he has gone to his other sister at Keighley. And Mr. Smallside has left tHe mill and gone to Manchester."

"What about Garridge?"

"I haven't seen him since the fire; I do not know where he went."

"Well," said Lady Murgatroyd, "perhaps old Mr. Scatcherd would tell us if we asked him."

"Why are you so interested in these payments, *Grand'mère?*"

"Oh—I am just curious."

"Smallside, Garridge, Towzer, Scatcherd," said Mr. Oakapple thoughtfully, "I wonder what those four could have in common?"

Ten days went by during which the invalids continued to mend. Anna-Marie went to the mill; Lady Murgatroyd sometimes gave lessons, Lucas wrote an immense amount in his brown book and played with the baby, who had taken a violent fancy to him. In the evenings, those who could, sang, and those who chose, listened.

Anna-Marie ran lightheartedly down the hill one morning, observing that no more snow had fallen for three days. And the wind was a little less icy. The days are getting longer, too, she thought. When the winter is over, and Luc is better of his cold, and Monsieur Ookapool is quite well again, how happy we shall all be together!

Arrived at the combing shed, she skipped gaily along her grating, tweaking out the wool waste with her pincers at such a rapid rate of progress that she saved herself three and a half minutes' rest time at the end of each row.

"Champion!" said a dry voice behind her.

Anna-Marie was so startled that she spun round violently, dropping the pincers, which clattered onto the floor.

There, behind her, sat the pale-eyed Bludward in his

wheelchair, with little Newky Shirreff sidling up behind him.

"Let's have a look at t'pincers, then, Newky; pass them here, lad," said Bludward. "A little lass called Biddy told me aboot these, an' I thowt I'd have a look for mysen." He inspected the pincers with slow and thoughtful thoroughness.

"Now let's see thee using them again, lass."

Anna-Marie felt very uneasy. She remembered Rose Sproggs's warning. But she could hardly refuse, so she cleaned along the row of claws again, rather reluctantly.

"Nay, lass, tha was doing it a lot faster than that afore. Let's see thee speed oop a bit."

Luckily at that moment the noon whistle went and Rose appeared to eat her dinner.

"Eh, Rosie! This little lass o' thine has happened on a grand notion," said Bludward agreeably.

Rose did not look at all delighted at this praise. She cast a look of burning reproach at Anna-Marie and said shortly, "Oh, aye. Happen it'll work. Happen it won't."

"Nay, but it does work," Bludward said. "I was watching the lass afore she knew I were there, an' it works very well. The only thing is, it won't do."

"Why will it not do?" demanded Anna-Marie, who did not see why she should be left out of this conversation.

"Because we can't have woon working faster than all the rest. That's not fair on them that are slow. T'manager'll expect iveryone to work as fast."

"Yes, that is why I have already showed Prue and Hetty and Sarah how to make pincers for themselves; Prue lost the tip of her finger last week, so she was glad to have them," returned Anna-Marie composedly. "Now we all work as fast as one another."

"That won't fadge, lass; tha's forgettin' the teams on t'other claw-racks. Ye have to think of iverybody in a factory, not just thysen. If t'claw-cleaners work faster, then t'managers'll ixpect ivery soul in t'Mill to work faster. Nay, it won't do. Tha'd best throw those tongs away and forget about them."

"That is the most stupid thing I have heard in my life," said Anna-Marie indignantly. "And I certainly shall not throw them away."

'Nay, lass, ye have to pay heed to Mester Bludward," said Rose, giving Anna-Marie an imploring glance. "Let *him* have the tongs, luv—that's best. Happen he'll be able to persuade t'manager that 'tis a'reet for t'claw-cleaners to use them."

"I think it would be best if *I* go to the manager with the tongs," said Anna-Marie.

"Art tha stark mad? A lass o' thy age canna go—" Rose began.

At that moment Davey Scatcherd came by, carrying a large oil drum.

"I want a word wi' thee, Bob Bludward," he said as soon as he saw the man in the wheelchair. "I see while I've been away t'swivelers has started using t'press operators' tack space to stow their trolleys in. I've said before that's dangerous, an' I'll not have it. Let 'em find another spot to stack their gear—"

Then he noticed Anna-Marie, gave her a brief friendly grin, and said, "Hey, lass! I didn't knaw as tha worked in t'Mill."

"Coom back from jail too big for thy boots, eh, David lad?" Bludward said silkily.

The smile vanished from Scatcherd's face. "I do my job; tha can take care o' thy own," he said curtly. "Only tell those men to shift those trolleys afore there's an accident," and with a glance full of dislike for Bludward he was moving on when Anna-Marie exclaimed, "Mr. Scatcherd— Davey!"

"Aye, lass? What's to do?"

"I have made this tongs, *voilà,* to clean out the claws better and quicker, and it works very well, so we need not pinch our fingers, and now Monsieur Bludward come and say we must not use it, or all in the factory will have to work faster. He say, perhaps he will show my tongs to the manager. But I think, if he does show them, it is to pretend that he has made them himself. And I do not see what right Monsieur Bludward has to give us orders. *He* is not the foreman. So what do you think I should do?"

Into the thunderstruck silence that followed these words the half-past-twelve whistle sounded.

"Back to work, everybody!" Rose shouted with relief.

Davey Scatcherd was carefully examining the tongs which Anna-Marie had handed to him.

"Let's see thee use them, then, lass," he said, passing them back.

She started to work. He nodded, as she moved rapidly past him. When she was at the other end of the row she saw the two men have a short, rapid exchange, which she could not hear, then Davey nodded to her again, and walked away.

Bludward's chair slid in the other direction. He did not look at Anna-Marie again.

Anna-Marie took a detour on her way home that evening to call in at the Scatcherd house and present Mrs. Scatcherd with a piece of Lady Murgatroyd's handwoven cloth as a thank-you present for her kindness to Lucas.

"Those Scatcherds are *une famille très gentille,*" she said, when she returned to the icehouse. "How they all fit into that small house I do not know, but they are very nice. We have all been singing songs together. Oh, and the old monsieur, he says he has a thing to tell you, *Grand'mère,* and he will come up here and relate it when the weather is a little bit warmer. *Eh bien,* Luc, *comment ça va?*"

Lucas said he was a great deal better and intended to start work tomorrow.

"Meanwhile isn't there anything I can do for you, *Grand'mère?*"

Lady Murgatroyd was rapidly and skilfully putting together a jacket out of more handwoven cloth.

"Yes, I have just the job for you," she said, biting off a thread. "When I undertook to look after Bess Braithwaite's baby I promised that I would write the poor woman monthly reports on Bet's progress. But I am a very bad correspondent, and I have not written for six weeks. I should be extremely obliged, Lucas, if you could write for me."

Lucas was somewhat taken aback, for this was not at all the kind of job he had expected. At first he looked rather blank. However he supplied himself with a sheet of paper, a pen, ink made from soot dissolved in chestnut spirit, and a stump to write on. For a moment or two he sat chewing his quill, and staring at the baby. Then the pen began to move. It moved faster. It raced. An hour had gone by before he was aware of it, and Anna-Marie was jogging his elbow and saying, "Luc! *Grand'mère* has told you three times that supper is ready."

Anna-Marie was a little subdued and thoughtful at the meal.

Mr. Oakapple and Lucas had been talking about the Deed of partnership between Lucas's father and Sir Randolph.

"So does that mean that after all you may own half the Mill, Luc?" Anna-Marie asked hopefully.

Mr. Oakapple thought not. "Because in a partnership each partner is equally responsible for the debts, and even the sale of the Mill did not pay them off. Sir Randolph had been taking money from the Mill and using it on bets. I fear your father should never have let himself be persuaded to go to India and leave Sir Randolph in charge."

"No," Lucas said. "But Sir Randolph and my mother disliked each other—that was why they went. I have often heard her say so."

"Anna-Marie, my child," said Lady Murgatroyd, noting that her granddaughter appeared unusually grave, "how is your job going at the Mill? Do those pincers work well that we made?"

"They work well, *Grand'mère*," Anna-Marie said in a troubled voice. "But I am not sure that I shall be allowed to use them."

"Why not?"

"There is a man called Bludward who makes difficulties. He says if I use this tool then it is not fair to all who do not have it."

"Nothing to stop them all having it."

"Well I think that is not his real reason. Rose, who is my foreman, says he wishes to show the tongs to the manager and take to himself the credit for having invented them."

"Well you don't really mind that, do you?" said her grandmother. "If the work gets done better and people's fingers aren't pinched?"

"Yes I do mind!" said Anna-Marie indignantly. "Why should this Bludward—who is not a good man, *du tout, du tout!*—take other people's ideas and say they are his? Rose says he does this often and the people are frightened to complain because he is very *malin*."

Now Lucas looked troubled. "I know that Bludward," he said. "I should steer clear of him if I were you, Anna-Marie."

"*Quoi?* To steer clear?"

Mr. Oakapple explained the phrase, and then began a discussion as to whether tools were a bad or a good thing; he was inclined to think they were bad. "And the more complicated they are, the worse. Before people invented tools, they could not hurt each other very badly, but with tools they became able to kill."

"But still, you can make useful things with tools," objected Anna-Marie. "You can weave cloth, like *Grand'mère;* you can dig. A flute is a tool, so is a violin; you can make music."

"Yes, but I see what Mr. Oakapple means," said Lucas. "We use tools too much, and ourselves not enough. That's why it's good to do things that don't need tools at all."

"Like what?" demanded Anna-Marie. "I cannot think of many."

"Walking—talking—singing—dancing—telling stories—playing our game of scissors-paper-stone."

"I have noticed a thing that is very ridiculous," said Lady Murgatroyd. "People invent themselves tools so as to get their work done faster. Then what do they do with the time they save? They spend it in looking after their tools."

"A tool can give one person too much power over other people," said Mr. Oakapple.

"Is that bad?" Lucas said, to himself more than to the others.

"Of course it is bad," pronounced Anna-Marie.

"Well, perhaps you had better throw away your tool after all, my child," Lady Murgatroyd said. "If it is only going to cause trouble."

"Perhaps I had, *enfin.*" Anna-Marie stuck her bruised thumb into her mouth and sucked it thoughtfully. Redgauntlet left his spot by the fire and lumbered over to lean heavily against her.

"Talking about tools"—Lady Murgatroyd opened the wooden chest and took out a cloth-wrapped bundle which she had brought back from the market with her earlier that day—"I found this at a secondhand stall—Not Mr. Hobday's. It is not a good one, it is very old, but it will do for you to make a start on, Julian. You will have to hurry up and practice—then we shall be able to have some fine concerts."

And she laid an old violin on Mr. Oakapple's lap.

"Off you go," she said smiling.

He sat motionless, looking up at her, paralyzed by doubt and self-distrust.

"Go on, Monsieur Ookapool," Anna-Marie said gently. "Not one of us here can play the violin, so we shall not know what mistakes you make. Just try! I have a good idea, we will sing some songs and make a lot of noise, so you can play a bit and we shan't hear you."

So Mr. Oakapple tuned the violin, laying it on his right shoulder and holding the bow in his gloved left hand. Presently he became impatient with the glove and took it off.

Anna-Marie and her grandmother were singing.

> When, when shall I meet you
>> When shall I see your face
> For I am living in time at present
>> But you are living in space.
>
> Time is only a corner
>> Age is only a fold
> A year is merely a penny
>> Spent from a century's gold.
>
> So meet me, meet me at midnight
>> (With sixty seconds' grace)
> Midnight is not a moment;
>> Midnight is a place.

Anna-Marie glanced quickly at her grandmother once, but Lady Murgatroyd smiled a warning and laid her finger on her lips. Mr. Oakapple was very softly joining in, playing a chord here and a chord there.

LUCAS ANNOUNCED next morning that he was well enough to work, and that he intended to go down to the Mill; if Anna-Marie could find employment there, so could he.

Lady Murgatroyd looked at him with a considering eye and remarked that he was remarkably headstrong and self-willed but she didn't think it would kill him to go down to the Mill. "Still, I daresay you'll regret it before the day is over."

"No I shan't," said Lucas stoutly. "Anyway, it's a Saturday. A lot of the shifts stop at noon."

"What about Mr. Hobday's thirty pounds that we have hardly touched yet?"

"Keep it for a rainy day."

Mr. Oakapple pointed out that Lucas would find it much harder than Anna-Marie to avoid recognition.

"I've thought about that. But perhaps if they know I've been working as a tosh boy they'll understand that I just want to earn a living."

As it happened, the first person that Lucas and Anna-Marie encountered, when they approached the Mill gates, was Sam Melkinthorpe, who glanced at Lucas, glanced again, and then gave him a broad grin and said, "Well, by gar! I've often wondered what became of thee when owd Tight-Fist died. Niver tell me tha'rt coming to work in t'Mill?"

"If they'll take me," said Lucas. "Will you put in a good word for me, Mr. Melkinthorpe?"

"Aye, I will, by damn! I'll say tha'rt the quickest-footed lad atwixt here an' Grydale, with a reet head on thy shoulders. I'll say a word to Mester Gravestone. They needs hands in t'winding room, I knaw."

"I'm not using my own name," said Lucas. "I'm calling myself Luke Minetti—In case of hard feelings."

" 'A'reet; 'tis true feelings against Sir Randolph is still mortal bitter, but that's not *thy* fault."

"Do you think people will recognize me?"

" 'Appen not," said Mr. Melkinthorpe, stopping to scrutinize him. "Wi' t'different clothes, an' all. An' tha's changed, too, soom way; I cannot say joost what t'differ is, but tha looks older."

"Well, good-bye, Luc," said Anna-Marie, turning off toward the combing shed. "I will look for you at dinnertime."

"Is she a friend of thine, yon little lass?" asked Melkinthorpe, when she had gone.

"She's my cousin; yes; why?"

"Tha'd better keep an eye oot for her; I hear tell she's put herself well an' truly into Bob Bludward's bad books."

"What did she do?" asked Lucas uneasily.

"Gave him the rough side of her toongue; I canna blame her, but 'twas a foolhardy thing to do. Tha knaws what Bludward can be when he's crossed; let alone by sooch a little snip of a thing."

Melkinthorpe was as good as his word and gave Lucas a high recommendation to Gravestone, the new manager, who said, "All right, we'll try you," and sent him off to the winding shop.

Mr. Melkinthorpe nodded good-bye and said, "Don't forget what I told thee now; I'll keep an ear to t'ground mysen."

Meanwhile Anna-Marie had arrived at the combing shed and was about to go to her place when she was stopped by Rose. "Tha'rt not working here any longer."

"Why not?" asked Anna-Marie in surprise.

"Tha's been transferred—that's all," said Rose shortly.

"Where to?"

"T'pressing room. So tha'd best goo on over."

"Why have I been transferred?" demanded Anna-Marie.

"What for should I know? Ask t'manager, don't ask me." And Rose turned her back and started instructing a new claw-cleaner.

Rather discomfited, Anna-Marie took her way over to the pressing room, where a red-faced man like a drill sergeant was haranguing nine or ten somewhat undersized boys and girls.

"Now, remember: t'Mill doosn't want ye to be bashed by t'press ony more than ye do; for that only means a spoiled carpet an' a lot o' wasted time. So I want ye to step lively, keep yer balance, an' foot it quick: in—out—like a fullback taking t'ball away from t'goal. Some o' you lads plays football, I reckon?" Several of the boys nodded.

"What aboot us lasses, Mester Blaydon?" called one of the girls.

"Don't tell me none on ye's ever taken part in a football game in t'street? Well if ye haven't, try an' make believe 'tis a game o' Puss-in-t'Corner—see how quick ye can get across. Now," he said, looking round, "t'press is being greased for an hour, so let's have a bit o' practice. I'll toss a wipe on t'floor, an' let's see which of ye is quickest at getting it back. Take it in pairs—quickest from each pair tries agen wi' soombody else."

He divided the children into two groups, one group on each side of the pressing floor, and tossed a swab into the middle of the big space.

"Now—when I blow my whistle—first pair—go!"

A boy and a girl dashed toward each other. The girl triumphantly whipped up the swab from under the boy's nose, ran on past him, and flung herself up the steps on the opposite side.

"Very good, Martha Dunnett. Bide there an' we'll try you agen in a minute. Next pair!"

Two more ran out. This time the boy was the quicker. On the whole, the boys and girls were fairly evenly matched.

Anna-Marie, as last comer on the fluff-pickers' gang, was left till the final pair. Then she was matched against a thin, rather miserable-looking draggle-haired fair child, whom she easily beat.

"Anna—what's thy name?—Minetto? Try again wi' Martha Dunnett."

This time Martha, who had been so quick on her first attempt, seemed unaccountably clumsy, and slipped on the polished floor. Anna-Marie won again.

"Very good, Anna Minotto. We'll try thee agen in a minute against woon o' the boys. Now Saul Ramsbotton an' Geordie Hicks."

Geordie, who looked like an embryo center forward, easily won, but later when matched against Anna-Marie, he was not nearly so fast, and she was able to snatch up the swab before he could reach it.

By the end of the practice Anna-Marie somewhat to her own surprise, for she had thought several of the boys much quicker—had emerged as the winner of the snatching matches.

"Now we'll have a bit o' sweeping practice," announced the red-faced man. "Take oop yer brooshes. I want the floor marked out into squares—here's a bit o' chalk, Geordie, you do it. Fair shares, now, one each. Right? Each stand by your square. Now I'm going to choock oot a handful of cotton waste, an' when I blow t'whistle, I want to see who can get his square clean first. I doon't want to see woon thread left! Ready—go!"

They all rushed out onto the floor and each swept his square with feverish speed. Again Anna-Marie had her square perfectly clean quite thirty seconds before anybody else. She had thought her square was smaller than the others, but everything had been done at such a speed that it was hard to be sure; nobody else appeared to have noticed this, if it was so.

"Anna Minotti wins again. Well doon, Anna. Boys, are ye not ashamed of thiselves, to be beaten by a lass?"

Some of the boys did look rather shamefaced.

"Right, Anna Minetto. Tha seems to be t'quickest, although tha'rt new to t'gang, so tha can be snatcher for today."

None of the other children seemed to envy Anna-Marie this distinction. Some looked glum; others looked scared. Most of them tended to glance away if they chanced to meet her eye.

"Now ye can all have five minutes for a breather while t'floor is prepared and t'first carpet's put doon. Anna Minotto, coom here."

She did so, and he gave her some special instructions about the best place to stand, how to receive signals—"Can't have more than woon snatcher, ye see, or there'd be the risk o' boomping, but watch all the oothers, an' they'll signal if there's a bit o' floof in their square. Now, there's a temptation to stand wi' knees braced, but ye doon't want to do that—knees joost nicely flexed is best, an' hold t'tongs in thy right hand—so—keep quite relaxed."

Anna-Marie did not feel very relaxed. The men who had prepared the floor had finished and were climbing the steps. Another group was pulling along a dolly with a rolled-up carpet on it.

"Ready, then, lads?" called Mr. Blaydon, looking up.

Lucas, in the meantime, had been taken to the winding shop, where the duties were not difficult, though rather monotonous. Here, some of the wool, which had been pulled out and double-twisted by great spinning wheels in the next room, was fed through holes in a screen and wound on to huge steel drums, which constantly whizzed round and round with a steady peaceful hum.

"T'main danger here is ye may go off to sleep an' topple on to woon o' the bobbins," the foreman who was instructing Lucas told him. "Stay awake an' tha'll be all right."

Lucas's duties were to keep an eye on three of the steel bobbins, to see that the wool fed onto them evenly and did not lump or form ridges; to stop them when they were wound full, shift them off the spindle on which they rotated, and replace by an empty drum. They needed changing every twenty minutes or so, and were arranged so that they filled up in sequence, never two at the same time. The full bobbins were then rolled away along a gallery and down a gentle ramp into a huge store where they were kept until required for the weaving process.

The winding shop was quite a pleasant place to work, for it was open on three sides, not too hot, not too noisy, and there was constant variety in the color of the wool coming through from the spinning-shed. Nevertheless, Lucas was profoundly uneasy, and had some difficulty in keeping his mind on his work.

His anxiety was not allayed by hearing a snatch of talk between two men who walked past him.

"Seems as Bobby Bludward is fixing oop woon o' his little booby traps—"

"Nay, is he, then? Who for, does tha knaw?"

"Soom lass as gave him a bit o' sauce—joost to teach t'oothers to toe t'line—"

"Woon o' these days soomone'll booby trap *him,* an' aboot a hoondred chaps'll toss their caps in t'air for joy—"

They went out of earshot.

I wish Anna-Marie were out of this place, thought Lucas. It's not good, her working here. She's such a hothead; she won't watch her tongue.

One of his bobbins was wound full with bright violet

wool. Who could possibly want a carpet of such a color? But perhaps it would be mixed with something else, made into a pattern when it was woven. He pulled the lever which gave a signal to the men in the next room to stop spinning, broke the wool, fastened it off, and hoisted the bobbin off its spindle. This was an operation needing both skill and strength, for the bobbins were six feet in diameter from rim to rim—higher than Lucas as they rolled—and heavy in proportion. His foreman had helped him at first, but there was a knack, as Lucas had soon discovered, of swinging them off the spindle and over on to their rims all in one movement. Now he could do it alone. He checked his other two drums, to make sure they were winding smoothly, and was just starting to roll the violet bobbin along toward the store when he heard Sam Melkinthorpe's voice in his ear—loud, urgent, full of horror: "Lad! Quick! Coom to t'pressing room!"

"What's the matter?" Startled, Lucas had given the bobbin a shove; it rolled on ahead of them as Melkinthorpe grasped his arm and almost dragged him along.

"Yon bloody murderer have fixed it so's the press'll slip—they've owergreased it—woon o' my mates as works on the press told me, Bludward got them to do it—"

"Why?" panted Lucas, giving his bobbin another shove.

"Why? Acos they've fixed for yon lass to be t'snatcher—that friend o' thine—that's why!"

"*Anna-Marie?* The snatcher? But I thought she was in the combing shed—"

"Not any more!"

They had arrived at the pressing floor. The spreaders were just finishing their operation of smoothing out a great pale-gray and green carpet. The little snatcher was standing ready on the edge of the steps, holding her tong—Lucas saw that it was Anna-Marie with a resolute, intent expression on her face—

And there in the middle of the gray-green carpet, as the men unrolled the last couple of yards, was not one wool clot but two. Two of the other fluff-pickers, higher up the steps, signaled and pointed, each in a different direction.

Anna-Marie hesitated, then sprang out.

"Anna-Marie!" Lucas shouted. "*Stop!*"

But there was too much noise, with the tremendous whine of the press overhead, for her to hear his voice. She snatched up one lump of wool in her tongs—turned toward the other. . . .

With a wild burst of energy, which he would never have believed he commanded, Lucas hurled himself after the violet bobbin, turned it at right angles to its course, and sent it bowling down the shallow steps onto the pressing floor. Not an instant too soon. With a terrific silent downward rush—so fast that the ground seemed rushing up to meet it—the press came down. Anna-Marie looked up and went white; she took one faltering step toward the side. She would never have reached it in time. But the bobbin had rolled into the middle of the floor; the press came down and collided against it—six feet above her head.

Anna-Marie's legs gave way under her and she crouched down on the gray-green carpet like a partridge that sees a hawk fly over.

"Watch oot!" shouted Sam Melkinthorpe. "It's crackin' !"

A sharp, violent sound came from just above them. Lucas bounded slantways down the steps, grabbed Anna-Marie round the waist, and sprang back to safety, just before the two halves of the press, which had been cracked across the middle by its impact with the steel bobbin, tipped slowly down until each end rested on the floor.

"By gum!" said Sam Melkinthorpe, awestruck.

Lucas sat down weakly on the steps by the side of Anna-Marie and put his arm around her.

Men came running from all over the factory—in twos and threes, then in dozens.

"Look at that!" someone said wonderingly. "Snapped like a stick o' toffee!"

People formed a group round Lucas and Anna-Marie.

"Are you all right, lad? Was tha hurt at all, little 'un?"

"No—no—it is nothing—I thank you," said Anna-Marie scrambling to her feet, among all the helping hands. "It was just—it was so—so sudden."

But when she stood up her knees began to tremble again.

"I'm going to take you home," Lucas said.

"Aye, better," approved Mr. Melkinthorpe. "She's shook oop bad. 'Appen she'd be the better for a nip o' summat."

Lucas began to draw Anna-Marie through the crowd; she went with him docilely. In the middle of the mass of people they met Mr. Gravestone the manager, angrily elbowing his way forward.

"Was it you?" he demanded, laying hold of Lucas's collar. "Were you the boy who broke the press by rolling a wool drum under it? Do you realize what that is going to cost to put right? Thousands upon thousands—you have put half the Mill out of action for at least three weeks. The owners will sue you—you will have to pay for this—"

Lucas burst out laughing. He found something irresistibly comic about Mr. Gravestone's red face and red hair and blue outraged eyes.

"All right," he said. "Send us a bill. Come, Anna-Marie."

But a little farther on, by the swiveler, they walked into a more serious scene.

Bludward was there in his wheelchair. His pale eyes expressionlessly took in the fact of their arrival.

Rose Sproggs was standing in front of him, shaking her fists, and shouting, "I don't care who hears me speak! She were a good lass an' a bright lass, an' it was murder, Bob Bludward: there's no oother word for it. Tha's doon it oonce too often. I'll speak my mind if it's the last thing I do—"

Suddenly she saw Anna-Marie and stopped, struck speechless. After a moment or two she said: "I thowt tha was dead, luv."

"No," said Anna-Marie. "Luc—" She was unable to go on.

Scatcherd had come up behind Rose and was facing Bludward over her shoulder. "I towd thee, Bob Bludward," he said gently, "I towd thee before—remember?— when Fred Tebbutt were found i' the dye vat—I said sooner or later tha'd leave tracks behind and then I'd get thee. Tha's gone too far now."

"Aye, he has!" shouted Rose hysterically. "There's chaps on t'press who'll talk—"

"Ah, howd thy hush, woman," Bludward said impatiently. He seemed quite undisturbed by these accusations. Looking at Scatcherd, he said, "Tha'll fight, then?"

"Fight? Who said owt aboot fighting?"

"Art scared o' fighting wi' a cripple?" Bludward said contemptuously.

"Nay, no man calls me a coward—"

"If tha doosn't fight I'll call thee a soft soomph. Well? Bolt guns an' stackpins?"

"Eh—very well—if tha wants to fight—I'll not say no." Scatcherd seemed to have been shaken from the position he had established for himself. "When—an' where?"

"Three this arternoon—oop by t'lake i' Midnight Park."

"Fighting!" cried Rose furiously. "Isn't that men all over! Fighting! What does *that* get a'body?"

"Luc," said Anna-Marie in a small voice. "Luc, I am very sorry, but I think I may be sick. Can we go home?"

But outside the factory Anna-Marie felt a little better. They were amazed to find that it was a beautiful day—fine, and even a little warm. The sun shone. Birds sang in a startled manner. The snow dripped gently off the trees in dazzling drops.

Near their turning point off Milestone Hill they overtook an elderly man; when they came up with him they saw that it was old Mr. Scatcherd.

"I'm coom to see thy gran," he said. " 'Tis a fine day for a ramble. Reckoned 'twas time I tabored oop to put matters straight wi' her."

"Mr. Scatcherd," said Lucas, as they went slowly on at his pace, "did you know that your son Davey is going to fight Bob Bludward in the park this afternoon?"

"Nay, is he though?" said the old man with lively approval. "Not before time, either. How? They can hardly fight wi' clogs, seeing Bludward's a cripple."

"No," said Lucas. He had heard about the duels, often to the death, which the men of Blastburn fought, using no weapons but the steel-tipped clogs on their feet—dancing round each other like gamecocks, hands on hips, till one of them had his legs kicked from under him.

"Pity," said the old man, taking his pipe out of his mouth and banging it against a tree. "Davey's lightning-quick on his feet; plays goal for the Blastburn Wanderers. Reckon it'll be bolt guns, then?"

"Yes, that was what they said."

"That Bludward's a dead shot," the old man said, and relapsed into silence until they reached the icehouse.

The fresh air and the walk had restored Anna-Marie to something like herself, and this was as well, for inside the icehouse they found another unexpected guest—the lawyer, Mr. Throgmorton, looking, for once, rather less than his customary neat, trim, gray, proper self.

"I am come in answer to your letter, ma'am," he was saying. "I must confess I was surprised—greatly surprised—to find you installed here. I had believed you dead, firstly! And secondly I doubt if you have any but the barest squatters' rights to take up residence here, in Midnight Park, which as you know, has been sold."

"We'll come to that in a minute," said Lady Murgatroyd equably. "Why, Mr. Scatcherd! The very person of all others that I could have wished to see. Do please sit down—have a stump. . . . Now, Mr. Throgmorton—you are acquainted with Mr. Oakapple here—and you know *me*. Now, we should be obliged if you would be so good as to inform us for what reason you have been withholding from Lucas Bell here—whom we both confirm to be none other than Lucas Bell—the income he should have inherited at his father's death?"

"Why," began Mr. Throgmorton in a harassed manner, "—if the young man can prove that he is Lucas Bell—and if he can produce his father's will—I do assure you I never had the least intention of withholding anything due to him—er—an income of twenty pounds a year I believe—once a reasonable claim was established of course."

"I am delighted to hear it. Fortunately we have the will here—together with some documents that you may not have been aware you had mislaid, Mr. Throgmorton—some receipts for payments to various persons."

The lawyer's gray complexion paled to a greenish color; his mouth opened in dismay as he saw the papers that Lady Murgatroyd held in her hand.

"Lucas and I will come down to your office and go through his father's accounts with you on Monday, Mr. Throgmorton," said Mr. Oakapple.

"Yes, Mr. Oakapple—that will be quite convenient," stammered the lawyer. "Happy to see you better of your injuries, sir—happy indeed; I had not understood that you had survived the conflagration—"

"I should probably not have survived if this boy, whom you so strangely failed to recognize, had not worked as a sewerman to pay for my treatment," said Mr. Oakapple.

"Now, Mr. Throgmorton," said Lady Murgatroyd gently. "Just one other point. The payments made by Sir Randolph to Scatcherd, Smallside, Towzer, and Garridge. What were they for?"

Old Mr. Scatcherd got up from his stump and hobbled forward. "Maybe 'tis for me to speak now, my lady. Dear knows, it's been a fidgety thing on my conscience for twenty-odd years. But times was hard, and I'd dunnamany mouths to feed, an' no use chooking away good brass. But if I'd properly knowed i' th' first place what it'd lead to, I'd niver, niver ha' doon it. Joost a bit o' fun, we thowt it were, when we said we'd do it."

"What did you say you would do?" Mr. Oakapple's voice was very quiet and sad, as if he could see the answer ahead, like rocks.

"Why, I was to supply a gurt bit o' Clutterby Pie—I was a master baker i' those days—an' Gabriel was to put it in Sir Quincy's bedroom—an' Garridge was to ride woon way through Canby Moorside, dressed like Sir Randolph—an' Smallside, he were to ride back—

"Eh, but if I'd knowed Sir Quincy would die o' the business, an' young Mr. Denzil go off an' get drowned i' furrin parts—an' you, my lady, we heard tell as you was dead too, otherways I'd ha' blown the gaff long ago.

"Garridge an' Towzer an' soom other chaps went on an' did anoother dirty job for Sir Randolph, trying to stop yoong Mr. Denzil sailin' off; woon o' them scuttled the boat so it would sink; but I wouldn't have owt to do wi' that; I'd had enow by then. An' they did theirselves no good; two on 'em got killed. An' Towzer's niver been the same since; his heart's gone from him."

Old Mr. Scatcherd fell silent, staring at the fire, as if he saw a great slice of Clutterby Pie in it.

"So you see, Mr. Throgmorton," said Lady Murgatroyd, "it is probable that the sale of Midnight Park is null and void, since Sir Randolph had obtained the estate by fraudulent means. If you received any commission on the sale, you would be well advised to return it."

Mr. Throgmorton looked really appalled. "I very much

doubt if you would be able to get other witnesses—" he began.

"I think we could get old Monsieur Towzer," said Anna-Marie. "I am sure he is very sorry for what he did."

"And Smallside might consent to help if he knew we had the receipts; Garridge, too—" Mr. Oakapple said. "Of course, if it was proved that you knew of the original fraud it might be awkward for you—"

Mr. Throgmorton had had enough. "Well, ma'am, I'll look into it, I'll look into it. I know *nothing*. I can promise nothing. It is a very complicated legal situation—very. I will bid you good day."

He departed at great speed, looking, Anna-Marie said, as if somebody had hit him with a sack full of snow.

When he was gone Lady Murgatroyd turned to old Mr. Scatcherd and said, "It was kind of you to come up, Mr. Scatcherd. I am very much obliged to you. Won't you take a bowl of soup with us?"

"Why, thank you, my lady." The old man suddenly looked rather tired. "I won't say no. Not so stout on my pins as I reckoned. An' I want to stay on to watch t'fight."

"Fight?" said Lady Murgatroyd. "What is that?"

Lucas explained to her why the men were fighting and, like Rose, she sighed and said, "What good will that do?"

"I do not at all like them fighting because of what happened to me," said Anna-Marie.

"They would ha' fought onyway, lass, soon or late," said the old man. "Those two has always been at odds. Half the town follows yon Bludward—acos he puts 'em in fear wi' his Friendly Lads—an' the oother half's for my Davey. They even calls theirselves Bluddites an' Scatchers. So it were bahn to coom to a fight i' the end."

Anna-Marie, who had wandered to the door, exclaimed, "Why, what a lot of people are coming into the park. And, Mr. Scatcherd, there goes your son!"

She ran out to meet him across the thawing snow.

"Hallo, lass," he said smiling. "Art cooming to see me fight, then?"

"Perhaps," said Anna-Marie. "I do not much like it, though. Davey, your papa is here—do you not want to come in and see him?"

"My dad? Here?" He was very surprised. Old Mr. Scatcherd, evidently somewhat relieved that he had got his awkward confession over before his son arrived, clapped Davey on the back and said, "Now, mind tha doos us all credit, Davey, boy. I haven't allus fought straight, but mind tha do, now. Stick 'im right i' the gizzard, we'll all be watching."

Lady Murgatroyd said she was not going to watch any fight, but Mr. Oakapple went out with old Mr. Scatcherd. Anna-Marie and Lucas walked with Davey across the park toward the site that Bludward had chosen. The lake was in a dip, at some distance from the ruins of the house, beyond a slight ridge.

On the ridge they turned to look at Blastburn which lay down below, damp and glittering and smoky, its chimneys black against the unwonted sunshine.

"Aye, it's a moocky old hole," Davey said affectionately. "There's a lot wrong, but still, it's lively! It takes a howd on ye, if ye live there. Luke, lad, I want to ask thee summat."

"Yes of course; what?" said Lucas.

"You're a good friend, I can see that—you an' I might be friends, happen. But if yon Bludward doos me in, I hope tha'll take on the job o' seeing that he an' his mates doosn't have things all their own way i' the place."

"You're asking *me?*" said Lucas, surprised. And then he said, "Yes; all right."

"Shake hands on it," said Davey, and they shook.

"What about me?" said Anna-Marie.

"I doubt I don't have to ask thee!" said Davey, rumpling her hair. "Tha'rt a fighter born. I've summat to give thee, though; kind of a keepsake to pass on, ye might say."

"Oh, what is it?"

"My mam tells me as tha has a rare sweet voice for a lass thy age. Now, my owd gran, she come of gypsy stock, an' she taught me a way to sing wi' mouth closed, so the sound seems to come from a' round aboot. Like this." And he demonstrated.

"Oh, it is strange!" cried Anna-Marie. "But I thank you. I am sure not one person in a hundred knows to sing so. Not even Monsieur Ookapool."

She had several tries at it without success, and then suddenly achieved the knack. "I feel as if the sound was coming in at my ears instead of going out!"

"That's it," said Davey, satisfied. "Just the way my gran used to do it. I wouldn't like not to have told somebody how."

By now a large crowd had collected in the park; evidently half the town had got wind of the fight and come out to watch.

Lucas even observed Mr. Hobday, who, catching sight of him sidled up and said, "Hey, Luke, boy, I've 'eard tell as 'ow your gran 'as a famous owd tuning fork as used to belong to Orlando Gubbins. I know a cove what would be prepared to pay thousands and thousands for that-ere fork; 'ow about it, eh? Think your gran would sell?"

"No," said Lucas. "I'm quite certain she wouldn't. It is not even worth asking her."

Mr. Hobday, much dashed, looked as if he intended to try more persuasion, but at this moment they saw Bludward in his chair being pushed over the snow by Newky and his fuzzy-haired brother Joe. They wheeled him to a spot about ten yards from the lake, and then Lucas noticed that Joe went round among the crowd offering odds of twenty to one against Scatcherd. But there were not many takers; Bludward, it seemed, had too high a reputation as a marksman.

The ground for the duel was marked out: twenty-five yards. Scatcherd, with a little group of friends, stood nearer to the frozen ruins of the Court; Bludward's chair was not far from a big chestnut tree.

The seconds carefully checked over the bolt guns. These were a kind of metal bow, wound up by a spring; they fired the stack pins, which were used to skewer labels to the big bolts of wool in the mill. They were deadly weapons because the pins, although only four inches long, were fired with such tremendous force.

Not at all the sort of tool Mr. Oakapple would approve, Lucas thought, noticing the tutor studying one of them.

"Right? Ready?" called the taciturn Jobson, who was organizing and umpiring the duel. "When I drop this swab, both fire!"

He dropped the hank of wool. Everybody heard the *spang* of Bludward's bow, and saw Davey start as if he had been bitten; but he still stood straight, with his bow unfired. Then he began to take aim, very deliberately; Bludward, seeing this, suddenly gave his wheelchair a vigorous shove to shift it out of the line of fire. It catapulted backward down the slight slope, and out on to the frozen lake, where a number of people were standing.

The crowd scattered—some to one side, some to another—and the chair flew along the lane thus formed. And then an awesome thing happened: jarred by the sudden pressure from the people moving all at once, the ice began to crack down the middle of the lake. A dark, widening gap appeared: Bludward's chair rolled straight into it and vanished from view.

There were screams and shouts as the people on the sloping ice saved themselves by scrambling to the bank; but by the time anyone had thought to try and rescue the man in the wheelchair, it was too late.

Then they heard the twang of Davey's bow.

Anna-Marie and Lucas ran to him. He was leaning against a tree.

"Oh, are you all right?" she cried. "Did he not hit you?"

"Nay, lass, I'm doon for. Owd Bob got me right here." And he laid a hand on his breastbone.

"What for didst tha not fire?" said Melkinthorpe.

"Nay, I did. I aimed for yon chestnut tree, an' I hit it too!" said Davey grinning.

Old Scatcherd came hobbling up. "Hang on, Davey lad—tha did well—hang on!"

"Nay, I can't Dad. Owd Bob's fixed me proper. Give my love to Mam—an' the little 'uns. Remember what I taught thee, lass—"

"Oh, *don't* die!" cried Anna-Marie.

But he did die.

Sam Melkinthorpe and other friends carried him home, and old Scatcherd walked alongside. The crowd slowly melted away from the park, leaving the snow blackened and trampled and thawing, with patches of green visible for the first time in weeks. Lucas walked slowly after the mourners.

Anna-Marie spoke to nobody. She walked back to the icehouse with her lips pressed tightly together, and, once inside, sat down on the floor with her arms round Red-gauntlet and cried very bitterly for a long time.

"I don't *want* him to be dead," she wept.

Her grandmother and Mr. Oakapple watched her sadly in silence.

But, much later, she finally sighed deeply, and sat up, and blew her nose. "Well—he *is* dead—like Papa and Sidi. So that is that. But it is such a waste! He was so nice. And he p-played for the Blastburn Wanderers—"

"Yes, it is a waste," said Lady Murgatroyd.

There was a tap at the door.

"May I come in?" said a tall thin man, and did so. "I

heard a rumor—so I thought, if it was true, that I would come to pay my respects—Why, Eulalia! It *is* you. What a pleasant surprise. So you have not been dead all these years?"

"Why, Gus—good afternoon," Lady Murgatroyd said, "Let me introduce my friend Julian Oakapple. And this is my granddaughter, Anna-Marie. My cousin, Lord Holdernesse."

Dabbing her eyes, Anna-Marie studied Lord Holdernesse and saw that there was a strong family resemblance between him and Lady Murgatroyd. They both had the same tall bony thinness and grayness. But where she looked firm, and full of thought and decision, he looked like a dreamy old scarecrow. He gazed about him absently, murmuring, "The old icehouse; yes indeed. I can remember playing hide-and-seek here with Quincy and his sister when I was eight or nine—now what was her name?"

"So I hear you have been trying to buy Midnight Park, Gus," said Lady Murgatroyd. "I hope you weren't too upset to hear that the sale was off. I daresay you'll get your money back—if that wretched Throgmorton doesn't abscond with it. You had better watch him pretty sharply."

"Oh?" he said vaguely. "The sale's off, is it? Why is that, Eulalia?"

At this moment Lucas came silently in. He looked pale, but collected.

"Why? Because Sir Randolph won the estate by a fraud."

"A pestilent fellow; never liked him. I am not at all surprised. So to whom does it belong?"

"Why—to us, I suppose. All of us here. Let us go and look at it."

They walked outside, all of them, into the cool vaporous sunshine. Anna-Marie carried Bet, hugging her tightly. The smoke of Blastburn lay like a cushion on the horizon.

"Well—I'm sorry for you that you didn't manage to buy

the park, Gus," said Lady Murgatroyd. "But I am glad for us."

She looked away from Blastburn over the great, bare, dirty, beautiful stretch of land, with its sooty trees, and its trampled snow, and the lake full of cracked ice.

"Oh, I don't begrudge it to you, my dear Eulalia—not at all. I have got the Mill, after all."

"Have you, sir?" said Lucas, with interest. "Are *you* the British Rug, Mat, and Carpet Manufacturing Corporation?"

"I do own that company, yes."

"Then," said Lady Murgatroyd, "you are going to have your hands full setting things to rights there. But there is someone here who can advise you. My young cousin Lucas Bell. He has been studying the Mill and knows a great deal about it."

"I'll be very glad of your advice, my dear boy."

"Well—" Lucas ventured, "I had been thinking of becoming a writer—now that I have my father's twenty pounds a year to live on—"

But then he thought of his promise to Davey Scatcherd.

"Naturally you can be a writer as *well*," said Lady Murgatroyd briskly. "But you must certainly advise Gus."

Must I? thought Lucas. Do I know enough about it? He thought, *Industry is a good thing because it is better to work in a carpet factory than to be out in the rain with nothing to eat.*

"I'm sorry I was obliged to break the press in your factory, sir," he said to Lord Holdernesse.

"Did you, my dear boy? I was not aware of it. Well, I daresay it can be mended."

"I'm not sure that is really a very good way of making carpets, sir."

"No? You must explain it all to me by and by."

"Oh, and there's another thing, sir, that perhaps you should know," Lucas said. "When I was down in the town I overheard a couple of people talking very wild and saying they were going to breach the dikes and flood the lower part of the town—It was Joe Bludward and Newky," he told Anna-Marie—"So I went round by Haddock Street and warned the Scatcherds and everyone there. Apparently the Bluddites live mostly up at the Clutterby end of the town, so they thought they would be safe. But old Mr. Scatcherd says they have probably forgotten that the tides are at springs and most likely the whole town will be flooded; Joe Bludward always was a stupid lad, he says. So the Scatcherds are going to warn everybody to be on the lookout, and I mentioned it to Mr. Gravestone at the Mill, as that is fairly low-lying."

"It sounds," said Lady Murgatroyd, "as if we shall have everybody camping in the park. Well there will be plenty to do. How fortunate that the weather is a little warmer."

"That old Gudgeon!" said Anna-Marie in sudden alarm. "He is sure to be drowned if there is a flood!"

"I warned him too," said Lucas. "I went round that way."

"By his boat? *Mon Dieu!* Were you not afraid?"

"It was all right. He hardly seemed to remember me. I'm not sure whether he really understood what I was telling him though. He just said, 'The end thereof shall come in with a flood; but neither can the floods drown love,' and then he wandered away and started hunting for tosh on the bank."

"Oh well," said Anna-Marie, "you did your best."

Lord Holdernesse and Lady Murgatroyd had strolled up onto the ridge and were looking down at the town. Scraps of their conversation floated in among Anna-Marie's sad thoughts.

"It is no use *telling* people to change, Gus. But if their lives are better—I think there is a younger Scatcherd brother who might—"

"—Encourage the notion of fair play, start educational groups, inculcate higher principles—that sort of thing, eh, Eulalia?"

Groups, principles, Anna-Marie thought, but *people* are more important. *I* am important, me: I am going to make up tunes that will be cheering people for hundreds of years.

"Just the same," Mr. Oakapple said, standing beside her, as if he had heard her thoughts, "if you went away from here, what would you remember most? Not any of the people singly, but this great dark town with all its hardship and trouble."

"Davey said it was a m-moocky old place but he loved it." She wiped her eyes again.

Lady Murgatroyd and her cousin were talking about Sir Denzil.

"Ah, he was a wayward, reckless boy—but everybody loved him. He had a way of looking at you and smiling—Quincy was rather a hard parent, y'know, Eulalia. If he had been more understanding, now—"

Lucas thought sadly about the life and death of Denzil Murgatroyd. What a waste of that gifted, lively, inventive boy, he thought. If he had meekly done what his father wanted, and devoted himself to the Mill, would things have turned out better? What good did it do, that everybody loved him? If he and Sir Randolph had not quarreled, would Sir Randolph have been a better person, not left such a trail of destruction behind him? Does Anna-Marie take after her father? No, Lucas thought, she is herself, no person is a continuation of anybody else. And then he thought, perhaps I could write about Denzil Murgatroyd. Perhaps I could write his story.

Once upon a time, he thought, *there was a boy* . . . and then stopped short in astonishment as the two images overflowed across one another, the image of Greg and the image of Denzil. They were the same person, and I never guessed it till now.

"So what will you do with your park, Eulalia?" said Lord Holdernesse.

The sun was low on the horizon, the shadows were long, it was becoming chilly.

"Well," said Lady Murgatroyd, " what shall we do with it, my dears? Build another great house?"

"No, no, let us not," said Anna-Marie. "Besides, we have no money. I have thought what I shall do: I shall collect snails. I have seen a sign saying that doctors at the infirmary will buy snails—with shells—for fourpence a quart; people want them for cage birds, also. And I do not believe the Friendly Boys will be able to say they have the rights to the snails in Blastburn. Also the doctors want frogs, one penny each, and worms are required by the men who sell turf. I shall get the other fluff-pickers to help me too; I think they did not look happy and will be glad of a change. And Luc can help me and we shall do quite well."

But Lucas thanked her and he thought he would have enough to do.

"And we'll write, read, sing—run a music school—"

"*Avec le diapason de Handel, alors!*"

"Just live here," said Lucas.

"Do come and call on us, Gus, whenever you like," said Lady Murgatroyd, as he raised his hat to them and took his departure.

They went into the icehouse where the fire smoldered gently and there was a warm smell of woodsmoke. Redgauntlet thumped his tail.

"I think perhaps this evening it would be a nice thing if you were to play your violin a little, Monsieur Ookapool, *n'est-ce pas?*" said Anna-Marie.

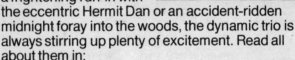